I0550600

DIETODAY

a novel

DIETODAY

MARK HAWKINS

Copyright 2018 Mark Hawkins

All rights reserved. Reproduction, distribution, or transmission of the
contents of this book is prohibited without prior written permission from
the publisher, except as permitted under the U.S. Copyright Act of 1976.

This is a work of fiction. Any similarity of the characters or events to real
persons is coincidental, and not intended by the author.

Science, Religion & Law, LLC
An Arizona Company
www.sciencereligionlaw.org

ISBN: 978-0-578-41058-6

To the people who love Heart Mountain

To live, or not to live, that is the question.
We cannot help but be.
Life begins with wonder. Our early months are marked by
light; we are swaddled and suckled. We hear voices of music,
words of love sung in our praise, not merely for being, but
for living. In the beginning, admiration of us is inevitable.
Time passes, and one day we become a voice of music,
singing our admiration for the living. Today I sing with joy
burning so bright it scorches me.

CHAPTER 1

A FACE IN THE DUST

I WAS ALONE.

An instrument arrived that day. We installed it into the particle field generator at the National Strategic Hadron Collider, or NSHC, in the desert, west of Phoenix, Arizona. We would move forward quickly now. We were done waiting.

We'd stabilized dark matter two months earlier. Tests showed that many of the atomic elements we know had a counterpart in stabilized dark matter: Gold, and Gold II, Copper, and Copper II, Uranium, and Uranium II.

I had an uneasy feeling being there alone, but this was my equipment. I knew it better than anyone. I switched on the equipment to start the process. I didn't set a level for shutdown. I wouldn't need it.

Uranium II had a dangerous characteristic: the possibility of nuclear explosion without enrichment. An instability was inherent in this new type of element--one not based in atoms. We didn't know what it was based in. Electron microscopes showed us atoms in Uranium I. We understood atoms to the quark level. We didn't understand Uranium II, or any of the stabilized dark matter, because when we looked at the particles, we saw no atoms. We saw no strings. We saw

1

something we didn't understand. Where's Niels Bohr when you need him? Or Einstein? All the great ones were gone, half a century ago.

We'd stabilized 1.2 kilograms in the initial test, but now we could stabilize larger quantities, and, in the next couple of days, we would run a strategic test to see how much more. There was no time to lose. I shouldn't have felt guilty about staying late and working. No one should have cared. There were the usual night security guards in the building complex, somewhere; but no one else was there.

I'd been running the equations to make sure the instruments were going to function properly. I got caught up in the numbers, and it took longer than I thought, but, finally, I was ready to make sure it was working. This was really exciting, but I still had a nagging feeling. An uneasiness.

Dr. William Griggs, the Director of the National Strategic Hadron Collider, said the strategic testing would occur as soon as the generals and dignitaries could arrange to be there. We would have short notice, so he wasn't going to mind.

The particle generator was warmed up.

I watched as the particles formed. Amazing! No matter how many times I watched the process, it was still remarkable that this process worked.

My palms were sweating. What was wrong with me? I watched a sweat droplet roll down the back of my hand. Time was strange. Why didn't I wipe the sweat off?

From nowhere came an odd thought, *What if I didn't shut the stabilizer off in time--on purpose?* A metropolitan area of four million people would evaporate, that's what would happen. Starting with me.

Dust. There was more dust than there should be.

Why was there so much dust? Why couldn't I move?

Too much dust. Time stopped.

I couldn't move. How could particles be forming if time had stopped?

The particles were piling up on the floor. I just knew something horrible was about to happen. What was it? A nuclear explosion? No. That wasn't it. It must be something else, something unseen.

I tried to shout, but my tongue was stuck, my jaw tight. Fear. This wasn't possible. I'd never had a seizure. I wasn't sick.

I wished I were asleep, and that this were just a nightmare. I knew better. I shouldn't have done this alone. What if it wasn't just stabilizing matter? What if we had opened a door, and something unseen was coming through, feeding me maniacal thoughts? Something with the power to stop me from moving. We, as scientists, had been watching twenty percent of the universe, the part made of atoms. What if the other eighty percent, the part piling up on the floor, wasn't nice?

The dust was still gathering on the floor. More and more of it, growing thicker as I sat there.

The dust on the floor began to move. Instead of settling to the floor, the particles streamed upward. They began to form a shape.

I heard behind me a knock, and someone opening the door. "Sir, is something wrong?"

It must be a security guard, but I couldn't turn to look. I was still rigid, unable to move. I felt a hand shake me. That broke the trance. I could move again.

I reached out and flipped the switches to halt the testing, my hands trembling and sweaty. I watched to make sure the dust settled. It wasn't supposed to stream upward. That had never happened before. Combined with the fact that I had been frozen, it was terrifying.

3

I turned to thank the security guard, but he had already left. I jumped up and hurried through the door. The hall was empty. I ran back and forth, looking for him, checking other rooms. I never found him. The guy had just averted a disaster, and I'd never even seen him.

I didn't want anyone else to know what had happened. It would sound crazy. I'd have to figure out a way to explain it, if anyone asked, as they surely would. Why was there a huge pile of dust? They'd want to know. Why had I run the strategic test without everyone present? I would tell the truth, that I made a mistake.

Spooked, I gathered my things to head for home. Home. Oh, no. Today was my son, Sam's, sixteenth birthday. Now I felt nausea and bile burning in my throat. This night meant a lot to Sam. We'd gotten him a telescope with computerized charting ability. How many times had I talked it up? It ached to try so hard, and still hurt someone I loved so much.

■ ■ ■

It was ten o'clock when I got home. I heard the television in the family room. My wife, Marie, was sitting with Sam on the couch and, in a rare moment, she was holding him. There were tears on his cheeks. That's when I knew how much I'd hurt him.

His gift was sitting on the coffee table. The box was opened, but he hadn't assembled it.

Our ten-year-old daughter, Emily, was on the sofa as well, clinging to Marie.

I put my satchel on the counter.

Sam got up and walked past me, headed for his bedroom. He roughly wiped his cheek as he passed. "Sam," I said, wanting to explain. He didn't stop. It was like watching him crash his bicycle when he was five—I was cringing inside, in fear of how bad he was hurt.

"Marie, I…."

"Whatever you have to say, don't," she said.

I waited. Silence only made my anxiety worse.

I had to try. "We just got word today that we are going to be doing some important testing," I explained. "We had to jump on getting things ready."

"And why would I care, exactly?"

"We stabilized dark matter. That's been announced in a press release. You know what this means."

"You care more about it than your son," she said. "That's all I know. That's all he knows. Everything else is classified."

"Maybe he couldn't leave, Mom," Emily said. She was ten and forgiving. She didn't like conflict, especially not from her parents. No child did.

"Emily, time for bed.," Marie said.

"It is not!" responded Emily. Marie and I weren't particularly strict about bedtime, unless it was convenient for us. There were two sides to manipulation. Some children were gifted at it.

Marie took Emily off to bed, over Emily's protests, and I scrounged in the fridge for what was left of chicken enchiladas, Sam's favorite. Must have been a nice meal. I didn't really have to miss it. The reality was, I got excited and forgot. I felt so bad for Sam. My appetite was gone.

Marie came back downstairs.

We had a discussion. It involved several pillars of American family life: the first was neglecting family for other things; and the second was excessive debt, especially credit card debt.

The real issue, though, was how insecure and isolated Marie felt. I just didn't know how to help her. My life seemed just beyond my control, in the midst of, or maybe because of, the success I had at work.

Marie brought up divorce. If she wanted a divorce, she should have realized that she and our children were going to see me less, not more. Divorce wasn't the answer, we just needed to get through this. Things would get better.

Or maybe not. She asked me to leave, and go to a hotel that night. I hated leaving, but it was better to respect her request.

At first, my biggest concern was what it would be like to go to church on Sunday, recently separated from his wife. I needn't have worried. My church leader was kind, sympathetic, and understanding when I called him the next day to explain what happened. I'd had a dual major in college-- physics and divinity--before I started my graduate work at Stanford. We were good friends.

The next few days at work were hectic. When they asked why there was so much dust, I told them the truth, that I'd made a mistake, without the scary part: I had been physically unable to move.

I called my children every night. Marie and I talked, as well. She didn't let me come back home, though. She was really struggling, and I didn't know how to help her. I knew she'd been unhappy for a long time. She'd been telling me how low her self-esteem was. I just didn't know how to fix it.

At church on Sunday, we ignored the fact that I was living in a hotel, and we didn't tell anyone. Our church leader was the only one who knew.

Marie told the children they wouldn't be seeing me over spring break that next week, because she needed time with them. Sam retaliated by inviting himself to go boating on Lake Powell for a few days with his best friend's family.

Marie then decided to go to Sedona for several days with a couple of friends, elementary school teachers, who picked spring break to go to Sedona because they had the time off. She also wanted me to have some time with our daughter. She allowed me to stay at the house with Emily while she was in Sedona.

"Are you ready to storm the castle, Sir William?"

"I am, Your Highness." Storming the castle sounded like a great idea, as opposed to waiting. Emily was filming us in a medieval scene of a castle with orcs. The camera had auto-focus and motion detection, so we were both able to be in the action while the camera rolled.

"We must advance before the orcs reach the unicorns," Queen Emily said. "There is no sign of Rasgon, our dragon. I'm sure he'll come to our aid."

Emily led the attack. Emily reached the top of the stairs, where she began slashing at pretend orcs.

"The unicorns are safe!" Emily cried.

Emily had always loved fantasy. She owned an impressive herd of toy unicorns, ranging from the size of a dime to the size of a cat. We had never passed a store that had a stuffed, porcelain, or glass unicorn without an investment in Emily's stable. Her imagination was expansive and pervasive, and fanciful creatures were her particular delight. They were her favorite movie theme.

She acted as though she were greeting the dragon, who was just arriving.

"Rasgon! I knew you'd come!" she cried out.

Emily stood tall and triumphant, with her stable of unicorns and her fierce dragon. I bowed on one knee by her side.

"And now, Sir William, I order you to return to the castle. You will no more be banished."

Uh-oh. That was a little too close to reality. I was only at the house for a couple of days while Marie was out of town.

"I'm sorry, milady," I responded, "but that won't be possible. The Queen's mother and I must remain at peace."

The corners of her mouth descended in a well-honed pout.

"But there can be peace," she said.

"The finances of the castle are in disarray. We must raise some gold coins from the peasants, or we cannot sue for peace."

Actually, it was just one peasant—me. But that peasant was ready to find a way, whatever it took to get back to the castle, back to the Queen and her mother.

"Now off we go to the banquet hall, to celebrate our glorious victory!" I swept her up and held her securely, one arm behind her knees, and the other holding her shoulders. I carried her down the stairs.

"Wait! Dad, I have to turn off the camera."

I put her down at the bottom of the stairs and watched as she hit the off button on the video camera.

I had forgotten this was all on video, and her mother would definitely see it. She would hear every word I'd said about peasants and gold coins. It's just so hard not to express how you feel, when there is so much hurt and anger inside, so much fear and loss.

■ ■ ■

While Emily and I were eating lunch, I received a call that I was needed at work immediately. We were going to do the strategic testing. The team I led at NSHC had successfully stabilized 1.2 kilograms of dark matter. Now we were attempting to stabilize a larger quantity. I had chosen 50 kilograms because the tests we were running on the particles showed Uranium was present, or more accurately, Uranium II, which had peculiar characteristics equating to being naturally enriched, and unstable. Preliminary tests had predicted the possibility that the substance could spontaneously react, leading to explosion, if it reached critical mass of 200 kilograms. We had cut the number by three-fourths as a precaution, until we could test the danger more thoroughly.

For ten years I had thought this scientific success would

be the great and grand moment of my life—the elusive success—and the moment had finally arrived. Life didn't follow my daily planner, however; the generals and the senators had more important schedules than me. I was forced to find someone to leave my daughter with. I couldn't ask Marie. I should have already told her about the likelihood I would get called in while she was away. The time with Emily was too important for me to imperil with any conditions, and Marie wouldn't have accepted any of my excuses, so I naturally hadn't told her. Now that the likely had become certain, I needed someone appropriate for my daughter to stay with, particularly if the committee began some of the inevitable meetings and required us to stay overnight at a hotel near the accelerator location.

"Hey," I told Emily, "I found out I have to go to work." The details of what we were doing weren't common knowledge, and Emily wouldn't understand, anyway. "I need someone for you to stay with if I have to be gone overnight."

"No problem, Dad. Call Aunt Sarah."

"Aunt Sarah and I don't exactly get along." At least, not since Marie and I separated. Sarah was fiercely loyal to her sister.

"Okay, well, I'll call her," she offered.

I called, disregarding my discomfort, expecting that after a chilly conversation, Sarah would agree to have Emily stay the night at her house. The line was busy.

We finished lunch, put the dishes in the dishwasher, and I went to get ready to go to work.

I kept trying to call Sarah, but the line remained busy. I waited longer than I should have, and finally told Emily to and keep trying to reach her aunt as soon as the line was free. If the line was busy, Sarah was in town, so I wasn't worried. I rode my motorcycle as fast as I could, but I was going to be late.

A snowbird is a person who lives in the cold north and

likes to go south for the winter months. They find Arizona more comfortable than places south of the U.S. border. Snowbirds don't fly. They drive. Slowly. Their real purpose is to interfere with nice people on motorcycles, especially ones who are impatient even when they aren't running late.

On my way north to the freeway, I had to stop at a red light. There were two lanes, a car in each. I was behind one of them, and a cop pulled up on my right. When the light turned green, there was a noticeable pause—from both the front cars. Then they rolled forward, one only slightly slower than the other. Snowbirds are a minority, so you always hope to encounter one at a time, and everyone else can buzz right past them. Not this time. They gradually reached a speed that was ten miles per hour below the limit, and there they held. I could see the officer shaking his head. Finally, he turned on his blinker, and made a quick right turn. As soon as he was out of sight, I blasted right between the snowbirds, barely made the next light, and was on the ramp to the freeway.

■ ■ ■

Anxiety roiled inside me as I watched the strategic testing. The generals from the Defense Department were across the lab from me, behind shatterproof glass an inch thick. We were all in rooms behind glass, on both sides of the testing area, but if this thing blew, they'd never find the glass or any of us. We had attempted to convey to these really important people how dangerous this was. I had limited the quantity to 50 kilos, but still, this was an unknown substance. We were guessing. In his wisdom, my boss hadn't spread the word about danger. These were government dignitaries. A few senators, a few congressmen, but not the vice president. Representatives from Lurich, Inc. were there, including the CEO, Sky Lurich. Sky and I had gone to school together years ago. The fact that his company was the chief private investor in our project stemmed from his personal interest in it, as well as from the fact that Lurich, Inc., was a contractor for strategic weapons.

There were no foreign dignitaries. Even though most of the projects at NSHC were international, this one was classified.

We had my team, assembled from graduates of the leading physics programs, which, for decades, had mostly been the same: Stanford, Harvard, Berkeley, and MIT.

We were in Arizona, in the middle of the desert, in the longest and most powerful particle accelerator in the history of the world. Thirty-four miles long, twice the size of LHC in Switzerland. The length was not to increase the speed of the particle collisions; LHC had already achieved virtually the speed of light. The purpose was to expand the capacity for testing and related lab space. We'd had choices on where to build it: Nevada, Wyoming, Arizona, or Alaska. New Mexico had unequivocally declined—they'd already put up with nuclear bomb testing a century ago. They must have learned their lesson.

The dark matter we hoped to condense would be stabilized by a quantum processor which looked like a large chrome box the size of a refrigerator, with a one-way mirror on one side. Across the white-walled testing room was another identical box. The boxes generated a field in between the one-way mirrors. Dark matter particles were skimmed off the particle accelerator and shot into that field.

We had 70-inch monitors displaying the activity in the particle field. We would be able to see the particles shooting into the field, where they stabilized. The life spans of these particles used to be measured in decimals with powers of ten, as miniscule fractions of a second. In the stable field, they stayed put.

Four-fifths of the matter in the universe had been called dark matter. It wasn't dark anymore. We would see it, lighting up our screens, even before we could see it in the field. We would also hear it, like a Geiger counter, ticking upward as the mass increased. The screen would show the total mass in the field. We had new elements. We tested the 1.2 kilograms we stabilized months ago, and the results were impressive: stronger, more resilient kinds of matter. New kinds of matter, with which we could build new kinds of worlds. Not just Gold, but Gold II. Our tests showed that every element had a more powerful counterpart.

I was highly distracted, due to the fact that I'd just realized I'd forgotten to call Sarah to make sure she'd been able to pick up Emily.

Dr. Veronica Fraticelli, or Ronnie, as we called her, was standing next to me in the booth. We'd been working together on this project for ten years. It wasn't lost on me that she was one of the most attractive women I knew; she and her former husband were friends with Marie and me. We had often enjoyed barbecue at their house. A year ago, they'd divorced. They'd never had children. She'd engrossed herself in our project after the divorce, taking time off only for rock climbing. She attacked that sport like she did everything else, which is why she was slender and athletic.

"I can't believe this," I whispered.

"That we really have this test underway?"

"No. That I forgot to check on my daughter. She was at the house when I left, and I planned to have Marie's sister, Sarah, pick her up."

"So, you moved back home?"

"No, Marie is in Sedona for a few days and Sam is at Lake Powell with his friend."

"I'm sure Emily will be fine. You can call her as soon as this is over."

If I was honest with myself, I knew that underneath my verbalized concern for Emily was my worry about Marie kicking me out of my house and talking about divorcing me. There was also the anxiety that the dust had streamed upward the night I was there, and I hadn't been able to move.

This was my moment, though; it was the moment for our team. There was one dream I had never let go. I only wished my older brother Brett would have lived long enough to see this. He had been really excited about what I was doing, and so proud of me.

I looked over at Sky Lurich, in a booth to my left. He had a slight smile. To him, this was a cloud of alchemistic glory. What ancient magicians couldn't do, Sky had paid for us to do. So what if we couldn't make gold out of thin air? We could make Gold II, so very much more rare and valuable for the person who paid for it all.

The yellow warning lights ceased flashing, and the green lights came on, signaling the test sequence would begin.

Ronnie was nervous; I could see her moving her right heel in and out of her shoe the way she always did. Her brown hair, almost shoulder-length, hung to one side as she cocked her head. One of our team members tapped at the keys on the huge computer panel in our booth. It looked like a synthesizer or a sound mixer, but it was the complex controls for very powerful computers. There was a whir like a thousand bees in a microwave. The particles would be changed in an oval area, seven feet wide, between the machines. The red light came from the machines, meaning the particles were being diverted into the area. A strong sense of foreboding returned.

A fine dust appeared in the air inside the oval, settling towards the floor. There were murmurs of approval. I felt a shiver streak up my spine. Senator Strong had his prodigious, unkempt eyebrows raised, and his mouth slightly open. I was glad he was impressed.

Another electrifying shiver coursed through me.

The dust stopped settling to the floor, and began to coalesce, at about the height of a person's chest. The particles continued to appear, with more and more particles. Then they spread out, and formed the shape of a person. I felt tingling in the air as the people around me tensed. The figure, indistinct at first, clarified. It wore white clothing like fine linen, middle-eastern in style. Its hair was shoulder-length. Its feet and hands were bare. The surreal form increased in clarity until we could discern a recognizable face—masculine, but shimmering, unstable. The person's gaze was intense, his eyes intelligent.

The whirring stopped as the sensors in the particle field recognized the 50-kilogram limit had been reached. The particles stopped accumulating. The shimmering increased, and the form became unrecognizable. Gravity prevailed, and the figure sank in a cloud of dust.

We all knew what the dust meant. We expected it. The dust of new worlds, of unknown knowledge—dark matter stabilized. Now there was more, a being, a person.

One of the generals broke the silence. "Who the hell was that?" he demanded.

CHAPTER 2

PASS OR FAIL

PANDEMONIUM BROKE LOOSE as we all rushed from our compartments and spilled out into the hallway that connected them. There was shouting and commotion as we scurried down the hall to the conference room. I could hear the general shouting, "What kind of security breach was that? We've got someone breaking in here in the middle of our test!"

The chaos continued in the conference room.

"Get me the president on the line!" the general demanded. "We want this place locked down. We are going into quarantine! Who is supposed to be in charge here?"

There was an answer to that. Chuck Griggs was in charge. In theory, he was my boss. Well, not just in theory. He was the executive director of the NSHC. At a moment like this, when I was supposed to make him look good, instead, I had likely produced a national crisis.

Dr. Griggs stepped to the podium and waited for silence. He looked out at the group and bobbed his head up and down several times, the way he does when he can't figure out which part of his trifocals to look through.

"We all thought we saw a person in there. We don't any

of us, I don't think, have a clue why or how. We came here to watch matter being stabilized, and it was a great day. It is everything we hoped for. We'll be running further tests to learn about the chemical nature and compounds we've gathered. What we don't know . . . what was a complete shock to us all . . . was the appearance of what looked to be a person. We are going to need to study what happened here. It is too early to draw any conclusions."

"We know what we saw!" The general's face looked like a ripe tomato being squeezed to the popping point, the veins in his neck bulging. "How do we know that thing was a person? It could just as easily have been an alien showing up as a person!"

Everyone started talking at the same time, and chaos once again prevailed. Dr. Griggs had the microphone, and he was finally able to get enough of their attention to say, "But the fact is, this person . . . or alien . . . is not here. He, or it, did not fully materialize—"

"Yeah, why is that?" The general asked. "And what if it had? We'd be sitting here with an alien in our midst, gawking like a pack of tourists. We have no idea what we're up against!"

Dr. Griggs' eyebrows were knit together in panicked reflection. He paused, the way he always does when one of us asks him something he should know but doesn't.

He said the first thing that came to mind. "Will??" It must have seemed like a fine idea, to bring me up there to get him out of the hot seat. He cleared his throat. "Yes, Dr. Will Johnson, why don't you explain?"

The room was silent as I made my way to the podium. "My team designed the stabilizer for automatic shutdown if we reached a predetermined mass of matter. After the original test with 1.2 kilograms, we discovered we had stabilized Uranium II, which behaves as though it were already enriched to weapons-grade Uranium, and, more importantly, it was unstable in a way that normal uranium is not. We calculated the potential for nuclear fission occurring spontaneously and estimated the theoretical danger would begin at 200 kilograms. We designed a shut-down if the matter reached 50 kilos to avoid the risk of a nuclear explosion. Recently, we refined that and added extra instrumentation to track the Uranium II being stabilized, so the machine would shut down as needed."

"Did you have any estimates of payload for this material?" the general asked.

"We estimated the payload would be 100 times normal uranium, but that is theoretical, based on the properties we saw. The payload of an explosion would be as much as the largest device ever tested--Russia's 50 megaton Tsar Bomba."

"What if your calculations were off?" Senator Strong asked, his bushy eyebrows twitching. "We could have been blown to kingdom-come here today! You didn't have a problem with that?"

I felt uneasy and angry, like I had the last time I was at the lab. I hadn't told anyone about the night I was alone at the lab, unable to move, as I watched the dust piling up. Should I tell them now? "I had the utmost confidence the test would go well today, sir," I explained, "and I'm pleased with the precautions we took. As you can see, this allows us to address the question of whether we are going to do this again anytime soon and invite our unknown guest to come back. The reason he didn't succeed in staying with us this time is that he didn't have enough mass to hold together. If we up the limit to 100 kilos, he might stay around."

"We'd all be fascinated to meet him, I'm sure," Senator Strong said. "We have no idea what we are dealing with here."

We continued the discussion but, ultimately, got nowhere.

Eventually we left the conference room, and Sky Lurich approached me in the hall. "Fascinating development, Will. Weren't you expecting a visitor?"

"How could anyone have expected that?" I asked.

"I was expecting it," said Sky. "In fact, I'm disappointed you weren't. You were always one to think of the unconventional, particularly if it was religious. Don't you believe in angels and spirits and hosts of unseen beings on this planet? Why would you be surprised to see one?"

This was Lurich—always stretching things, always maneuvering, almost always full of bull. I wasn't going to tell him, or anyone else, about the night I was alone, or my sense that we had opened a door, and it wasn't just stabilized dark matter coming through.

Sky and I had been in the same undergraduate physics program, although he eventually dropped out. Some people would have seen our discussions in college as religious persecution, but I always felt I gave more than I got. My religious theories were highly speculative, but at least I had a theory. In fact, it was the idea that dark matter equated to the religious concepts that got me interested in the project in the first place.

"If this really didn't surprise you," I said, "then for the first time in your life, you thought of something before I did." If someone was going to try to tell Senator Strong we just saw a religious being, it wouldn't be me. I wasn't going to say it to Sky, either.

He laughed. "You and I need to have a little chat," Sky said. "I'll be in touch." He walked briskly forward with his employees ahead of me down the hall. I could talk to him for thirty seconds, and feel like we had sparred a round. Eventually every match ends.

■ ■ ■

We all stayed in a hotel that night at the NSHC site. I

guess it wasn't a quarantine—that would be for diseases. The general had the right idea, since information could be more lethal than a disease, but the quarantine of information never happened. Somebody with a cell phone had captured the whole thing on their grainy little cell phone camera. Security breaches happen. One dusty face makes great world news. After it was on television, the U.S. president eventually made a public announcement.

In the meantime, we weren't allowed to make any calls or leave the hotel, even though we never ended up having any meetings. I asked several times to call my daughter, and tried to explain why, but I didn't get permission to do anything. I tried to walk out, but I got stopped by security before I could leave. Finally, at 1:00 p.m. the next day, I was allowed to leave NSHC and use my cell phone again. I tried several times to call Sarah, but there was no answer. My only consolation is that Marie was in Sedona.

When I got back to the house, I couldn't get the key into the lock. The week I was supposed to spend with my daughter wasn't half over, and Marie had allowed me to possess a key for that week only. I peered at the doorknob. It looked to me like a key was broken off in the lock. I rang the bell.

Marie answered the door. She looked great, with her blondish hair blown back, and nails done by a stylist, probably in Sedona. Except that her blue eyes looked like Hurricane Frieda.

"Do you know what you did, Will?"

"Marie, I—"

"Emily was home alone, Will. She was terrified last night. She was crying when I got home."

"How did you get home?"

"Oh, you're surprised I came home! You were at the

world-important event, your daughter was home alone, and you didn't think I'd come home? It took three hours."

I saw my daughter peeking around the corner from the kitchen, her chin lowered, watching us, her eyes wide.

Anger and resentment welled up inside me. Why did she have to do this in front of our daughter? Why did she have to be so critical? Why did she kick me out of my own house?

"Tone it down, would you? Emily is right there."

Marie turned around, walked toward Emily, and gave her a hug. Marie whispered something in Emily's ear, and took her to her room. I went in and sat down on the couch. As Marie came back, I could see the recent time at the gym had added tone to what was already an attractive figure. She'd never before been particularly athletic, but she understood nutrition, and all of us stayed thin and healthy because of it. Her face was taut.

"Don't you dare act like this is my fault," she said.

"I'm sorry. Sometimes I have a big mouth."

"Is it big? Let's see, is the Grand Canyon big? Is the ocean big?"

"I'm trying as hard as I can," I said. "I'm doing everything I can. And it's not as if I were failing. We finally had the breakthrough—and more. The implications of this person appearing are huge, they could change the world, we barely have any idea . . ."

"Oh, stop being so dramatic," she interrupted. "I never asked you to change the world. I just need my children to have a father, and to have a roof over their heads. How much extra are they paying you for this breakthrough?"

"You know they aren't paying anything extra. But, it doesn't matter. It is still huge."

"It's only huge in your mind, Will. To me it is worthless. It isn't making things better; it is making them worse!"

The anger was simmering, ready to boil. I had hoped so often that we could get through this, but the obvious answer was for her to change. She wouldn't. My anger at her grew into even greater anger at God. On the one hand, giving me the greatest professional success of my life, while, at the same time taking my wife away. I was at the point where I could either start arguing angrily with Marie, or I could back off. We had been here before, so the terrain was familiar, and so was the searing pain of arguing with her. Usually, I would hold back my words, because I didn't want to hurt her, I wanted to make things better. But something within me still demanded that she change, too.

"I'm sorry, Marie. What can I say?"

"There is *nothing* you can say, Will. Or, maybe there is one thing. When you get divorce papers, just say 'yes.'"

CHAPTER 3

LURICH'S MASTER

THERE WAS A TIME, right before I woke in the morning, when I would dream. Or maybe that's just the only time I remembered it. Most of my dreams made little sense; they were a jumbled mix of my subconscious mind. After a fitful night trying to sleep, still angry at Marie, I finally drifted off and started to dream.

The dream was dark and full of conflicting impressions. It seemed, strongly, to be more than a dream. It was as if a door had been opened and, now, confused information was streaming into my mind. We should not have stabilized dark matter. No, of course we should have! This was an achievement, an advancement of mankind. It would bring the destruction of mankind. How could that be an advancement?

The dream started with Sky Lurich and ended with the world. Like many dreams, I couldn't tell it was a dream until I woke up.

I saw Sky alone at night in his glass-walled city-tower office. He walked towards a wall and placed his hand beneath his company logo. A seamless door unlatched. He entered a chamber with wood-paneled walls. I was with him, but for some reason, he could not see me. There was an indistinct sound as he entered the chamber. The music that had been playing in his office outside was silenced as he shut the door. The room was hidden, sealed, and sound-proof. The light was hardly sufficient to see clearly.

There were two figures in the room. One was a remarkably lifelike replica of Sky, dressed in a black silken robe, with a hood.

The other figure was a replica of the devil, as our culture portrays him. His torso and face looked like a man's, except with red skin. He had horns protruding slightly from his head. The lower half of his body was covered with fur, like a satyr, with hooves and a tail. In his hand was a trident.

The two figures were facing each other, ten feet apart. They stood lifeless, their eyes closed.

Ten feet to the side of the figures was a column, the height and width of a person. It was black plastic on the side facing the figures. There was a panel of controls on the other side.

I watched Sky step up to the controls. He began attaching electrodes to his forehead, chest, arms, and legs. Then he stepped forward and pressed his eyes against a viewer.

He pushed a button.

The eyes opened on the replica of Sky. The figure looked around. He was eerily lifelike, almost alive. He took a deep breath and exhaled. He flexed his well-defined muscles. He placed his hood over his head, leaving his face visible. He took another breath and began to hum.

I stood, watching. It was hypnotic. The figure of Sky began chanting in a language I didn't understand. I looked at Sky and could see he was chanting, as well.

They stopped chanting. Sky's replica gazed at the devil figure. The replica knelt, placing his hands on the ground in obeisance. The replica spoke, looking at the ground. "My lord, I come before you this evening. I beseech your presence. How often I have called you, and how seldom you answer. I need you now, and I believe you will answer." I could see Sky's lips moving, at the controls. His voice and words were being amplified as the replica's.

I watched the devil figure. The lights dimmed. A mist of vapor hissed forth around the figure, shimmering with surreal red light.

The devil's eyes flicked open. He seemed to look directly at me, even though I wasn't really there. It was a dream. I had to be invisible. Then he smiled, acknowledging me. My jaw felt stiff, and I realized my mouth was gaping open in a noiseless scream, almost the same as the night I was alone at NSHC.

The devil looked down at the initiate before him. He exhaled, a throaty rumble of sound, like an airlock.

"Yesssssss. You do well to call upon me. The latest developments have been as I hoped. We have much to talk about. Yet you complain that I rarely talk to you. Do you not think I have other servants? There are so many, they are beyond your comprehension."

"My lord, why can I not see you, without this contrivance?"

I had been intently watching the two figures facing each other and had forgotten the real Sky at the controls. Now I looked back at him.

"Your contrivance was resourceful, and it pleases me."

There was irony, I thought, that Sky would be secretly building machines to try to the talk to the devil, when he belittled me for believing in God.

I saw Sky's lips moving, but the sound was magnified and synthesized to be the devil's throaty voice, coming from the lips of the devil figure, vivid and alive. Sky was voicing both parts, like a split personality.

"Look upon me now," the devil said.

Like an initiate to an evil rite, the replica of Sky looked up from his obeisance.

"The testing was a success, and the figure appeared, as I told you it would," the devil said.

Sky's claim of not being surprised now made some sense.

"Yes, master, but you have not told me the meaning," Sky's replica said. "What is your purpose?"

"You understand so little of who and what I am," the devil said. "You designed this form, and you have imagined me to be the devil. You believe you are simply voicing the thoughts I put in your head. Creating this form shows me you are just as silly as the religious believers—worse, in fact, because it is easier for you to believe in a hellish caricature than in who I really am."

"Then tell me who you are," said Sky's replica.

"If I told you anything, you would have no way to know it was true," said the devil. "You will see me with the rest of the world, when they conduct the test again." There was a pause and then the devil spoke again, "I would tell you what I want you to believe, but what do you really know?"

"I know nothing. But, I believe you are a being of limitless knowledge, residing in another dimension, unseen, but communicating powerfully to me as a voice in my mind. You are a being with awesome power, controlling the destiny of this planet."

"Yes, and the time is near when all mortals will understand my true power," the devil said.

"Will you not reveal it to me first?" asked Sky's replica.

"Why? Do you doubt me?" said the devil. "Yes, I doubt you. I feel your power. I feel your mind. But there is nothing in this world that I need. You must offer me something beyond mortal wealth or knowledge."

"Must I? If you wish to remain alive, you will cease your insolence," the devil said.

The initiate bowed his head, still kneeling.

"Yes, master."

"How old am I?" asked the devil.

"You are eternal, my lord," said the initiate.

"Is there any knowledge I do not possess?" asked the devil.

"You possess all knowledge."

"Yes, and I share with you this knowledge: Will Johnson must serve me. He has already opened the door, albeit unwittingly. There is more he will yet do, but his work as a mortal is done. You will kill him," said the devil.

"I can't kill him!" protested the initiate. "I *need* him. What good would he be to us dead? I want him to run my labs. He is the key to production and control over stabilized matter. The government, the university—no one else can control him if he's in my employ."

"Hah! Your labs do not interest me, nor the production of matter, except for my purposes," said the devil. "You do not fully understand who he is, or those who would help him. He has served his purpose for you. I must communicate with him more directly."

"I can bring him here, master."

"No," said the devil. "You will keep the secrets of this chamber or you will be destroyed."

"Give me more time," begged the initiate. "I need him alive."

"You will obey my will."

The real Sky threw himself back, away from the machine, and the blazing eyes of the figures drooped shut. The figures froze, lifeless again. Perspiration dripped from Sky, and he gulped air.

"Like hell I will," he said to the empty air. Then he walked right through me and out of the room. I swear I could almost smell his sweat.

■ ■ ■

The scene shifted in my dream, and I saw Sky, dressed in dark robes, at the head of an army. Battle fire decimated the mortals near him, but the bullets passed right through him, without leaving a trace. The scene spun, and I could see modern Jerusalem, with its stones, walls, domes, and minarets. Two men stood before the city. Now, the battle fire came from Sky's countless army, but it was being turned back against them, the bullets and missiles destroying the soldiers sending them.

The army stopped firing and Sky gave orders to surround the city.

■ ■ ■

I awoke. In my heart—in my core—there was terror. In my mind was the cause, an idea. This wasn't a dream. It was data, recordings of the future. I was the only one who understood. How could that be, when I was so confused? Something unconscious, things that had bothered me for years, were there. Impressions of America. The world. At a zenith. On a precipice. Did these things bother everyone, or was it just me? School shootings. Contention. Racism. Opioid epidemic. Technology was irreversible, it was the dark horse of apocalyptic evolution. Digitization. Atomic bombs were time bombs. How long until terrorists used them? And now, the final piece. Stabilizing dark matter had opened a door. Dark matter had come through, but so had data. There was a vast database, flowing, full of fear and evil, and I had upgraded to a high-speed connection.

CHAPTER 4

CONGRESSIONAL HEARING

I AWOKE DRENCHED in my own perspiration. The dream remained vivid. I got ready for work. My phone buzzed as I was about to start my motorcycle. The number was unlisted.

"Dr. William Johnson, please."

"Speaking."

"Hello, Dr. Johnson, my name is Rebecca Smith, assistant to Senator Thomas Strong, Chairman of the Senate Committee for Homeland Security and Governmental Affairs. Senator Strong asked me to invite you to attend an emergency hearing to be held the day after tomorrow. It will be a joint meeting with the house and senate committees to review recent events at the NSHC. Dr. Griggs and Dr. Fraticelli have also been invited. It will be a public hearing, with members of the press in attendance, as well."

"What if I can't make it?"

"You will lose the opportunity to defend your project."

Becky gave me the details, although she had to repeat some of them, because my phone was cutting out. The battery was low. I could never remember to plug my phone in a computer, and I'd been meaning to replace my wall charger but hadn't.

■ ■ ■

When I called Marie to tell her I was going to Washington, she was pleasant. She told me the children were upset that I wasn't around more, and she suggested I have dinner at the house with the children that night. When I asked why, she said she had just closed a deal, and she wanted to go out with her friends. She had a history degree, but that was back in college. In the past two years, she had worked hard to become a real estate agent, starting out as an assistant in a real estate office, and getting the training she needed for her license. Now, she was starting to see some success. It might have been part of the reason she had decided to separate—she had the confidence that she could make it if she needed to. For my part, I was glad for her success, either way.

Emily answered the door when I arrived that evening.

"Hi, Daddy!" She gave me a hug. "Mom made your favorite—lasagna."

We went through the hallway, lined with our family pictures. She hadn't taken down the ones of me. Was that a good sign? When we got to the kitchen, Marie was at the sink cleaning up some dishes, and I could smell the aroma from the oven. Around the house she often wore sweats, but tonight she was wearing jeans and a blouse. She had always been more of a shopper than an athlete, but she ate right, and she looked really good. She met my gaze when we came in.

"Hi," she said.

"Hi, honey. Did you get highlights? Your hair looks great."

"Thanks."

I moved towards her, wondering if she would kiss me, but she turned back to the sink.

"Why don't you and Emily set the table?"

"Sure."

I got some plates from the cupboard, and Emily got the silverware. I asked Emily about how our film turned out, and we talked about her plan for filming with her friends as we finished setting the table.

The beeper on the oven went off.

"Will, would you take that out? The pan is heavy."

She handed me the hot pad holders and opened the oven. It felt good just to be near her.

When everything was ready, Marie called for Sam. He was in his room doing homework. I knew he didn't normally come when he was called, usually because he had music playing on his iPod, so I went to get him. I knocked, and then opened the door. He was playing his keyboard, using headphones. He unplugged the headphones and played a riff from "Stairway to Heaven."

His room was a mess, as always. Several pairs of his size 14 shoes were scattered around.

"Great song," he said. I put my hands on his shoulders and squeezed.

"Hey, the lasagna's ready. Let's go."

I sat in my usual place at the table. Marie called on Sam to say the blessing, and for once he did it without complaining.

"So, what really happened at the testing Dad?" Sam asked. "The news never tells everything."

The news channels had been playing the camera phone video of the incident non-stop.

"I can't remember, I was too worried about forgetting Emily and what Mom was going to do to me," I joked.

Sam and Emily laughed, and Marie smiled.

"Everybody there was stunned," I said. "I've never seen anything like it."

"Nobody has," said Marie. "It really was amazing."

Her acknowledgment was a ray of sunshine after a storm.

She often didn't acknowledge my achievements because she didn't want me to get caught up in my own importance. I knew that was her real reason, but it still bugged me.

I couldn't say anything more about it, so we moved on to other things: Sam was on the track team and had done well in the high jump. He was talking about the kid who from East Valley High who had jumped 7' 2". Emily was talking about the spelling bee coming up. She had almost won the last one.

"Hey, Dad," Sam said when we were done eating, "why don't we take the telescope out to Usery Mountain Park?"

I glanced at Marie. She was looking at her food.

"What about your homework?"

"I started it early tonight. I'm almost done. Emily did hers already, too."

We wouldn't be able to stay out very late, but even a quick trip would be fun.

I smiled. "Sure, that sounds great."

While the kids were getting ready, I helped Marie clear the dishes. Our hands brushed as we were putting dishes in the sink. It felt wonderful just to be near her when she was happy. I grabbed her hand and squeezed.

She squeezed back, but then let go and turned away to grab more dishes. She looked back over her shoulder. "What are you going to say at the hearing?"

"Why, are you worried I'll be too dramatic?"

"Who? You? You'd never be one to suggest this would change the world or anything." She smiled.

"There is such a huge range of possibilities about what it could mean for most people. To me, religion says there are other types of people than mortals: spirits, and resurrected beings. Eighty percent of the universe is made of dark matter."

"You can't explain religion at a congressional hearing,"

Marie said. "They won't listen. Be a scientist. You're good at that. Stick to the scientific possibilities and leave religion out of it."

She looked in my eyes. It was great to be talking to her. She was wonderful, when she wasn't angry. "I love you, and I always have," I said. "Can I move back home?"

Tears welled in her eyes. "Why did you have to bring it up? Our children needed time with us. I was having a pleasant evening. You don't get it, do you?" she said. "I'm drowning. My life is lost. I can't do this, and I'm done trying to explain it."

"What do you mean, you're lost? You have me, we have great kids. Your real estate career is doing well."

"We've talked about this," she said. "Everything is about you; now, more than ever. You aren't here, emotionally. You haven't been. My self-esteem is gone!"

"I don't understand what you mean...."

"I know you don't. I can't do this. I won't argue with you." She was sharp now, angry, and tears rolling down her cheeks. "I just can't do this." She turned and left the room.

Sam came in, ready to go. He yelled at Emily to hurry up. Then, he went in to play the piano. He'd been able to play with emotion since he was very young, unlike most children who are always hurrying to show how fast they can play a song. He played "Rhondo alla Turca," by Mozart. He knew it was one of my favorite songs.

We drove up to Usery Mountain Park to the backside of a hill, where the city lights were blocked, and Sam set up his telescope.

"What are we looking for?" asked Emily.

"We are going to look at the constellation, Sagittarius," said Sam. "In the spring, the center of the Milky Way rests towards the southern horizon near it."

"Oooh, we get to see the center of the Milky Way?"

"We can't." Sam replied. "It's blocked by interstellar dust. All of the stars in our Galaxy are in orbit around a super-massive core, probably caused by a black hole and super-sized stars."

"How do we know what is there if we can't see it?"

"Scientists can measure how much stuff is at the center by figuring out how much it would take to hold all the stars in the galaxy in orbit," Sam said. "Plus, they use infrared photography to see how bright the center is."

"Is it as bright as the sun?"

"It's way brighter than the sun."

I decided to chip in. "The infrared photography shows the core is like a giant cluster of huge, blazing suns, and the suns get smaller as they get further out. The suns at the center are the oldest ones of all."

We looked at Sagittarius for a while. There didn't seem to be any indication that an intensely bright core of the galaxy was there; it was completely hidden from us. Then we leaned against the back of the pickup, and looked together at all the stars, and the splendor of the vast clusters of distant galaxies.

"Hey, Dad?"

"Yes, Sam."

"You're going to Washington, D.C., tomorrow, right? So, do you think maybe Mom will change her mind? I mean, this could be like a big deal, right?"

I noticed Emily looking at me, her eyes wide.

"I don't know, Sam. Mom and I have had problems for a long time. I'm not sure anything can change that."

"I just don't get it," Sam said.

After all these years, it was clear to me that Marie was serious about wanting me to change. I didn't believe she was serious about divorce, though. I could guess she was thinking that, even with a major breakthrough, I wouldn't take advantage of the benefits it would offer. I'd let the opportunity pass me by, and we would still be bankrupt. She'd probably be right. What Marie wanted was a fundamental change in the way I thought, and I wasn't sure I was capable of that. But, in my heart, I believed we would make it through this.

"I can't explain it to you, Sam. It's not anybody's fault. Sometimes it's just the way things have to be."

Sam pounded his fist against the side of the truck. "That's a bunch of crap." He started walking rapidly up the road in the darkness. I watched him go, knowing he wouldn't go far. He just needed a little space. I certainly understood that. Emily and I would wait for him to come back.

How was I supposed to explain to him what I didn't understand myself? If Marie really wanted to divorce me, I couldn't stop her. Maybe God could fix things. He's supposed to be omnipotent. I certainly wasn't.

I sat on the tailgate and Emily climbed onto my lap. We sat there in the quiet until Emily fell asleep. I put her in the back seat. When Sam finally came back, he let me give him a hug, but he didn't say anything.

■ ■ ■

On the flight to Washington, I thought of everything that had happened at the NSHC. Making contact with aliens couldn't be like this, could it? They were supposed to come in spaceships, weren't they? Not that I believed in aliens. In my view, everything is in order, everything has a pattern. There are trillions of stars, and possibly just as many earths like ours. To me, our world is one of countless numbers of planets, populated in a systematic way over the course of billions of years.

My views were a combination of religion, science, and common sense. Science is true. Religion is true. My hope was that people from various world religions, not just Christians, were going to be caught up into the heavens at judgment day. Not that I could fully grasp it. If judgment day had been the next day, we'd all have died of shock. No one can really comprehend that God is going to appear. I sure hoped it would happen. It would be awesome; unimaginable even. That was really the problem. Hoping for something beyond my imagination. Still, it had to be scientific. God didn't contradict science, he gave us science. If we were all God's children, He should have good news, even for atheists, when the time came. They'd ask, "Why did you hide yourself from us?" And he'd explain.

I had spent a lifetime studying religions of the world. I'd studied divinity in college, as a dual major. My views on all aspects of religion were skewed by science. I didn't try to teach my personal views in church.

What was I supposed to say to members of congress at this hearing? Was I supposed to tell them what I really think? That it wasn't an alien we saw? Based on what I believed, it could only be a spirit, taking physical form; the equivalent of a resurrected being, or maybe a being like Elijah, caught up physically into heaven, and changed. A being like that wasn't made of atoms. There might be a better technology than mortal atoms, and it took us several thousand years to figure that out.

My experience at the lab, and my dream of the incident in Sky Lurish's office, bothered me. If we were going to see an angel, we could all be excited about it. What I felt was dread, in my gut and in my soul.

There was no proof of what I believed. The notion of aliens was a more scientific explanation than what I thought it was and was far more likely to be palatable to a congressional committee. No doubt, most of the members of the committee would profess to be religious, but even most religious people didn't really believe it was possible for angels to appear. None of the committee members was likely to want to seriously discuss angels as an option.

■ ■ ■

Before going into the hearing, I was able to talk to Dr. Charles Griggs, my boss from NSHC. We were in the hallway, and we stepped around a corner for a few moments to talk. He was looking through some papers he held in his hands. He bobbed his head up and down as he looked at them. Then he pushed up his glasses and held the papers a foot from his face.

"Did I ever tell you trifocals cause dyslexia?" he asked.

"No, you didn't," I responded. Then changed the subject. "Any last-minute suggestions before we begin, Chuck?" I asked.

"Frankly, I don't like our options," he said. "Do we call this thing a person? Was it an alien?"

"How about if I tell them it was the devil," I said, "and he plans to take over the world?"

He laughed. "I think we need to leave angels and devils out of the options, don't you?" Then a thoughtful look crossed his face. "I did have an interesting discussion with Sky Lurich. He warned me to stick to science and avoid nonsense and speculation. He wants us to strengthen our credibility, and he wants us to move forward with a repeat test. He believes we have absolutely nothing to fear. Since I'm testifying first, all you need to do is follow my lead."

It was not surprising that Sky Lurich was trying to influence what we said about the incident. His company was the biggest investor, and he'd been at the strategic testing. I thought of the dream I'd had about him. It seemed crazy. It is rare that anyone has a dream that conveys a real event, a premonition of something that has happened or will happen, and I'd certainly never had one. Of course, no one had ever wanted me dead before, either. A few times I'd had déjà vu, and it was always a creepy feeling. Sky's office was in New York, and I'd never seen it. I couldn't help being somewhat curious about whether it really looked the way I had seen.

This didn't seem like a good time to mention the dream to Charles—in fact, I doubted there ever would be a good time. If the dream had any truth, I didn't want to follow Sky Lurich or Charles, both of whom were anxious to proceed with a second test, regardless of the potential hazards. On the other hand, maybe my job, and my hope for a thaw with Marie, depended on it.

■ ■ ■

We moved into the hearing room and took our places. I smiled at Ronnie, seated several rows behind us. She was immaculately dressed in an ivory business suit. The hearing room was the largest available, but it was still packed. I'd heard the rumblings from many of the people who had been left out.

After the introductions, testimony started with Dr. Griggs, who briefly described the strategic test, what we expected to happen, and what did happen. A senator cut in with a question before Griggs had finished his explanation.

"We've all had a few days to think about this, Dr. Griggs," Senator Strong said. He had a ponderous voice that matched his eyebrows. He was from New York and had long enjoyed financial contributions from Sky Lurich. "There have been all kinds of speculation about this event. Was this personage human? Was he an alien? Was he from a different dimension, or even a different time? We know what we saw. It was a male, he had long hair, and he looked like he was wearing a long garment, like a dress. Who do you say he is?"

"He appeared as part of a scientific experiment. There is no reason to suppose that there is any explanation other than scientific. We know, precisely, the types of particles he was made of because we still have the particles. We've already tested them enough to know they are the same types of particles we produced in the previous test.

"What I don't think we have any reason to assume, scientifically, is that he came from somewhere else, that he existed before our test." There were murmurs of surprise in the room.

Senator Strong's eyes narrowed, his eyebrows nearly touching in the center of his brow. "You are suggesting he came from nowhere? That during this test we were essentially creating a new being?"

"That is the only assumption we can safely make. Science gives us no reason to think otherwise."

I was thunderstruck. It was the antithesis of what I thought. Had Lurich put him up to this?

"If what you're saying is correct, then what do you think we'd be dealing with if he hadn't dissolved? Would he have had any memory? Would he have language skills?"

"He would have the same knowledge and skills as a newborn babe. He would be a new being, open to our suggestions, to our teachings, and to our culture. He would likely be, however, physically different from us, not in outward appearance, but in the molecules from which he's made. Humans are composed of basic elements, including carbon, hydrogen, oxygen, nitrogen, and others. He would be made of carbon II, hydrogen II, etc. We would find out through testing what his characteristics would be; what his DNA would look like."

"How, exactly, are you going to test him? You're assuming he'd cooperate with you sticking a needle in him?" Senator

Strong asked. There was a murmur of laughter from the crowd.

"I've been wondering what happened to him when the test stopped—whether he was injured or killed by the act of partially materializing," Senator Strong said. "Do you think he came into existence, and then ceased to exist, in a matter of seconds? We gave him birth, and then we killed him?"

"I'm not suggesting we killed him. We just failed to make him permanent."

"Hold on there, Doctor." A popular senator from Georgia, Harry Stewart, was speaking. His drawl slowed the conversation like brakes on a train. "Let us be clear. If what you suggest is true, at this moment, does this person, or being, or whatever he is, exist, or not?"

"I'm suggesting that, at this moment, he does not exist," Dr. Griggs replied. "He came from nowhere."

"I beg to differ with that notion," said Senator Strong. "I think he came from somewhere. But before we get to that, let me ask this: If what you suggest is true, and he came into existence in that moment, why was he standing there looking at you all? Why wasn't he in a fetal position on the floor?"

Laughter sounded again through the room.

"The fetal position of a newborn child results from his position in the womb—" Dr. Griggs answered.

"Well, pardon me, sir! Let me rephrase: Why wasn't he flat on his back, lying on the floor? You get my meaning, don't you? If he came from nowhere, he wouldn't be able to stand on his own, much less speak to us. If his mind were as clear as a newborn babe's, then he could provide us with no knowledge or insight, since he himself would remember nothing. I certainly hope you are wrong about that."

"Well, sir, I agree with you," said Dr. Griggs. "If he was newly created, he would have no insight into his past. However, he would be of tremendous scientific value. Suppose he doesn't grow old. Suppose he can't catch a cold, not to mention cancer. Suppose he's physically much stronger than we are . . ."

"Sounds like you think we're creating Superman," Senator Stewart interrupted. "Turns out he's a nice guy, once he learns how to talk, so are we going to create more just like him? Is it your plan to start a new race?"

"Not a new race like him; a new race for us. Suppose we can copy his DNA, or genetic code, and use it to enhance our own. Maybe we could cure disease and aging. The scientific potential is enormous."

They continued their questions with Dr. Griggs for some time. The more Charles talked, the less I liked the direction he was going. It was a great argument for proceeding with a retest—here was a benign, perfectly ignorant being upon whom we could conduct experiments. He would be the ultimate lab rat. We'd all become supermen and cure our ills with no risk whatsoever.

Eventually, they finished their questions and it was my turn to testify. By that time, I was thinking that Dr. Griggs and Sky Lurich had planned this out as their strategy of choice. I didn't like it.

Senator Strong welcomed me and started the questions. "Dr. Johnson, I'm a little surprised at Dr. Grigg's explanation, but I like it. Do you agree that this being came from nowhere?"

I doubted Senator Strong was surprised at all. He had likely discussed this entire line of questions with Lurich ahead of time. It would be easy for me to play along. But there was clearly opposition to this idea, and if they were going to get any support, it would have to come from me.

"I think we need to discuss the other logical possibilities you mentioned earlier, Senator Strong," I answered.

I saw Charles shift back in his chair. That was all the warning I was likely to get, but I wasn't nearly ready to join the party line.

"First, an extraterrestrial," I continued. "We've long searched the heavens using radio waves, spacecraft, probes, and anything else we could think of to contact intelligent life beyond Earth. This might be our first contact with a being from another planet."

"Frankly, that is still hard to believe," said Senator Strong, his eyebrows lowered. "First of all, he didn't look like an extraterrestrial. He looked like a hippie, or someone from a Christmas play."

"I agree with you, senator. We've always assumed that, when we made contact with aliens, they'd come in spaceships because that is our own primitive means of travel. But that notion is outdated. We know that no spaceship will ever travel faster than the speed of light, and the distance from us to the stars is, well, astronomical.

"Perhaps we stumbled on the technology for a wormhole," I continued. "I think that aliens are a lot more likely to come through a wormhole than in a spaceship. Our concept of what they look like is our own speculation. There is a possibility, however unlikely, that every intelligent being in the universe looks just like us."

"But where does your speculation get us?" asked the senator.

"The starting point should be the possibilities. Let's look at another: Perhaps this was a being from another scientific realm—let's say he passed through a dimensional rift—rather than from another planet."

"I'd like to address that," said Senator Stewart. "But first, let me say that your team, in developing this technology, has accomplished a very exciting thing, one that we were all looking forward to seeing developed. Congratulations, by the way. You've done a marvelous thing in stabilizing dark matter."

"Thank you, Senator."

"Now the question," Stewart said, "is whether there is any basis to believe that there could be beings in another dimension, or whether the idea of multiple dimensions is even plausible."

"Certainly, the idea is plausible," I said. "We've had years of advances in string theory. Still, the reality is that our concept of alternate dimensions is really only theoretical. If this being were from another dimension, I would expect his knowledge to far surpass ours."

"Either way," Senator Stewart said, "if this being were an alien or a being from another dimension, I'd agree he could have knowledge far superior to ours. That's why I don't trust this notion that he was created out of nothing. We have to consider the potential risks."

"Dr. Johnson, you've suggested aliens and beings from other dimensions," said Senator Strong. "Is it your testimony that you think this being was an extraterrestrial?" His voice had an edge.

I could see Dr. Griggs from the corner of my eye, watching me, his eyes narrowed.

"Actually, no. What strikes me is that his appearance was dependent on us doing something that had never been done before. We created the particle field, and he showed up in it, which suggests to me that he was already here, and the particle field simply allowed him to manifest himself. If he had the technology to come from some distant planet, or any technology which would be so enormously advanced over ours, why does his appearance require the use of our technology?"

"Then, in fact, you agree with Dr. Griggs that the mostly likely explanation is that this being came from nowhere?"

There it was. I had hoped to avoid directly confronting what Dr. Griggs said by politely reviewing other scientific possibilities. What I really thought wouldn't sound like science. I took a breath and answered. "For us as scientists, or for you as senators, we have a difficult time believing in things we can't see. The scientific evidence is limited at best. However, I do think that we need to consider the possibility that there is a very large number of unseen beings in our world, and that they may be hostile."

"Dr. Griggs made the suggestion that this being came from nowhere," said Senator Strong, "therefore, he couldn't be hostile. Even if this being were an alien, even if an enormous number of them were out there, our contact with them would change our view of everything we know. It is hard to understate how profound this would be. Would you forego the chance to make contact with them on the mere speculation that they might be hostile?"

"No."

"Even if they were hostile," the senator said, "it seems to me we've already got an answer for that. If I recall correctly, the test stopped because you designed it to shut down when it had stabilized a preset amount of dark matter. I understand you've already run tests on the matter. We know how much it weighs, what it's made of. If we want to repeat the test, all we have to do is increase the mass threshold. And if we want to preclude other beings from appearing, all we have to do is limit the threshold to the weight of one such being. Then we don't have an alien invasion, am I right?"

"Yes," I responded, but couldn't help wondering what that one being might be capable of.

Dr. Griggs' countenance was somber, like the prospects for my future.

The testimony and questions continued for hours, with

other witnesses called after me. At the end of the hearing, the members of the media were allowed to ask questions.

A woman with a media badge was the first at the microphone. "Senator Strong, do you intend to repeat the testing procedure to allow this person, whoever he is, an opportunity to return?"

"That's not something we've decided yet," the senator replied. "After this hearing, members of this committee will be meeting with the president to make our recommendations. I can tell you that we certainly want to know who this being is. We are trying to calculate the risks, but the truth is that none of us have ever seen anything like this. It will take time to digest it and make the right decision. Next question."

He pointed to another person. The man was smartly dressed in a jacket, button-down shirt, and slacks. His face was strikingly handsome. He was clean-shaven and immaculately groomed. A press badge was clipped to his pocket. He paused at the microphone for several seconds, looking at Senator Strong. His silence was uncomfortable.

"I know who he is. We should all know. We've had the writings for thousands of years. There was a war, and a powerful being was cast into the earth, with a large number of his followers. He was not a mortal. We would call it a technological war, although that doesn't fully describe it. These people were isolated on this planet and are attempting to advance. You've seen one of them for the first time. I warn you that you are not to allow him to return."

The senator raised both eyebrows. "Would you repeat that, in English? I heard you, but I have no idea what you are talking about." There were chuckles from around the room.

"You are oblivious to what is hidden in plain view. Yes, it has been masked by religion. Revelation, the book in the Bible, says a powerful being, with all his followers, was cast onto this planet thousands of years ago. Religion calls him Satan, so you think of him as mythically religious. He is not a mortal, so mortals have been free to ignore him, unseen. Now, a door has been opened and the unseen has come through, in the form of stabilized dark matter. You believe in stabilized dark matter because science has proved it. You see it as a technology, and it is. Revelation speaks of a war. You need to understand it was a technological war. Stabilizing dark matter uses a technology that will allow this mythical figure to become a physical person. If that happens, it won't matter whether you are religious or not. Such a being will bring with him the practical application of that technology, and it will lead to the destruction of mortal civilization."

That was what I had felt in my dream about Sky Lurich, a darkness, a powerful foreboding. It wasn't just me. I wasn't alone. Although, I'm glad it was this guy who was saying something and not me.

There was laughter and murmuring throughout the room.

Someone said, "You've got to be kidding me!"

Senator Strong raised his eyebrows. He nodded to the security guards. They approached the man and asked him to go with them. He didn't try to fight. He simply left the room with the guards. Maybe he was sophisticated enough to know what he said wasn't likely to be well-received.

The media deluge resumed. When it was finally over, Ronnie and I returned to the hotel the senator's office had arranged for us. The TVs in the lobby already had the cable news coverage of the strange man from the hearing. His name was Eli Matheson. The media badge was real. He was a freelance reporter who only wrote on occasion for a small newspaper in Missouri. Even his editor had no idea how he'd gotten into a congressional hearing. He'd been questioned, but the

FBI announced, within an hour, that they had released him. They said he gave no statement and immediately requested an attorney. Since he hadn't committed any crimes, there was nothing to charge him with. He didn't say a word to the cameras as the agents escorted him past the media to a waiting taxi. Only the cabbie knows where he went.

The media coverage jumped into the debate over whether we should actively attempt to retest, to allow the person we had seen to materialize fully. The hearings had gotten into the super-strength possibilities of such a being, made of stabilized dark matter, with inherently stronger qualities than our normal elements. As I watched the coverage, I wondered, along with everyone else, about the implications. Humans are infinitely vulnerable; a being formed of stabilized dark-matter elements may not be. We had tested the properties of the matter, but we didn't know how they would hold together in a being made of it. Could you chop off his arm? Would he bleed? Would his organs be the same? Would his DNA be immune to the deterioration that causes human aging? Dr. Griggs was right about one thing. We could only speculate until we did the retest.

■ ■ ■

Ronnie and I agreed to find a place to eat. We had a lot to discuss. She was the only other team member besides Griggs who had been invited to the hearings, and even though I was the team leader, I needed someone to commiserate with. It turned out it wasn't our disappearing cosmic man that I needed to commiserate about.

I tried several times to call my kids before I left for the restaurant, but they didn't answer. Eventually, my phone died. I'd forgotten the cord to charge it. A knock came at the door. I answered, thinking it was Ronnie. A man in a blue shirt with an EZ Run logo stood there. He handed me an envelope. He didn't even ask my name. No doubt he had seen my photo. I thanked him and watched him walk towards the elevator. I closed the door.

I looked at the return address on the envelope—a law firm.

I didn't have to open it; my intuitional certainty said it contained divorce papers. Why did Marie pick today, in Washington, D.C., after Eli what's-his-name's little tricks? Actually, Marie wouldn't have known what Eli was going to do, and she didn't care what the congressional committee did. Her lawyer picked when and how to serve me, and he probably had a glass jar with the air sucked out where his heart was supposed to be. I sat down and read the papers. All she wanted was the house, the cars, ten years of alimony, and my children. I felt electrocuted.

I wasn't just hurt, I was angry. My anger was at the God I believed in, for letting me lose my wife, even when I was trying my hardest. There was nothing between me and the torrent of pain.

I was still weeping when I heard a knock. I yelled, "Just a minute," blew my nose, and splashed some water in my face. This time it was Ronnie at the door.

"Is something wrong? Your eyes are puffy."

I wanted to answer, but my voice box wouldn't do its job. When I, finally, found the ability to speak, I croaked, "Marie just served me with divorce papers."

"I'm so sorry. I know what that's like."

After Ronnie's marriage ended last year, she had been quiet about her social life, at least with me. Her vague answers had stopped questions. I enjoyed working with her because she was extremely capable, but there were many things we did not agree on, particularly religion. She was an atheist.

"Perhaps you need some time alone?" she asked.

"No. Actually, being alone is the last thing I need," I told her.

We walked down to the hotel restaurant. Ronnie was wearing a white starched button-down blouse with detailing and a black skirt. Ronnie looked great, as good as I'd ever seen her. Being at dinner with her made it hard to put that from my mind. It struck me as odd that she was a colleague, but other people would not see us that way. On the other hand, I enjoyed being with her. It was a small plus sign after the huge minus sign of a divorce petition.

We took our time with the menu before we ordered, since neither of us had been to the restaurant before. Ronnie ordered red wine with her food. She had always been comfortable with conversation, but now I saw that she was equally comfortable with the silence that had settled across our small table.

"Have you ever tried to pray?" I asked.

"It's been a while," she stated.

"Prayer meant the world to me. Only now do I realize how much I relied on it. I loved God. I loved the idea of God, a perfectly loving being. He was always there for me, throughout my life," I explained.

"You loved God?" she asked. "Have you stopped?"

I looked down at the table.

"Right now, I feel anger. Tremendous anger. Shock. Betrayal," I said.

"Why?"

I looked up from the table, into her eyes. "What kind of being is he? I knew him as a loving, comforting, perfect being. Suppose you believe in the story of Abraham sacrificing Isaac. What did Abraham say to himself, standing with the knife, ready to plunge it into his son's heart at God's command?"

She shook her head and shrugged. She wasn't going to venture a guess, but I knew. I found out tonight.

"Abraham was asking God, 'Who are you? I thought I knew you, but I don't. You are telling me to do something wrong. What kind of being asks this of a man?' If we had looked in Abraham's eyes we would have seen the shock of betrayal. That's what I learned tonight."

"Marie is the one who is divorcing you," Ronnie said. "I felt the same kind of pain, the same kind of grief, and God had nothing to do with it. I loved my husband, but I knew he was like an addiction dragging me down, because he was so negative most of the time. When he finally filed for a divorce, the pain was horrible, but at the same time, I was relieved it was over."

"Marie is a flawed human," I responded. "We are all so flawed, we make so many mistakes. God has got to help us. He has got to be there for us when it is important, and marriage is important. I don't think it is my fault, or even Marie's fault. I begged for help, pleaded for help, and the more I prayed, the less I heard. It makes me so angry at God. We are kidding ourselves if we think we are in control. He could control some of this, and He doesn't. He just lets it crash around us. I grieved that my wife would threaten divorce, even before she served me papers. It's like my life, my career, everything is a failure. I am a failure."

"Oh, come on. You just led our team to stabilize dark matter. You testified before a congressional committee today. You are not a failure." Ronnie picked up her wine glass, looked at the wine, brought it to her nose to inhale the aroma of it, she took a sip. After a few seconds passed, she said, "I know you are a religious person, and I respect the way you live your religion. I could see, as we worked together, that it was helping you, making you a better person. And you are a good person."

She put down her glass, reached across the table, and squeezed my hand.

"You are one of the best people I know."

We finished our meal while we continued chatting. I enjoyed talking to her and felt some comfort when she shared with me how hard her divorce had been, and how, in some ways, it was a relief. After an hour and a half, the restaurant was still full, and our waitress was glancing at us each time she passed us.

We went back to Ronnie's room, to check the itinerary for the next day. Senator Strong's office secretary was supposed to e-mail it to us, but my phone was dead. Ronnie had a laptop.

They were planning to start again at 10:00 a.m. I wrote down the information on the hotel-provided notepad on her desk.

As I leaned over her shoulder, I noticed for the first time how close we were. I could smell her shampoo. It felt so comfortable being with her. It was so natural and wonderful that, at this moment, there was someone as amazing as her in my world.

I finished writing and sat on the edge of the chair next to the small table where her computer rested.

The entire evening, she had been professional and proper; she had been a listening friend.

She met my gaze.

She was watching me.

She wasn't kicking me out.

She wasn't looking for an excuse to get rid of me.

She was moving her heel up and down in her shoe, the way she did when she was nervous.

I put my hand on her shoulder.

She put her hand over mine and caressed it. Then she moved my hand, pulling me towards her until my lips touched hers.

CHAPTER 5

OFFERS

AFTER THE NEXT day of congressional hearings, with much debated but nothing decided, I flew back home. Ronnie and I were on different flights.

Alone in my hotel room that night, with all the lights out, I stared out through the open curtains into the darkness beyond the window pane. Marie's filing divorce papers was a betrayal, but mine was worse. It would affect my children, and how they thought of me, for a lifetime.

Never in my life had I done anything remotely as serious as having an affair. That night I recognized grief as never before. Not only was Marie divorcing me, but now she had a good reason. A man who had an affair must deal with a cargo ship full of problems, starting with the grief and shame it would bring to his wife, even if she was divorcing him. Even if he doesn't get a divorce, he'll deal for years with the pain and insecurity the affair caused his wife.

Forgiveness takes time, but how long wasn't certain. A month? A year? An eternity?

I went back to my office the next morning. We had been given orders to meet as a team and determine what it would take to ensure an environment where we could conduct a retest, if the government decided we should.

At 11:00 a.m., I was in my office when Sky Lurich called.

"Hello, Will, this is Sky Lurich. Glad I caught you in the office."

"I'm glad you did, too. Things have been hectic. What can I do for you?"

"Listen, I'm really excited about the potential production of stabilized dark matter," he said. "We are planning to move forward with everything we've got to a production phase. I'd like to discuss with you what we're doing, and frankly, I'm interested in having you join us. Please keep that confidential."

"I understand."

It seemed odd he was more excited about production than about the being who appeared—then again, this was Sky. To him, production is money.

"I want to discuss this with you in person. I'd like to fly you out to my office."

Wow.

He had me talk to his assistant to make the arrangements.

I called Ronnie to let her know I wasn't going to be able to meet with our team that afternoon.

"Lurich has invited me to fly to New York and meet with him."

"Did he say why?" she asked.

"He wants to talk about the production of stabilized dark matter," I explained.

"If he's flying you out there, he might end up offering a job."

He'd said to keep it confidential, but she'd gone right to the issue.

"Yes, he said he was interested in having me join them. But he said to keep it confidential."

"That's fine," she said. "I'll tell the others you're sick. For what it's worth, I don't trust Sky. He's been hard to deal with the whole time, rushing our schedule, demanding deadlines, ignoring safety issues. Everybody says that's how he runs everything."

"I know. I've known him a long time, but he and I don't have much in common. There was something else that happened." I told her about my dream.

"Dreams don't mean anything," she said, "and that one is really bizarre. Most people find it hard to believe in the devil, even people who are religious, never mind someone like Sky. He's always felt a little creepy to me."

"It will still be interesting to see whether his office looks the way it did in the dream."

"I'm sure it will be completely different," she said. We chatted a bit longer and then ended the call.

I went to the airport, boarded Lurich's private jet, and flew to New York. Lurich's guards patted me down, and then took me into Sky's office suite. It was huge, with a panoramic view from windows the length of the office, and, to my dismay, identical to my dream. I could see the wall that in my dream had covered the secret chamber. Sky came out from behind his desk, and we sat on leather couches looking out over the city.

"Congratulations, Will, on stabilizing dark matter. From what I hear, it was ten years of exhausting work before you finally had a breakthrough."

"Thanks. It turned out to be even bigger than we expected, when that figure appeared."

"Very true. Now let me ask you—our testing shows advanced elements corresponding to many of the earth's substances—as many as 60 elements already, some in trace amounts. What the media is calling dust was really more like silt—a variety of elements in very small particles. So, do you expect the quantities of these super elements, if we end up calling them that, to be in consistent amounts?"

"Not necessarily. Each time we run the test, we may get a different mix of elements."

"What I have in mind," Sky said, "as you've heard before in our meetings and proposals, is to find ways to harvest whichever of these super elements turn out to have the most commercial value to us. Do you think that is going to be possible?"

"We've considered for some time what it will take to gather dark matter in commercial quantities," I said. "I think it is very possible. It is also very dangerous."

"The dangers are there, yes, but we've got them under control. We'll take every precaution we need to."

"I'm not exaggerating when I say we don't know that much about what we're dealing with," I said. "Read about the cancer rates on the military personnel who were on Bikini Atoll, or the other nuclear testing sites. I think we'll be ready for commercial production in about ten years." My negativity was fueled by my sense of danger and evil, but I couldn't say that.

His lips grew thin, and his cordial conversational tone disappeared. "Will, let me be straight with you. I'm already modifying one of my research sites for this, and I'm going to throw everything I've got at it. I don't want production in ten years, I want it immediately. I've already got a contract with NSHC. I want to hire you to be part of our team. I'll triple your salary, and yes, I know exactly what you make. I'll also give you stock in the company. What I don't want is negativity or nonsense about it taking ten years. You already spent ten years getting to this point. Frankly, I don't really understand how you did it. What I hear from the university and the industry is that you're too nice a guy to run the show. You know what I'm talking about?"

"Yes, I've heard some of that talk." I knew exactly what he was talking about, and he hit a nerve. My wife was divorcing me over a similar sentiment.

"You ever watch teenage kids playing basketball? Aggression is ninety percent of the game. Offense is, 'This ball is going in that basket, and you can't do a thing to stop me from putting it there.' Defense is, 'That is my ball, and I'm taking it back.' Every time you meet someone, they size you up. I want you to change. I want aggression from you. I want to change the way you think, from scientific equations to profit potential."

"Money is not the most important consideration here," I said. "The real power is in the impact of this scientific breakthrough on humanity, and I think you know it." There are things a man like Lurich would never understand about me: why I believed in God, why I served in my church, and why I didn't aspire to aggression. I was a person of principles and belief. Except that I just had an affair. He also wouldn't understand the near certainty I felt that something would go terribly wrong if we did a retest. It might even be too late already. And I wasn't the only person who thought so. Eli Matheson, the stranger at the congressional hearing, had been clear. He said this technology would destroy our society.

"I'll tell you what I do know, Will. You're broke. All your hard work has gotten you a mortgage you can't pay, and your credit cards are nearly maxed out with a huge debt on top of that, considering your income. I had a very thorough and perfectly illegal credit check run on you. What I want from you is to have you totally committed to what we are doing. Expect long hours. I want you to lose yourself in your work."

I didn't like being around him. It had been easier in

college, when we were younger. A lot had happened since then. His company had a reputation for being ruthless. "Being lost in my work hasn't exactly helped my marriage."

"You don't have a marriage. Your wife served you with divorce papers, and you slept with Dr. Veronica Fraticelli— the very night you received the papers, in fact."

My heart stopped beating. Unfortunately, it started again.

"Oh, the look on your face! Priceless. If you are going to start sleeping around like a politician, you need to think like a politician. Have you never heard of electronic surveillance? I need you, you need the money, and I really don't think you have a better option. You will have other offers. But I promise you that you won't get a better offer than this one."

■ ■ ■

When I got back to the Phoenix airport, I dialed Ronnie's number to talk to her about it. As I was dialing, I realized I was calling Ronnie before I'd called my wife, and I tried to hang up before it rang, but didn't quite make it. I hung up anyway and waited a few seconds. I was relieved when Ronnie didn't call back.

I dialed Marie and told her about the offer. She sounded more excited than I'd heard her in months.

"How do you feel about it?" she asked.

"Sky has never been the kind of person I'd want to work for. His company is constantly in the newspapers for lawsuits and accusations. I don't feel good about it. But there is one other thing." I told her about my dream, and that his office looked exactly like it had in my dream.

"I just can't see any reason why you would have a dream like that. He can't really have a room where he tries to talk to the devil. It's just too crazy," she said.

"It was an eerie feeling though, déjà vu, like the time I was hiking in the Grand Canyon, and I came on that waterfall I felt I had seen before."

"Maybe so," she said, "but that doesn't mean the dream meant anything."

"You don't have a bad feeling about it?" I asked. During our marriage, Marie had often shown uncanny intuition, and I still trusted that, even though I didn't think she'd been making a wise choice when she filed for divorce.

"No, I don't. It sounds like a great opportunity. It's the same work you love doing, and for a lot more money. You are strong enough to maintain your own standards while working for him. He's not going to ask you to do his dirty work because he has plenty of other people who can do that. You earned this. You've accomplished something important, and Sky recognizes that."

Were other considerations clouding her normal intuition? I didn't feel comfortable asking if she would reconsider the divorce, but she might. Until she found out about Ronnie, that is. Then again, she might want me to have the job with Lurich so she could get triple the alimony.

We talked a while longer, and finally she said, "You decide, Will. I'm sure you'll do the right thing."

When we finished talking, I called Ronnie. She asked if I wanted to come to her place for dinner to talk about it. I hesitated because I didn't feel right about being with her again.

The truth was, I wanted to see Ronnie again. God probably didn't care much what I did at this point, and I wasn't sure I cared what he thought.

Ronnie had dinner ready when I got to her house, and I was hungry. She had me get some juice from the fridge, while she put the food on the table. I told her about my conversation with Sky.

"Wow," she said. "He doesn't mess around, does he?

Three times the salary. At least he's frank about his expectations. But I don't see how you could ever work for him."

"You think I'm not up to it?"

"No! That's not it at all! It's because I think you're better
than that. How long have we worked together—ten years?
You are completely predictable."

I started to protest, but she interrupted me.

"I mean that in a good way. It's one of the reasons I've
always admired you, even when we disagree. It's not just
respect for you having ideas that led to breakthroughs with
dark matter. It's the kind of person you are. You are predicta-
bly serious about serving people, about pursuing what's good
for humanity. You are so unlike Sky Lurich in every good way
I can think of."

While we were eating, she got up to open a window. I felt
a slight breeze, the pleasant stirring of night air.

"To tell you the truth, even though you are predictable, I
don't think I've fully figured you out," she said. "I've seen the
religious faith you have. I just don't understand why you
believe it. Science has so completely refuted religion."

I smiled, then chuckled. "I don't think you have any
concept of how wrong that is. Science is showing us who God
is in ways that were incomprehensible a few decades ago. In
fact, I've had a feeling about that. We are at a zenith in science
and technology, at the pinnacle of human society, and
America is the ultimate country. This is the very time when
God is showing us everything—not just how this earth
functions, but how the entire universe functions."

Even as I said it, I felt a pang of my own hypocrisy. Here
I was, talking to her about religion, after what she and I had
done.

"That makes no sense," she said. "We have the cosmic
microwave background recording the first moments after the

Big Bang. We know about the formation of suns, and how the destruction of suns provided heavier elements and metals. We know how gravity acted to form our planet from those metals. We have four billion years of earth's history, and evolution. Religious people are trying to say God created the earth in seven days. That isn't what the evidence shows."

"I've never felt comfortable holding God to our interpretations," I said. "To me, God is eternal because he existed before the Big Bang."

"There was nothing before the Big Bang…" she countered, then stopped and added, "If you are saying 'matter' or 'God' existed before the Big Bang, that's impossible. Everything, including God, would have been destroyed in the Big Bang."

"God is eternal because he has always existed as a mind," I said. "A mind is unaffected by the existence or destruction of physical matter. I'm suggesting he calculated the expansion of the universe and put in place the forces we know about to make everything happen—gravity, electromagnetic, strong, and weak nuclear forces. He used them to create suns, then planets. He left all the data of the microwave background and light from the stars for us on purpose. He was leaving us a record of what he did. He wanted us to know."

"Faith has nothing to do with science for a reason," she said. She got up and got two glasses of ice water and handed one to me. "The Bible doesn't match up to scientific realities. The story of the ark, for example, is utterly unjustifiable."

"Science and religion don't have to be incompatible. Noah was a person. He built an ark. He put animals in it. Believers don't need to assume more than that. A scientist who believes that miracles are a type of magic has already lost the war. If God were a scientist, how would he create a world? Or the species of life? There is good reason to think that Darwin discovered exactly what God wanted him to discover."

She laughed. "Like what?" she asked. "God wanted Darwin to show us that we don't need God?"

"God wanted Darwin to show us the process of natural selection. Now we see that there is another step beyond that, because we've discovered DNA modification. We see how higher levels of species could be biologically engineered from lower levels of species. There is a scientific way to do it, and God wants us to know. It doesn't mean we are descended from apes, let alone amoebas. It means the species are technological, and God had to develop them. DNA modification is a technology, a tool. Natural selection is also a tool; both were part of God's research and development billions of years ago, after he created the first planet like ours."

She narrowed her eyes.

"I think, in particle physics, we are just barely beginning to comprehend how strange our existence really is," I said. "Without the Higgs particles, matter wouldn't have mass, and we would all disappear, right? People don't have the faintest inkling of how complex religion becomes, if you view it in the light of what science shows us."

"It's all just in your mind," she said.

"Okay, what about dark matter?" I asked. "Two thousand years ago, the Bible stated that there were people who were spirits; there were people who were mortals; and there were people who were resurrected. Now, finally, science has figured out that eighty percent of the matter in the universe isn't physical matter made of atoms and molecules. That isn't unnecessary speculation, it is fact. It means that eighty percent of the universe may include spirits and resurrected beings who are very real, but who are not made of atoms and molecules. Religion was ahead of its time. Religion says the Ark of the Covenant was used to see the throne of God. What if it turned out that was scientific, a type of technology?"

She didn't answer. We finished eating, and I cleared away the dishes.

I looked under the counter for dish soap, and found it, making a point not to ask her. She watched me. Perhaps she was wondering if I were doing the dishes to impress her, but more likely, she knew that I liked working and helping better than sitting and watching. We had stabilized dark matter, and that took work.

"Well Dr. Johnson," she emphasized the word 'doctor', the corner of her mouth lifted in a smile, "off the record, who do you think the being in the dust was?"

"Based on science, I have no idea. Based on religion, it would be a spirit who was not given a body on earth."

"Like who?"

"A devil. There are supposed to be billions of spirits on this planet who are angels to the devil."

"Angels? Why would you call a devil an angel?"

"It's in the book of Revelation, the one that guy, Eli Matheson, talked about. The concept is that they once followed God, and were as the angels, and were cast out. But you have to understand that there are different types of angels."

"You mean seraphim and cherubim, and all that?"

I lowered my jaw in mock surprise. "Hey, how did you come up with those? I didn't know you read the Bible?"

"I wasn't always an atheist. We've talked about these possibilities before, because you wondered if those might be related to angels or the devil. It made you sound a little crazy." She looked at me coyly as she said it, so I wouldn't take it personally.

"I've looked more into what the Bible says about angels, though," she said, "after all that's been happening."

"Fantastic. Although those aren't the types I'm talking about. It goes back to what I said a few minutes ago. Some angels are in spirit form, meaning a mortal couldn't touch them. Others are resurrected beings, and you could. That comes from religion, when Christ was resurrected."

Her eyebrows narrowed. "You really believe in this, don't you? You, a scientist, believing in angels and devils. It's too much for me, though. I don't buy it."

"Don't you ever wonder where dumb ideas come from? I don't just mean drying-your-cat-in-a-microwave dumb, I mean life-altering dumb. For example, if you are violent and suicidal man, why would you shoot your wife, and maybe even your children, before you commit suicide? Why not just shoot yourself? The same is true for the mass murderers and shooters, on a bigger scale."

She was silent. She looked towards the dark window. Finally, she spoke, "I had a friend whose husband was violent. He was just filled with hate. Fortunately, he didn't kill anyone."

"As humans, we come up with a lot of stupid ideas on our own," I said. "But those strong compulsions and addictions are more than just us. There is addiction, with a physical counterpart. But much of it is a force of will, an evil presence, a malevolence that goes beyond our own mortal thoughts. To me it is obvious. We see evidence everywhere, every day. Those negative thoughts, 'I hate my job,' 'I hate my life,' or 'Why does everything in life have to be so hard?'"

"That reminds me of my ex-husband. Of course, he struggled with depression."

"Yes, and it isn't just people who are diagnosed as depressed. It affects all of us. Most of us go through life with a sense that life is of enormous value. Men who are starting shooting rampages have become convinced life has very little value, so much so that they will shoot children in elementary schools. They are mentally ill, yes, but it isn't random. They have been persuaded to believe in an idea. We all spend our time arguing. What if it turns out Satan is actually made from a different technology, a person made of something besides atoms, but just as real as we are?"

We talked for a long time. Finally, I told her I needed to go home. She rested her hand on mine. She gently took me in an embrace, and with silent lips invited me to stay.

■ ■ ■

The next morning, I called Sky's office and left a message declining his offer. I should have told Marie, but I didn't feel like it.

At eleven that morning, I received a call from Marie. She wanted me to have lunch with her at The Bistro. Even more surprising, she offered to pay.

The Bistro occupied a good part of the street level of the Wyndlas Hotel. Marie was already at a table near the window. She was wearing a new blouse, a sheer blue fabric over a beige shirt. She wore beige jeans. Her hair and nails were done, and she was wearing heels. This wasn't unusual for her, but she was making a point to me: she still looked great.

She smiled as I approached the table, seemingly relaxed, as we exchanged greetings. We talked about normal things: The children were at school, Sam had overslept yesterday, and she had a dentist appointment set up for them on Monday. It was easy to fall into our normal conversation.

I had baby-back ribs, she had a salad. She encouraged me to order dessert, and then she wanted to share it with me.

She was in the most pleasant mood I'd seen her in since— well, since before she'd kicked me out of the house. She insisted that I let her pay for the meal.

Finally, she looked at me and whispered, "I have a room upstairs."

I gave her a smile, but I was dying inside. As we got up from the table, she came close to me and slid her arm around my waist. We left the restaurant and walked towards the elevators. I could see the hope in her eyes, and I was trying to avoid doing anything to shatter it. My mind was numb. The truth? The truth was, I loved this woman. It was marvelous to see her this happy. As we rode the elevator up, I thought of how much I had wanted to heal our marriage—if only....

When we got inside the room, I finally pulled away from her. She looked hurt, but it appeared she was expecting some resistance.

"Look," she said. "I know I've been unkind. But you've been saying you wanted to come home. You can."

"One week you're serving me divorce papers, and the next week we're here?"

The words felt terrible coming out of my mouth. I didn't want to talk about divorce papers. They were the second thing that came to mind, and the first I couldn't bring myself to talk about.

She looked wounded. The happiness and hope were slipping from her eyes.

Her voice softened.

"I never wanted to hurt you. I just wanted you to change. I never wanted a divorce. We couldn't go on the way we were, and it would be so easy for things to change. In fact, they already have. I was trying to help you stand up for yourself. We can make this work. I love you."

I saw pain and pleading in her big brown eyes, and I never loved her more than in that moment.

The idea came into my mind to tell her the truth, right here and right now: I had an affair with Ronnie. But I love you, and there is nothing I want more than to be back with you, and my children, in our home. I'll give anything to do that. But you are going to have to forgive me to make that happen, and it will take some time. It can't happen today.

I struggled to say it. I searched for better words, but I found none. I had always thought that if I ever was in this position that I would just tell the truth. Had I changed? Had being with Ronnie compromised me enough for me to lie now?

I told her.

I watched her eyes and felt my insides cringe.

She didn't scream or shout; she crumpled on the bed and began to weep.

■ ■ ■

I walked out. I went downstairs to my motorcycle. I drove like a maniac, towards nowhere, in a city with a lot of traffic. There was a fury inside me that I shouldn't have allowed, but I embraced it.

I got stuck behind a slow-moving vehicle again, another snowbird. The other lane had an old pickup overflowing with palm fronds and yard waste. Once I got past them, I went that much faster.

It was not a great time for me to be driving around snowbirds. Sometimes snowbirds make driving errors. Sometimes they can't see the motorcycle weaving through traffic at seventy miles an hour in a forty-five zone, so they think they have time to make the left turn on the yellow light. A million times I'd played out in my mind how it would be to lay down my motorcycle, to kick free of it, or to swerve and avoid a collision entirely. Unfortunately, when I slammed my foot down on the brake, I heard an odd pop, like something had come loose, and the pedal went all the way down. The same thing happened with the hand brake. I didn't have time to do anything else. I just rammed unceremoniously into the side of the snowbird's sedan.

CHAPTER 6

HEAVEN OR HELL

DARKNESS. THERE WAS an odd buzzing, and the darkness. The buzzing was distantly familiar. I was alone. Nothing mattered. Was I dreaming? How did I get here? What time was it? Then I remembered. That buzzing. Once when I was a small child, I fell off a merry-go-round and smacked my head on the ground. I woke up on the couch at our house, with my Mom pressing a cool, moist cloth to my forehead. That's where I'd felt that buzzing before. That wasn't the only time. Whenever I had a serious injury or pain as a child, that buzzing would be there, comforting me. I hadn't felt it in years, though, not since I had grown up. There was something familiar about the darkness, even more distant than my childhood memories, but I couldn't remember why.

I saw a light in the darkness. It looked distant. I wanted to see it better. I seemed to be moving towards it. I wanted to be in the light, out of the darkness. When I reached the end of the tunnel, I moved into the light. There was peace, calm, and love in the light, and something else—data. Information.

The information was light and love. I felt the love of my mother, and my brother, Brett, and then the love of every person I ever met. It seemed as if every moment of my life came back to me, a flood of data brought to my conscious thoughts. But it wasn't my conscious thoughts, or my mortal body, it was just my mind, my own thoughts. This was technology, I thought. This was a recording of my life, which had always been in me, and now, without physical, mortal inhibition, it all returned to me, and this light was allowing it to come back to me, to make it accessible. There was the good, and the bad, from taking candy from a store when I was six years old, to being in Ronnie's arms. Religions and arguments faded; baptism, grace, all opinions became irrelevant. Race was a gift, a beautiful diversity of appearance and culture, with no reason for hatred; everything seemed healed. I had no sense of time, just extensive, universal understanding and peace.

Though I saw my adultery with everything else, it was with understanding, with simple reality, not condemnation. This was not a moment of judgment. This was not God. This was not an omnipotent, terrible judge. To me, as a scientist, the light had the objectivity of science, showing me the practical aspects of mortality.

Looking at my life, my wife was a highlight. From the time we met, to raising our children when they were small, there was joy with Marie. So many things we shared. There was remorse, misunderstanding, and loss, and my affair.

The question I felt, without hearing, as I perceived my mortal life as a whole, was whether my mortal life was valuable to me? Did I want to participate in the experiment of life and afterlife? It wasn't about judgment, it was all about experience. The overwhelming, humbling answer was that all my life's experiences were very precious to me. This I understood in every part of my mind.

I thought, "Am I going back?"

The answer was a feeling, not a voice, and I understood that I was not going back, not as a mortal. I was going to experience what all people do, as ex-mortals, and I would know soon enough.

I moved forward, surrounded by light, but everything was distorted, until gradually it things came into focus.

I was in the middle of an intersection not far from my house, back in the mortal, physical world.

A woman stood before me, extraordinarily beautiful. Her shoulder-length brown hair was swept away from her face, as if by the wind. She wore an exquisite white robe. Why was she standing in the middle of the intersection?

"Oh, I'm so sorry," she said. She gazed towards something on the ground. With a shock I realized it was me. Or at least, what was left of me. My mortal body lay prone on the pavement, my forehead bloody from the impact of the motorcycle crash. I was either dreaming, or I was dead. I felt like I should be nauseous, but all I felt was the buzzing in my head. It made it difficult to think.

"It's a little bit of a shock when you're new here, I know," she said.

"My head is buzzing. Something doesn't seem quite right." You die, and there is a beautiful woman waiting. Heaven certainly should have women greeters, if this was heaven. Heaven and hell happen after you die. What was I doing at a mortal intersection?

"Anyway, my name is Leilani, and I'm from the Association of United Religions."

"Nice to meet you," I said, absently.

I didn't feel right. Maybe I was in some kind of shock. Wrecking my motorcycle didn't seem like any big deal right now, and I couldn't remember anything before the crash. The buzzing. Dying in a motorcycle crash is huge. Why did the buzzing say it was okay? What day was it? The mortal street and buildings around me were still there. I could see the cars stopping and the shock on the people's faces, the mortals. Everything looked the same, except for this woman in a robe. Maybe this wasn't heaven. Maybe we were still on earth.

"I always thought when you died, your family members were supposed to come and meet you."

"They probably didn't know you were going to die. It's not like you died of an illness, where they would know it was coming. Maybe it wasn't your time."

How could it not be my time?

I was about to ask, when she continued: "Well, I know it might be a little soon for you to think about, but I'd like to invite you to our orientation for newcomers. We hold it at a nearby church." She told me where the church was.

That was hilarious. "So, you go out to hospitals and fatal accidents and invite all the newcomers to show up, is that it?" I laughed. My mind was in a haze. I shook my head, but it wouldn't clear.

She smiled but did not reply, and suddenly I realized that was probably exactly what they did.

"I'd love to go," I said. If this nice lady was going to be there, I should certainly go, too. The thought seemed blurred. "When is it?"

"The next meeting will be at 8:30 this evening."

"Okay, but it isn't like I have my watch. In fact, I think it got smashed...," I said, glancing towards my mangled motorcycle.

"It's pretty easy to find out what time it is. That paramedic has a watch, for instance. Or check the clock in that car going by."

How was I supposed to look at the clock in a car that was going by?

"Actually, I think I need to go check on my wife and

children—or at least my children." My children. The buzzing was fading, and now it occurred to me that my children had lost their father. I felt emotion welling up inside me. The haze started to lift. Oh, yes, my children. They were going to find out I'd died in a motorcycle crash. I didn't know how I could bear to see their faces when they found out. My throat felt tight—no, it wasn't my throat, it was something else. Something inside. I was feeling the anxiety that I used to associate with my throat feeling tight, but I felt nothing physical, only the anxiety itself. I thought of Marie, and I felt my head twitch as an electric shiver went through me. Something terrible had happened with Marie. What was it? A nightmare flashed in my mind, but it couldn't be true: an hour ago I was with her, and she wanted to reconcile everything; no doubt she had glimpsed the brightest future we had ever imagined, with our bills paid and time together, raising our children, only to find out instead that I had . . . How was Marie going to take this? What would it do to her? What had *I* done to her? I told her I had an affair, but maybe I shouldn't have. Ronnie wouldn't tell her, not now that I was dead, and maybe Marie would have been better off never knowing. I hadn't known how important that moment was—but then, who would really think they were going to die in the next hour? It was best I had told her; if it were me, I'd want to know the truth. I felt anguish boiling up inside me, ready to overflow in a burst of hot tears, and desperately hoped this vague recollection was a dream, part of the haze . . .

I heard Leilani say, "Now I feel terrible. I should have realized you have children."

I looked up and was surprised to see tears on her cheeks.

I swallowed my emotion and wiped my own cheeks with my fingers. I moved to wipe them on my pants, and then stopped. I too was wearing a white robe.

I took a closer look at woman in front of me. She didn't look like a ghost—she was simply a person in a white robe. The buzzing had made me forget to introduce myself to this Leilani, whoever she was, so I held out my hand and said, "I'm Will. Will Johnson." She shook my hand, and I could feel her hand in mine. It was different from a physical handshake, though: I felt only a sense of pressure, like the feeling you have after the dentist numbs your jaw with a shot—if you pinch the skin on your cheek you can feel the sense of pressure, but no pain. While things around me appeared the same, they didn't feel the same.

Leilani glanced over my shoulder and raised her eyebrows. "Oh, my," she said.

I turned and saw about forty people in white robes, both male and female, in a V formation flying towards us twenty feet off the ground. They closed a hundred-yard distance in seconds. They were standing straight up, with no indication of any wind resistance. They were all staring at me with a strange intensity that left me feeling like my fly was unzipped. I instinctively glanced down and realized the white robe I was wearing had no zipper.

The person at the front of the V stopped ten feet from me. He was athletic even in a robe, and his immaculate black hair showed that his barber knew what he was doing—if they had barbers here. "I'm Zinc, and I serve Azzoloft," he said. "He wishes to see you."

His voice was commanding. I felt dread.

"Who is Azzoloft?" I looked at Leilani.

Leilani stepped forward to stand at my side. "Leave him alone," she commanded.

Zinc smiled, his eyes glinting. He raised his right hand and motioned with his fingertips, and four men in white robes moved between me and Leilani, facing her in a row, shoulder to shoulder.

"Do you feel that you have the power or means to frustrate our purpose?" Zinc smirked at Leilani.

Leilani's lips tightened, and her eyes narrowed, but she didn't answer.

"I didn't think so." Zinc motioned again, and all the people flew towards me, swirling about me like a vortex, a blur as they took their positions. In an instant, I was surrounded by a sphere of bodies, like a huge white whiffle ball, all facing me. Their arms and legs were intertwined to form a complete barrier.

Panic arose in my chest. Why would they want to surround me? I began grabbing at arms and legs, kicking and pushing between the people, in a space between one person's shoulder and another person's foot. It didn't work. The ball of figures rose, and I rose with it, though I felt no gravity. I kicked off one side of the sphere towards the other and tried again, with no luck.

Finally, I moved over towards Zinc, who was part of the barrier, and swung my fist, hoping I would smash his nose all over his face. As I swung, he didn't flinch. He smiled instead. The moment my fist touched his nose, it stopped, with no impact, no satisfying crunch, and no howls of pain from my captor.

We were moving through the air headed northwest, hundreds of feet above the ground. I felt no pull of gravity. I could see where we were going through the gaps between robed thugs. They didn't speak to me, but I could feel their hostility, like a pack of large, muscular dogs cornering an intruder.

"So where are we headed?" I asked. I looked around at

them. They were all adults, but ageless in the appearance of young adulthood. Most wouldn't meet my gaze; those who did had eyes filled with disdain.

Annoyed that they didn't answer, I tried again: "How is Azzoloft these days?" I was just mouthing off, since I had never heard of anyone named Azzoloft.

"You'll know soon enough, you larvae-filled corpse," said Zinc.

"Hey! Why the animosity?" I asked.

"I have animosity because I know what a filthy mortal you used to be. Do you know why mortals take a bath every day? It's because they are such an inferior race of beings that merely existing for twenty-four hours causes them to stink. All their waste *excretions.* They are riddled with filth, disease, and decay. Do you think I'd appreciate such foul and vile things, or rather, that they'd disgust me?"

This guy was something else. I wasn't even in my mortal body anymore.

He continued forward in hostile silence. The trip was actually pretty short; we didn't even leave town. I could see we were approaching the grounds of the mortals' Camelback Passage Resort. Great. I loved that resort. I wouldn't mind playing a round of golf or taking a dip in a pool. Too bad I didn't have my swimming suit—on the other hand, it might look silly if I wore it over my robe.

As we approached the resort, I figured I'd have a chance to make a break for it. Seeing Azzoloft, whoever he was, didn't seem like such a good idea. A month ago, it would have been fine, no worries. But the timing was bad for all this, after I had slept with Ronnie. I hadn't repented. It was too late now—I was going to hell.

I'd had a bad feeling about Azzoloft for the last few minutes now, no doubt due to Zinc and his throng. I could see we were approaching a large building, and it looked like we were going to run straight into it. We were obviously moving too fast to stop. I moved my arms in front of my face in a defensive posture and watched the people in front of me disappearing right through the wall. In an instant, I was passing through the wall, as well...so fast, it was just a blur. I felt nothing, but we were inside the building now.

I was looking for my chance to bolt, and, sure enough, my captors started to move apart so I could get through. I pushed my way forward. What I saw before me as I tried to escape stunned me: I was in a tunnel, fifteen feet high, formed by people in white robes, all staring intensely at me. I stopped, gawking. Derisive laughter rippled up and down the tunnel. I looked behind me, and I could see they had closed in on me, a sea of white-robed bodies. I had nowhere to go but forward.

"Come along now," said Zinc. He had moved to be by my side. "We don't want to keep Azzoloft waiting."

Yes, I did. That's exactly what I wanted.

I moved forward in the tunnel of white-robed bodies with Zinc, filled with a dread like I'd never felt before. I felt like I was marching to my own execution. Every person forming the tunnel was staring at me. As we advanced, I heard a bizarre noise behind me, a rhythmic clicking. I looked back and saw the people behind me were opening their mouths and snapping their jaws together, making a clicking noise with their teeth. It had a maddening intensity. Moment by moment it seemed louder. I was entranced in the rhythm, hypnotized and paralyzed. They were closing in behind me, like a thousand rats coming down a tunnel to eat me. Was I losing my mind? I glanced down to see if my knees were shaking, and when I looked back up their mouths were gaping in laughter and derision.

I moved forward again and rounded a curve in the tunnel of people. The tunnel expanded ahead of me and opened up.

The resort is popular for conferences and has a large ornate conference room. I'd been to a physics conference there once before, so I recognized it. The physical surroundings were the same as mortals saw. A man was standing above the stage, his robe white, his shoulder-length hair dark and flowing, his features sharp and handsome, his bearing as regal as an emperor, shining momentarily with an unreal light that set him apart from everyone else. He had hundreds of people in white robes filling the space throughout the hall, around the walls and lofty ceiling, all showing remarkable reverence and awe, and cutting off any thought of escape. He looked familiar to me, but I didn't know why.

Zinc spoke. "Here is Will Johnson, as you requested, Master."

I didn't like the fact that he knew my name without asking.

Azzoloft raised a hand with affected graciousness. "Dr. Johnson, thank you for coming. I hope my friends did not disturb you too much?"

"No sir. They were fine." I gave Zinc a sickly smile. Why was he addressing me as 'doctor'? What difference did my college degrees make after death?

"Do you know why you are here, Will?" Azzoloft's look was musing, inquisitive.

I opened and shut my mouth several times. Every eye was on me, and those intense stares . . . I looked down at the little hairs on my toes. Finally, I spoke in the silent air of the hostile room. "Was it the adultery?"

Every person in the room burst out in uproarious laughter. Azzoloft laughed loudly, mockingly. Zinc's laughter was contained; belly chuckles, really. The laughter seemed to last for several minutes, and Azzoloft stood there, watching me and chuckling, until the laughter finally stopped.

"My friends," he said, "Will seems to be laboring under the mistaken belief that I," he paused to keep from laughing, "...that I am the devil." Laughter pealed again, resonating around us. "And he thinks he's been sent to hell for committing adultery!" Azzoloft battled to suppress his laughter, his chest shuddering, and lost.

Finally, the laughter died down again. "You'll be pleased to know, Will, that nobody goes to hell these days, especially not for adultery. The world is far too sophisticated for that." He took several steps and gestured towards his followers. "As my friends here all know, on occasion I find a post-mortal that I wish to speak to, and I have them brought to me. It is very unusual for me to invite them immediately after they die, which is probably the cause of your little, uh, misunderstanding.

"But you are different. I've been waiting for you. It took some persuasion to get you here. Do you recognize me?"

I looked at him more closely. He did seem very familiar. And then I understood.

It was him. The being from our test.

I was dumbfounded. "Who are you?"

"We are the Zolians, and this earth is our planet."

I raised my eyebrows. I thought the earth belonged to mortals.

"Yes, you heard me right. Mortals may think they own it, but the planet isn't theirs, its mine. This planet was once pristine and beautiful, our great jewel. We lived here, before any humans, as a great society, in perfect order and obedience. The earth is now befouled and polluted. There is haze in the air, poison in the rivers, and cities are in decay. Why is that?"

Why ask me? The answer seemed too obvious. "Humans have polluted the planet."

"Do you think we appreciate it?"

Why was he asking me? "No."

"What should we do about it?"

"I don't know." Mortals didn't know these people existed. I didn't know who they were, or how they got here if they hadn't been mortals. It was pretty obvious they hadn't stopped humans from polluting yet, so maybe they couldn't do anything about it.

"Oh, but you do know! You are lying to me, because you don't want to come out and say it. We should put a stop to it! In a few thousand years without humans, it will be pristine once more.

"It has been written that the earth will be cleansed, and so it shall. You have entered our world, even as you exited your miserable mortal existence, at a most remarkable time. We honor you today for leading the team that stabilized dark matter, as you call it." He reached out to his followers, his hand open, and they bowed towards me for a moment, every single one of them. Zinc was staring icily as he bowed. Azzoloft did not bow.

I nodded to them in return, out of courtesy and habit, but I was wary that he had just called me a liar and was calling my mortal existence miserable.

He looked around at the gathering of followers and reached out his arms to them. He closed his eyes. A light began to gather around him. It was as if particles of light were flowing toward him. He increased in brightness, and his followers appeared to dim, if only by contrast, until Azzoloft shined with a brilliant light. His eyes flicked open, and the surreal terror returned from my dream of Sky Lurich, except that I was not dreaming now. He gazed upon his followers intensely. As he opened his eyes, I felt an aching sense of dread, as though something were terribly wrong. His voice was powerful and eerie as he spoke, as if magnified and modified by electronic means, though I couldn't see any equipment. "My friends," he stated, "there has never been such a time as this. The things to come will fulfill all that has been spoken in ancient councils. All things will be subject unto me."

His followers moved into a prone position towards him, as if in worship.

He turned to me, and I shrank from his light as his eyes pierced me, so I could neither move nor speak. "In return for what you have done, albeit you did it unknowingly, I am offering you a chance to join us, voluntarily. In the coming days, mortals will choose sides, to be with us, or against us. The mortals who, like you, have died, and are among us now, will not be given such a choice. Most of them have already accepted an offer they can't refuse, but you? You will choose." With that, the shining around him ceased. His followers each returned to a standing position.

I didn't know what he was talking about. What offer had the others like me accepted? Right now, my choice would be to get as far away from him as possible. I was in no position to ask questions.

"The remainder of what I need to discuss with you doesn't concern all of my friends here," Azzoloft said. All his followers immediately disappeared.

It was like magic, and I didn't believe in magic.

"Why don't you and I go for a walk out on the grounds?" Azzoloft went straight to the back wall and passed through it. I walked to the wall, trying to keep up, but I didn't know how to get through. I reached out to touch the wall, and my hand disappeared into it. I felt nothing. I pushed my arm through,

81

and it also disappeared. Finally, I took an instinctive breath, like I was going underwater, and tried to step through the wall. I was wondering what the inside of the wall looked like. Once I was there, I felt silly. It was too dark inside the wall to see anything.

I emerged from the wall and followed Azzoloft out through the back wall of another room and onto the gorgeous lawn and grounds of the resort. In a strange way, I was elated to be able to meet the being from the dust. Or maybe I was elated because I wasn't going to burn in hell. But what had he meant by 'waiting for me?' Why were his followers so obnoxious?

"Did you know I own this resort?" he said.

"Do you, sir?"

"Of course. Do you know who has the deed to every mortal building in the world?"

"A really rich guy in China?" I suggested.

"No, Will. Don't you know what happens to an edifice when its owner dies? It is still there. But it isn't his anymore. In reality, it never was his. It is and always has been mine. Every great cathedral, palace, and government hall ever built in this world was constructed for me."

"Then why did you say mortals are polluting the earth?"

"They could build without the pollution. There are better ways to run things."

"Which brings us to several questions you have in your mind, some of which are worth answering. First, you are wondering who I am, and perhaps you are wondering where God is.

"I'll save you from asking and tell you plainly. Of course there is a God. He is a being ancient in wisdom, and yet more modern than all the fashions and science of the world. He is indeed omniscient. He owns all things. He is the only God this world will ever need. Do you know how I know God?"

"No, sir."

"I am going to share with you one of my people's truths," he said, "something that many post-mortals fail to understand. I know God because I am God. I was the first being on this planet. I own it by rights of discovery, and of conquest. This earth is what it is because of me. Every mortal who ever walked upon it is here to serve me. I own every building and every particle of it. During your mortal life you desired to see angels, and you thought when you died that you would meet them. And of course, you did. I sent my angels to bring you to me today. These followers of mine are angels, but not in the religious sense. This earth was formed by evolution. Humans were formed by evolution. But Zolians were not."

I felt my mouth slightly open as I looked at him. I saw a flicker of wrath in his eyes. I felt cold and clammy inside, emotionally.

"If you are God, is there a devil?" I asked. "I mean, there was a whole lot of laughing a few minutes ago when I mistook you for him."

"Of course there is no devil! Do you have any idea how preposterous the notion of a devil is? You can search the world over. You'll never see big caverns where the devils reside. You'll never see tridents, cloven hooves, horns or tails. Can you believe mortals are really that asinine? How can any of them possibly believe in a lake of everlasting torment, of fire and brimstone? It is such nonsense!" He paused, his face pensive. "It amazes me that mortals can believe in such outlandish fairy tales."

I thought of the figure of the devil in my dream, with its horns and tail. This being could not be God. I'd never seen God, but I knew how it felt to be near him. This was a being of fear, not a being of love. Science appeals to me with precision of thought and logic, but my religion gave me a constant sense that there is more out there, a light shining through the universe that is beyond the measures of science. My dream had shown me that there is darkness, danger, and very real reason to fear. Something was wrong here. The afterlife was not what I expected. Not what anybody would have expected, after millennia of being taught about heaven and hell. Why were there real people here? Azzoloft could call them what he wanted, but that didn't make them angels. Where did all these people come from?

I started looking around at the lush landscaping of the resort and noticed there were none of Azzoloft's guards in sight. I felt a very strong urge to fly away as fast as I could, to get away and never see him again. Would he send someone after me, or let me go?

He broke his silence before I could make up my mind. "Why is it that every person on Earth is even now not a scientist, rather than a believer in nonsensical mythology? There is no mortal on this planet who doesn't believe in nuclear explosions! They all believe because they have seen. They should all know how the earth got here, shouldn't they? Evolution and natural selection. Fourteen billion years since the Big Bang. Every thinking human now sees the great truths that science has revealed. And yet, Will, astoundingly, there are still multitudes who believe in Adam and Eve and a creation! How can you believe in nuclear explosions but not in evolution? Don't they understand the mapping of the genome provides incontrovertible proof of it? Do the believers now rush out en masse to proclaim the genius of Darwin? No. They will not believe the truth even when it is proved beyond any doubt."

Who was this Azzoloft, and what did he want with me? I needed to find a way to escape, but I was afraid. Being around him made me feel dirty.

"There is another question in your mind," he said. "You want to know what I want from you."

"Yes," I said. Was he reading my mind?

He faced me directly and looked straight into my eyes. His eyes glinted. "You saw a face in the sand, and you thought it was an alien; some being from another galaxy. You and the world were so very much mistaken. I am intimately closer to you than you realize. But you, of all people, should have known there was more to it. I expect great things from you, greater than that which you have already accomplished."

"Perhaps you will tell me then, sir, what your purpose was in appearing there? Are you trying to change your form? Would that even be permanent?"

"Do you really believe I would tell you unless it suited my purpose?" he asked. "Let me explain what I have in mind. Mortals have been losing control of their world as they gain information and technology. This has accelerated over the past century. You caused a triggering event, which will change everything. By stabilizing dark matter, as you call it, you opened a door. Events are going to happen quickly. I invite you to join me, and I expect your loyalty. I will have you speak to my followers. My followers will also be keeping track of you. I expect you will yet be useful to me."

I wanted to ask what he would do to me if I refused, if I wanted nothing to do with him, but I couldn't bring myself to do it. I remembered the feeling of dread and terror from the night I was at the lab alone, and felt it returning to me now. A power had been unleashed, and I sensed it in Azzoloft.

"Tomorrow I'll assign one of my followers to assist you in learning more about me and my people, the Zolians. I think I'll use Blitzer. Blitzer should do nicely. Be here at nine o'clock sharp to meet him." He paused. "And, Will, don't be late. I don't like it when people are late."

CHAPTER 7

POLICE NOTIFICATION

I LEFT THE Camelback Passage Resort on foot after Azzoloft dismissed me. Maybe the Zolians knew how to fly, but I didn't. After years of living in the East Valley, I knew how to get there from Phoenix. It was a long distance, unfortunately—about 20 miles, even though I never left the city. In Phoenix, like most metropolitan areas, the only thing marking city limits is a welcome sign.

Once I was off the resort grounds, I jogged down the street. Jogging seemed normal, except that I couldn't feel my feet hitting the pavement. I kept thinking about Marie and the children. This would be the worst day of their lives, at least for the children. For Marie too, I supposed. What a horrible time for me to die. Would she hate me worse, or love me more—or maybe a lot of both? My family was going to be getting a visit from the police, telling them I died in a motorcycle crash, and I wanted to be there.

When I got to Thomas Road heading east, I broke into a run down the sidewalk. There were a lot of mortal cars. It was strange to be in the middle of a mortal world, but none of them could even see me. What a bizarre thing, to still be here, in a mortal world, but to be invisible. I ran effortlessly. There was no muscle fatigue, no cramps, nothing to slow me down. But even at this rate, it was 20 miles back to Phoenix. How long would it take the police to get to my house and tell Marie of my death? Would she even be there? I reached the first cross street. The light was red, and there was a steady stream of cars, so I waited on the corner, uncertain what would happen if I stepped in front of them.

When the light was green, I started running again. As I ran, I wondered if I could speed up by jumping, like a long jump. I tried it, and I went about as far as I would have as a mortal. It didn't speed me up at all.

I continued running. I passed a park and saw a man in a white robe doing the backstroke in a fountain. The fountain was only about ten meters in diameter, so he was going around the fountain in a circle. He wasn't splashing in any water, nor was he wet. He appeared to be pantomiming swimming. He stopped and looked at me.

"Excuse me, sir," I said.

He smiled.

"What are you doing?" I asked.

"I'm waiting for you," he said. He stood upright and moved off of the water so we could talk.

"I'm Isaac, by the way. And you, of course, are Dr. Will Johnson. I talked to a nice lady named Leilani at the scene of your accident. She told me that the Zolians had taken you towards Phoenix. I followed in time to see where they were taking you and waited until you left the resort. I was just going for a swim here, waiting for you to come by, since you move pretty slowly."

"How do you know my name? And why would you be waiting for me?"

"Lots of people know your name. We watch the internet,

we just watch it over the shoulders of mortals, so to speak, since we don't have computers. I was waiting for you because I'm a fan of yours. You could say I'm into particle physics, as one of my many interests. I'm also part of the Science Association. We'd like you to come to a meeting with us. Your accomplishments in science are huge. More importantly, things are changing, since you stabilized dark matter. The Zolians are getting more powerful. We are studying what is happening, and some of us are hoping you will have some answers."

I didn't know I had any fans. This guy was pretty strange, but at least he was friendlier than the Zolians.

"Who are the Zolians? Why are they so hostile?"

"Theories abound, but nobody knows. They don't exactly carry ID. That's one of the things the Science Association doesn't agree on."

"You were acting like you were swimming in a mortal fountain, but you weren't splashing. Why were you pretending to swim in a fountain?"

"Most people here take themselves way too seriously. I happen to have a sense of humor."

That was fine with me, but the only thing I could think about was getting back to my house.

"Can you tell me how to fly back to the East Valley? I'm in a hurry."

"You do it the same way you're running. How are you doing that?"

"Well, that's easy. I already know how to run."

"Did it occur to you that gravity is what allows you to run? You can't possibly run, or even walk, without gravity—as a mortal, at least. Walking is merely falling forward and then putting a foot under yourself to keep from falling. Running is just fast walking—impossible without gravity."

"Okay . . ."

"You are able to walk and run because you believe you can, not because you are affected by gravity. It is your willpower that moves you. It is your belief, your expectation. If you expect to fly, you will. Here, try this. Put your arms out and will yourself to float off the ground."

I did as he said, but I didn't move.

He smiled again. "Looks like it's going to take you a while. Let's try something else."

He held out his arm. "Put your arm on top of mine, and I'll float up, and you'll float with me. Okay?" Here it was, like a scientific experiment, learning how to fly. Observation, hypothesis, and then the test.

I nodded and put my arm on top of his. We started floating up effortlessly, five feet, ten feet, fifteen feet above the ground. Then he moved his arm and quickly backed away from me.

"Hey!" I shouted. But I didn't move. I was standing in the air fifteen feet off the ground. I tried to walk forward in the air by moving my legs. I didn't move.

"I told you: you aren't moving physically, you are using your willpower to move. It is your mind."

"How can that be?"

"I have no idea. That's just how it is. A baby doesn't ask permission or directions to learn to crawl. He *does* it. But don't worry about it. I'll help you get to the East Valley now, and you can start practicing later."

I was grateful. Now it was a question of whether the police had already gotten to my house to tell my wife and children of my death, or whether I might still get there in time.

It took mere minutes to fly from Phoenix to the East Valley. We ranged within several hundred yards above the ground to just below the flight path of the commercial airliners on their way to the Phoenix airport. We must have been traveling a hundred miles an hour—far faster than the traffic on the freeway—but I did not have a sense of physical velocity, of acceleration or deceleration. It felt effortless, instantaneous.

When we got to the house, I saw a police car out in front. I cringed. I must be too late. I thanked Isaac as we touched down.

"Happy to help. Hey, whenever you're ready, we'd like you to meet with members of the Science Association. But for now, I'll leave you here. I need to go finish a murder investigation," he said casually.

More people looking for newcomers, like Leilani. I wasn't certain what he was referring to about a murder investigation, so I ignored his comment. "How will I know where to find you?"

"Don't worry," he said. "We have ways to find you."

As I approached the house, I noticed the police car was running and there were two officers still in it. Perhaps Marie wasn't there yet. The garage door was always locked, but it didn't matter now. I walked through the garage door. The garage was dark and Marie's car wasn't there. Good.

It was only a few minutes before she pulled up. Sam and Emily were in the car with her. She must have decided to pick them up after she left the hotel room. No point in leaving them with her sister once she knew she wasn't spending the night at the hotel with me.

I could see through the car windows that Marie ran her fingers through her hair as she saw the police car, her eyebrows slightly raised with concern. Samuel, on the other hand, was looking at the police car.

"I wonder why the police are here?"

Emily looked up from an article in *Entertainment*

magazine. She had a subscription to keep up with the latest in movies. I wondered briefly if my death would impact her film career. I hoped not.

The officers got out of their patrol car as Marie pulled into the driveway.

"We need to talk to you, Ma'am," one of them said as soon as Marie was out of her car. "Could we go inside?"

Once everyone was seated in the living room, I could see Samuel's lips were tight with concern. He was looking at his mother.

"Ma'am, given the nature of our visit, we won't delay," one of them said. His face was grave. "William Johnson is your husband, correct?"

She nodded.

"And these are your children?"

"Yes."

"Your husband was in a motorcycle accident this afternoon. I'm sorry, Ma'am, but he didn't make it."

Marie's face went white. She opened her mouth and covered it with her hand. After several seconds, her hand started trembling. "Oh, no . . ."

Emily blinked several times, then whispered, "Daddy?" I moved towards her and reached out to touch her cheek. Wouldn't my hand just go through her, the same way I went through walls? No, I was able to touch her cheek. It was the same as touching another post-mortal, which seemed strange.

I turned to Sam. His face didn't move, but tears started flowing down his cheeks.

I watched as my wife put her arms around them, and pulled them to her, bending forward slightly. They wept together. Marie began hyperventilating, sobbing in spasms.

The officers were somber. The grief was overpowering. It was a pain unlike anything I'd ever felt before, but I had no tears, no tightness in my throat, or no physical pains. My very soul ached, and now my mortal body wasn't there to mask it.

I was the cause of my wife's grief, in more ways than one.

I was also the cause of the lost look I saw in my little Emily's eyes. She looked up right at me, intently, but there was no way she could see me. Then I turned and saw our family picture on the wall behind me. I wanted to gather my daughter into my arms and comfort her, but it was impossible. I approached her and knelt. I put my hand to her cheek, but she gave no sign of recognition.

"Emily," I whispered. "Emily!" Her expression didn't change,

Sam wiped at his tears with the heel of his hand, but they were still flowing. I wished with all my heart in that moment that Marie and I still had a strong marriage. I wished we had never considered divorce.

My family was drowning in a sea of agony, and I couldn't save them.

Marie cried as though she would never stop. Hours before, we were at the hotel, and she wanted to reconcile. Instead, she found out I'd had an affair. And now I was dead.

Other people began arriving. The officers were very helpful. Glenda Wright, a member of the church board for our congregation, was there.

Our church leader arrived. Marie had begun to compose herself, but when she saw him, she broke down again. He put an arm around her, and she squeezed his hand. Glenda had retrieved a box of Kleenexes from the kitchen counter, and handed some to Marie, before grabbing a few for herself.

Adultery isn't good in any church. The church leader was a good friend to me, and he was a visual reminder for me of that stark fact. I felt ashamed as it occurred to me that I was glad he didn't know.

A police aide made arrangements for Marie to go the next day to identify me—my body, I mean. It could only add to the pain. Maybe it would help with closure. Not that there was going to be much of that.

Later, a police officer arrived and took her aside. "Mrs. Johnson, there is something I thought I'd better ask you about. There were no skid marks from your husband's motorcycle, and we've just confirmed that the brake cables were damaged by some type of acid. There was a remote-control device planted on the brake cables, which released the acid. Do you know of anyone who might want to harm him?"

Her eyes grew wide. She told him what she knew about Sky Lurich, and he had her write out a statement. Then he asked her to call Dr. Griggs, my boss, and put him on the line to speak with him.

Isaac had said something about investigating a murder, but he was so strange I had ignored him. Had he been talking about me? Was I not supposed to be dead? Had it not been an accident?

Marie reached Dr. Griggs and told him what happened to me. She told him she would let him know the details of the funeral once they'd been arranged. Then she put the officer on the line, and he made an appointment to meet with Dr. Griggs the following day.

Dr. Griggs had been a good man to work for. We had a wonderful group of people, and they were going to take my death pretty hard. He was likely going to be calling them right now, or sending out an e-mail notice. The first person he'd talk to would be Ronnie.

Over the next few hours, I watched as some of the members of our congregation gathered to help Marie and my children. The women had immediately organized a meal. Glenda Wright had Marie's phone and screened the calls.

Marie talked to her sister Sarah, who said she was on her way over. The people in my congregation were wonderful people, some of the best I'd ever known, and I loved them. It was humbling to watch them graciously help my family, full of love.

Several people in the congregation who had died came by, Ted, Denny, and others. Word had made it into the mortal world that I had died, and then spread to ex-mortals. From our conversations, they were very sorry I had died, but they didn't know I had committed adultery. I felt both guilty and glad that they didn't know. I was thinking about Ronnie.

I went outside and looked towards the west, wondering how I'd get to Ronnie's place. Isaac had helped me before, but there was no way to contact him. Even at a marathon pace, if I ran it would take hours to cover the distance. I thought about all the times I'd dreamed of flying, and how often I'd wondered if that was what it would really be like when I died.

All I could do was try. It was a matter of experimenting, something I had thought of when my children were one or two years old. They were constantly conducting experiments. They think they can walk like adults, so they start experimenting until they learn how. Their whole lives center on exploring their world. They start by chewing on everything they can reach, and soon they are opening all the cupboards. Two-year-olds have an ultimate mission: search and destroy.

My hypothesis now was that I could fly without Isaac. I began running west, at a rapid pace. If I stayed on the streets, I'd have a clear view, without running through any houses or fenced yards. On the other hand, it was a more direct route to just go straight, so when I crossed the main road, rather than turning, I leaped up on the wall and from there up onto the roof of a house, pleased with myself, because of how far I could leap. As I ran across the roof I realized how much of this was just in my head—I thought I was leaping from the wall to the roof, but the reality was that the wall could not have helped me, because my foot would just go through it. I jumped from that roof onto the roof of the next house, and from there I took off flying.

Exhilaration coursed through me, like electricity, as I rose above the rooftops, moving west. My arms were stretched out, and my head thrown back, moving at the same speed I had been running at. All the times I had done this in my dreams came back to me, with the surge of joy to see it a reality. I was flying. I felt like I had done this before, as if it were only natural.

Dr. Griggs may have already called Ronnie. If not, he would at any time. How could I speed up? I heard the whine of a plane engine coming from behind me. It was on a flight pattern into Phoenix Sky Harbor Airport, westbound. Instinctively, I started moving to get in front of it. Too bad I couldn't catch a ride. No doubt I'd just go through the plane like I did through the walls of buildings. Maybe there would be an airstream, like when a semi passes you on a bicycle and you speed up a little. But no, the air molecules shouldn't make any difference to me. I wasn't feeling any wind resistance.

As I was thinking about this, the plane caught up to me, as I was directly in front of the nose, and I prepared for it to pass through me. The nose did, but suddenly I was in the cabin, sitting in the pilot's lap. "Oh, sorry." I said it instinctively. He didn't react; obviously he was unaware I was there. I climbed out of his lap, wondering if, somehow, he was moving me, even though the walls of the plane weren't. I could see through the windshield that we were almost to Tempe already, and I felt a pang of anxiety, not wanting to go too far. Instantly I flew through the back of the cabin and into the stewardess who was standing on the other side. I put my hands on her shoulders and moved myself to the side, and flew towards the back through the passenger area of the plane, out of control. I tried to grab a seat back, but ended up grabbing the head of a bald man. I held on, trying to get my bearings. I looked over my shoulder and was staring into the eyes of a lady in a white robe, who was glaring at me. A Zolian was on the plane? I wanted to get off the plane, so I let go of the man's head, bounced off a lady coming out of the restroom at the back of the plane, and was out the back of the plane and in open air as the plane flew on.

Why did I go through the front of a plane, but stop when I came into contact with a mortal? Everything was like a new experiment, full of unknown variables.

I could see the ASU football stadium and Tempe Town Lake below me to the south, so I was close to Ronnie's house.

It wasn't far, and I was at Ronnie's in seconds. I went down through the roof near the front entrance. I could hear a television and followed the sound to the kitchen. Ronnie was preparing a salad while she watched a show consisting primarily of political commentary. She didn't appear to be upset, so I must have arrived in time. I watched her for a while. She seemed comfortable being alone. In a few minutes her cell phone rang. The sound was coming for a leather bag she carried back and forth to work. She pulled out the phone and answered. "Hi, Chuck." Her eyebrows narrowed, and her mouth opened slightly as she listened. Her eyes started brimming with tears. "Why would anyone do that?" She listened, lowering her chin as she wiped away tears. She grabbed the remote and turned off the TV. "I just don't see why they would want to kill Will." She listened a while longer, and then ended the call with a quiet goodbye.

She walked to the kitchen window and stared out towards the block fence and her neighbor's wall, her eyes full of loss, a forlorn expression on her face.

I moved towards her and put my arms around her from behind. "Ronnie, I'm here." She continued to gaze out the window, without tears.

"What am I going to do, now?" she whispered.

Had she wanted to spend her future with me? I thought so. I certainly would have wanted to spend it with her, except that I hadn't fully understood what Marie was thinking until the end. Now I would not be spending my future with either of them.

"The person I cared most about," she said. "The one person I thought might have the answers, who might actually figure out what it all means." Her tears began flowing, and she sank to the floor, shaking with sobs.

I stayed with her a long time.

■ ■ ■

When I started back towards the East Valley, I didn't have any trouble soaring up from the ground, and felt the exhilaration once again as I moved upward, looking down as the houses got smaller, but it was mixed with the somber pain of knowing what I had done to Ronnie. I thought of everyone I had seen today, and what I had done to all of them. It wasn't my fault I was dead, particularly now that it appeared it wasn't just my foolish speeding that got me killed. It was my fault, though, that I had betrayed who I was by a single act. My son didn't know I had slept with Ronnie, so his pain wasn't any worse because of it, but sooner or later he would know, and it would rightfully change how he thought of me. It had changed who I had become. It was almost easier being with Isaac and Leilani right now, because of the anonymity of strangers. Was it too late to meet Leilani at the church at 8:30?

I started flying in the direction of the church. I was still wondering why they held services so late. When I got there, I went through the outside doors, past the foyer and into the sanctuary. I passed mortals who were on their way out, who had no idea I was even there. Maybe the reason we were meeting so late was to not overlap with their service. It seemed odd that we were using the mortals' building instead of having our own, but then Azzoloft was using the resort, so he must not have had buildings either.

While the mortals stood around, chatting in their foyer, I went into the sanctuary, where I noticed the room had a high, wood-paneled ceiling that looked nice, and painted slump block walls that didn't. There was a large cross spanning the wall behind the pulpit, and stained glass with a large form of a dove behind the cross.

There was a group of about thirty ex-mortals, judging by their white robes, seated in the first couple of rows, probably more out of habit than anything. I saw one man who miscalculated and was sitting part-way sunk into the bench. Without gravity, and without being able to touch the pews, it was just as easy to stand. There were Hispanics among the group; evidently race was not affected by death.

I saw Leilani standing to the right of the podium with several other people. Our eyes met, and she put her hand to her mouth. Then she waved at me and smiled. A man, dressed in white like everyone else, approached the podium. He introduced himself as a pastor and welcomed us, explaining how great everything was in the afterlife. "Think about it," he said, "No more sickness, no more death, no more headaches, no more pains. Our friends, loved ones, and family members who have passed on are here with us. Our mortal worries are over."

My family members weren't here to meet me. Maybe they went somewhere else.

At about that time, I noticed there was one mortal lady in the room, a large woman wearing a white dress with a blue flowered pattern. She made her way to the organ bench and was positioning her music.

The afterlifer pastor was just starting to quote a passage of scripture when the mortal lady blasted the first chord of *Rock of Ages*, nearly blowing the pipes off the wall. She continued at a dramatic pace and a strong volume. The pastor's only reaction was to substantially increase the volume of his voice.

I was trying to keep a straight face. It suddenly occurred to me that we were here after the mortals' service only because someone knew this mortal would have the lights on to practice the organ. That meant the afterlifer pastor had no choice but to ignore her. I snorted with laughter.

The afterlifer pastor went on reading scriptures, and the mortal organist went on practicing, with a familiar version of *Abide with Me*. Then the pastor was admonishing us to continue in our faith in God and Christ. It finally occurred to me that, if that organ-playing lady finished before the long-winded pastor, we were going to get to listen to him in the dark, because she would probably shut off the lights and leave. Thankfully, she played on, sparing us the humiliation of trying to hold our meeting in the dark.

Eventually the pastor asked the newcomers if they had any questions.

The lady in front of me said, "Where can I get something to eat? I'm starving." Everyone laughed.

The pastor responded: "Obviously, you won't be eating anything for a while. When our Lord rose from the dead, we read that he ate some fish and honeycomb. That, however, was with a resurrected body. We aren't there yet. The reality of our current condition is that we don't feel hunger or thirst. Perhaps you thought you were hungry because you're new here."

A man spoke up: "I lost an arm while I was alive, and I

used to get those phantom itches in my missing arm. Maybe it's like that, only worse, because your whole body is gone!"

Then, in a more serious voice, he added, "It is marvelous to have my arm back, though."

The lady spoke up again: "Where are we supposed to sleep?"

"Some of you may find you don't need sleep. For the rest, you can sleep wherever you like," the pastor said, "and parks are popular because they are fairly quiet. Try to avoid sleeping in the middle of a street—the noise of the cars can be very distracting." A few people chuckled.

"Makes us sound like a bunch of homeless people," someone said.

"There's no need for us to look at it that way," said the pastor, "because we don't have any particular use for houses. The whole world is open to us as post-mortals, and we can go anywhere we like."

I raised my hand, and asked, "Where is Jesus, and when do we get to meet him?"

The pastor smiled. "I believe we'll all get to see him on the judgment day, but as of right now, we don't get to see him."

"You mean he isn't here? I thought this was supposed to be heaven?"

"I've been here for several years, and I've been around the world many times. As you've already found, we travel very quickly and have no need for cars or airplanes. We move where we want to go with hardly a thought. In all my travels, though, I've never seen Jesus, as much as I would love to."

"Well, what about Moses, or Peter, James, or John? Why don't we find them and ask them?"

"I've tried that also," the pastor said. "I don't really know whether they are here or not, but I've never been able to find them."

This was fascinating news to me. Why on earth wouldn't they be here? Where would they be? I spoke up. "Now, how can that make any sense? I'd say a lot of us thought that, when we died, we were finally going to get some answers. Are you saying we don't?"

"All I said was that I've never heard of Moses or any other prophet *here*."

The pastor then got to the point of the meeting, which was to invite newcomers to join with the ranks of believers.

A man asked, "What about hell? Do we know where it is?"

"We don't know where it is. That doesn't mean there aren't bad people here though, particularly the Zolians. They claim they were never mortal, and they argue that since God isn't here in the afterlife, he must not exist. Unfortunately, some people believe that. We encourage religious believers to gather together, as part of the Religious Association."

This couldn't be what most of these people had expected. Heaven and hell were supposed to be clear religious principles. Something was wrong. I remembered the feeling I had: A door had been opened. Something was happening, and none of us understood it.

■ ■ ■

Leilani caught me in the hallway after the meeting. "How did you get away?" she asked.

I raised my eyebrows.

"This afternoon? What happened with the Zolians?" she asked.

"They took me over to Phoenix."

She was staring intently. "What did they want with you?" she asked. "I've never heard nor seen anyone get taken by the Zolians like that, right after they died. They said they were taking you to Azzoloft."

"They did."

"And? They must have had a reason!"

"Have you heard about the testing out at the particle collider, where someone appeared out of the dust? I was the leader of the team that built the machine. That's why he wanted to talk to me."

"I see. Why was Azzoloft so interested?"

"He was the person in the sand," I said.

"Azzoloft!"

"If you don't like the sound of it, that makes two of us."

"What did he want?"

"He wants me to help him. He assigned me an instructor or something, a guy named Blitzer. I'm supposed to meet with him tomorrow at 9:00 a.m."

Her eyes narrowed. "Listen to me," she said. "When that instructor comes, Blitzer or whoever, you tell him to get lost. Avoid him. Don't go with him."

Staying away sounded like a smart idea, but maybe she was forgetting how that wasn't an option when they send forty people after you.

"I think I should talk to them," I said. "Think how much I can learn. And apparently, not all mortals get this opportunity." Maybe I could change the subject. "Hey, I haven't seen my mother or my brother yet. How do you find people here?"

"Go over to the state capital building. The lobby of the executive tower is set up with some volunteers who can help you find people. I volunteer over there sometimes, doing other things." Maybe I could try that tomorrow.

"One other question. Where's a good place to sleep?"

"Sleep isn't the same. You don't fall asleep and wake up eight hours later like nothing happened in between. You'll see. But anyway, I like to stay near my daughter. She's a mortal. And please, just stay away from the Zolians." She turned and was gone.

Her words reminded me of my own children. I started walking back to my house—Marie's house now.

When I got to the house, Marie's sister Sarah was there, and she and Marie were talking. Sarah was younger than Marie, and she didn't have much to do with our church. She was wearing a sleeveless blouse and a short skirt. I'd never felt very comfortable around her, but she and Marie had always been close. They weren't talking about me, of course. They were talking about the usual nonsense—stuff from the paper, and shopping, anything and everything but me, and they went on for hours.

My daughter wanted to sleep with Marie, which was good. Marie held Emily as they dozed off. When I checked on my son, he was already asleep.

CHAPTER 8

WELCOME TO HELL

WHAT DO CHILDREN do the morning after their father dies? Play video games, of course. I suspect Samuel was just doing what was familiar. What was he supposed to do, sit around and mope? They certainly weren't going to go to school, and Emily didn't want to be alone. My sister-in-law was at the house, watching TV. I didn't know where Marie was. I wish my sister-in-law had told my children not to play video games, but she probably would have let them do anything they wanted, even if they decided to get spray paint and graffiti our living room.

I watched my children play for a while, and they looked pretty dejected. It wasn't the abject grief I saw yesterday.

Perhaps I could communicate with them if I concentrated. I looked my son in the eyes. "I'm here," I said. "This is your father." Nothing registered on his face. For several minutes, I spoke to him, telling him how much I loved him, and reminding him of the good times we had.

I moved over near my daughter. "Emily, I'm here," I said. "I love you." She didn't react, but I continued to talk to her.

After a few more minutes, Samuel stopped playing video

games. I followed him to the piano. He began playing "Rhondo alla Turca." He didn't need any music. Tears dripped down his cheeks as he played. At the end of the song he bowed his head and sat there, eyes closed. I put my arms around him and held him.

■ ■ ■

I wanted to find my mother, and my brother, Brett. I moved in the direction of Phoenix. I was flying better now, although I still didn't go very fast. Eventually, I passed by the downtown area and the huge indoor ballpark. As I approached the mortals' Arizona State Capital Executive Tower in Phoenix, I could count that it was seven stories high in the central tower, with an extended lobby connecting to the historic portion of the State Capitol building. When I entered the lobby, I could see the mortal security guards at the entrances by the metal detectors. There were plenty of mortals about, just as when I had last been there as a mortal. I was amazed at how many afterlifers there were in that beehive of a lobby. They seemed to be organized in groups across the lobby. The moment I got past the doors I was greeted by a pleasant man who sounded like the guy from India who would assist you on the phone when you had computer problems.

"May I help you?"

"Yes," I said. "I'm looking for some people I know." I explained to him that I had gone to the police station and been directed here.

"You are new here, I take it? When did you arrive?"

"I died yesterday."

"Well, you could say you were born into this life yesterday; it does sound better."

"Where I come from, being born yesterday is hardly a compliment."

"Be that as it may, I think you will want to talk to Charlotte. Right this way."

I saw a distraught female afterlifer pass by, escorted by another, more somber, female. A scowling male was following them.

"What's going on there?" I asked the man assisting me.

"Domestic violence case, no doubt."

We followed them through an open door into a large office, where light was streaming through the large windows. The mortal who worked in this office must be important—it had nice paintings, a wooden desk, and an area for a dark leather couch and chairs. There was a black female afterlifer talking to several other afterlifers, but she turned when she heard the commotion from the still-crying woman.

Not only did individuals have accents, but race was still obvious. It made sense; we all looked essentially the same as we did as mortals, except we all wore white robes.

"Oh, my, honey, what happened?" We all looked at the black female as she moved toward the woman. Her presence dominated. It wasn't just her appearance, which was stunningly beautiful, although she wore a white robe like the rest of us. She seemed brighter, almost like she was shining. She controlled the situation, and it was going to be okay. She moved quickly to the crying woman, took her in her arms, and held for a few seconds, which appeared to have a calming effect.

"I'm so tired of him. I want him to go away." She was still crying, but less now.

"I know, I know, dear. Your name is Tracy, isn't it?" Tracy looked up, surprised this woman knew her name. "It's so good to meet you. We are delighted to have you here. I'm Charlotte. If this man is bothering you, we're here to help. Now tell me all about it."

"It's none of your business, lady," the scowling man said. "I don't care who you are." The perpetrator moved aggressively towards Charlotte. I was shocked when he reached out and tried to shove her away from Tracy. I wouldn't have had the guts to speak to Charlotte like that. She was taller than he was, and had a look of being physically powerful, muscular even. His shove had no effect. His hands stopped the moment he touched her shoulder. He tried again. She didn't budge a millimeter. His expression changed. His eyes had been narrowed, his jaw set, but now he raised his eyebrows in surprise, and backed away slightly.

"Perhaps you'd like to tell me what happened?" Charlotte looked at him, one eyebrow raised also, her voice accusatory.

"Nothing happened. There was a fire," he said. "We couldn't get out. Our bedroom was full of smoke, the wall was burning, and I passed out before I could get to the window. She never even woke up."

"When?"

"Last night, early morning hours."

"What about kids, did you have any children in the house?" Charlotte asked.

He looked away, his lips tight.

"We have two girls," Tracy said. "They were four and one, but CPA took them two months ago."

Charlotte nodded, understanding. "The Child Protection Agency took them. Turns out that was for the best, now, I'd say. At least they weren't in the blaze. And what caused the fire, do you think?"

Tracy looked at the floor. The man said, "How would we know? We were dead before we saw anything!"

Tracy started sobbing at the use of the word "dead."

"Is it true?" Charlotte asked her. "You didn't even wake up?"

"Yes. No. Well, I think I was dreaming about a fire," said Tracy. "I felt heat, I was terrified, I couldn't breathe, and I couldn't wake up. All of a sudden, I could breathe again, but I was looking down at my body. Oh my gosh, it was horrible! The flames! I could see my body was burning, but I couldn't feel anything. I wanted to get away, as far as I could, so I started moving away, but he followed me. I was shouting at him to get away, but he's been following me for hours. He keeps saying it's fine. It's not fine . . ." She sobbed.

"Come on, Tracy, this isn't helping. Let's get out of here." The man moved towards her.

"I hate you. Get away from me! Get away!" She tried to knock his hand away from her.

Charlotte looked at the man. "Bobby," said Charlotte. "I'll ask you one time, politely. Would you please leave?"

"Hell no! I won't!" He tilted his head back and laughed. "I'd like to see you try and make me. There isn't a thing you can do about it." Maybe he'd decided that, since he couldn't shove Charlotte, Charlotte wouldn't be able to do anything to him either.

Charlotte's face turned solemn, her jaw set, and her eyes narrowed. She drew herself to her full height, faced him and said, "Oh, yes there is." Charlotte nodded to the woman who had initially escorted the couple in. "Get a squad," she told the escort. The woman went out the door.

"A squa...?" Bobby's voice got stuck halfway through the word squad, and he swallowed before he could force out the second half of the word.

It was mere seconds before the woman was back with twenty other afterlifers. They swarmed around Bobby, flying very fast in a tight sphere of bodies. "Get away from me! Hey! Cut it out!" He flailed his arms at them. He was surrounded, in the same manner the Zolians had surrounded me yesterday. I could see Bobby's alarmed face in the gaps between bodies. I did not envy him.

Charlotte turned back to Tracy. "How would you like to go someplace safe, someplace beautiful?" Tracy wiped her eyes and smiled a little. "How would you like to see some family members you haven't seen in a while? Maybe your grandmother or grandfather?" Charlotte asked. Tracy smiled a little more and gave a slight nod.

"And you won't let him follow me?" Tracy asked.

"No, honey, we sure won't," Charlotte said. She nodded to the escort, who took Tracy by the arm. I watched them leave the room. I saw hope in Tracy's eyes. It was heavenly.

Charlotte now turned her attention back to Bobby. He was still surrounded on all sides by the other afterlifers, but they left a little space, so Charlotte could see him as she spoke. He looked like he might try to dart out, but they moved to tighten the gap, showing him an attempted escape would be fruitless. They, once again, opened the space for her to see him.

He evidently had regained his courage, and he wasn't happy at Charlotte's threat to keep him from following Tracy. "You forgot one thing. I know where all her family lives. If she goes around any of them, I'll find her. She'll never leave me. She's going to come looking for me as soon as you guys are gone."

Charlotte looked at the nearest squad member, a woman, and her look was suddenly ominous. "Did anyone tell him who I am?"

The women wavered, and her brow was wrinkled as she said, "That you're the president of the Greater Phoenix Volunteers?"

Charlotte had a sinister look now. "No." She gazed intensely at Bobby. "That I am the devil. Welcome to hell, Bobby."

CHAPTER 9

WHY AM I HERE

CHARLOTTE, THE DEVIL. I didn't believe it for a minute, but that didn't stop me from feeling tension. Azzoloft said he wasn't the devil. Charlotte said she was. I already knew Charlotte was a powerful being, a presence. I'd felt it from the moment I met her. I didn't know what Bobby had done, but it probably wasn't as bad as what I had done. Maybe the reason they sent me here wasn't to help me at all. Maybe it was a trap.

Charlotte's followers didn't blink when she said it. They were staring, somber. Were they all Zolians? Or something worse?

"You aren't the devil." Bobby spoke before I could, but his eyes betrayed his confusion.

"Oh, no? You think it wasn't me that persuaded you to use meth, Bobby?" Her voice was resonating again. "It wasn't me that talked you into setting up a meth lab in that house? It wasn't me that helped get your children taken away? And now you've killed her."

"Killed who? I didn't kill anybody! What are you talking about?"

"Tracy is dead, Bobby. Don't you realize? She is dead, and so are you." Charlotte's gaze was intense.

"It was an accident, it was . . ." From his protests, he at least believed it wasn't his fault, even if he was mistaken.

"You set up the meth lab, so you are responsible for the consequences. You killed her."

"I didn't . . . how do you know I set up a meth lab? You can't prove anything."

Charlotte was pacing the floor. "Your moment of truth has come; it is time *right now* for your judgment day." The words "right now" had a resonating ring as she said them." I'll speak the truth, and you will acknowledge it."

He stared, his eyes wild.

"You are poorly educated. You aren't working-class, you're lazy-ass. Your arrogance and your bluster stems from lack of self-confidence and lifelong ineptitude. You were controlling Tracy for years, even though she was the one bright spot in your wretched life; you got her addicted to meth, you kept her from going to college, you kept her from talking to her family and friends, and you made her life a living hell."

"I didn't. I love her. She didn't really want to break up."

"You beat her, Bobby. You bloodied her face. You gave her black eyes. You were brutal. That isn't love. It is *not* love." Charlotte was silent for a moment.

"What does the devil look like, Bobby? Did you expect him to have horns and a trident, and a big long tail? Is it that you can't believe I'm the devil because I'm a woman, and you've never seen any woman as your equal, much less your superior, no matter how much more intelligent and better educated than you they were?"

She was pacing again. "Tell me, were you relieved this morning to find out you weren't burning in a lake of fire and brimstone? You arrived in an afterlife which looked like the normal mortal world and found yourself in a white robe. Did you mistake yourself for an angel? Did you not realize that demons themselves are clothed in white robes? Did you not know they look like people? It isn't their appearance we abhor, but what they are. What they have become.

"No, Bobby, I am not the devil." Charlotte's voice was quieter now, but still intense. "But I can help you on your way to hell. You see, hell is a *mental* furnace, and the temperature is determined by wasted mortal opportunities. Yes, you are in hell, and you deserve to be there."

"What do mean I'm in hell? I'm in the same place you are."

"Look at your life, Bobby. All you needed to be was a good man. What if you had met your beautiful Tracy, and you had actually married her? What if you had worked at honest labor, and supported her, cared for her? What if you had caressed her face, instead of beating it? What if she had been your queen instead of your slave? Can you see her now, as your queen? Can you see what college would have done for her? Can you see her self-confidence blossoming as she learned? Can you see yourself as a good man, striving with all he has; to work, lift, and help his family, his two daughters? Can you see what might have been?"

Bobby had a rapt look on his face, as if he were somehow seeing and feeling what Charlotte was describing.

"Instead, you have a battered, terrified shell of a woman who died at age 27, killed by the meth lab belonging to the man she once looked to for safety, a man who is now a shell himself. A terrified, miserable soul, who will go out alone into this new world after death and learn to be a better person or who will remain in his misery, in the hell of his own shattered expectations of that glorious experience we call life.

"I said I am the devil. I'm not. I don't know if he exists. But if he were here with us now, he wouldn't be telling you the truth. He'd still be flattering you, lying to you, telling you that a little drug-selling never hurt anyone, that you are still a great guy, that you are wonderfully smart, and that Tracy was lucky to have you. I am not the devil, but I have introduced you to hell. I've explained to you the wretched truths that will be your companions from now on, unless and until you change who you are and the way you think."

Charlotte was silent. The squad members slowly backed away, leaving Bobby space to make his way out.

He glared at her, nastier than ever, hatred now burning in eyes, hatred from a deep, unacknowledged wound, as if she had stabbed him with a dagger and it was still jutting from his side. "This isn't over," he said. "You think twenty people can protect you. I'll be back with a hundred. I'll find every man you ever gave this little speech to, and I'll make you sorry." Charlotte met his gaze and smiled. Her eyes were clear, fearless, and sad.

Bobby left.

Charlotte dismissed the others. My guide introduced me to Charlotte and explained why I was there. Then he left, also.

"There are far too many like Bobby," Charlotte said. "He won't have any trouble finding a group to suit him. From white supremacists and gangs, to rotary clubs and feminist groups, people often stay in their favorite club, and they have more time for meetings than ever. Bobby will end up in the God Ain't Here Alliance. Oh, well. Come with me." I followed her as we moved up several floors. We went into a conference room with a nice view of the plaza, the green grass, and the Arizona Supreme Court building across the way. The conference room had plush leather chairs, paintings on the walls, and a large flat screen TV monitor. Potted plants filled one corner, all placed there by mortals as part of the decor. Charlotte sat in a chair against the wall. I sat against the adjacent wall.

"So, Will," Charlotte said, "I know you want to find your mother and your brother. I'd like to talk to you a little first, if you don't mind."

"I was curious about how your friends surrounded that person," I said. "I had a similar experience with the Zolians." I told her how they had surrounded me and taken me to Azzoloft.

Her eyebrows raised. "Fascinating. We've learned a lot from the Zolians, like how to surround another afterlifer, for instance. There is a lot you don't know yet about how Zolians communicate, and how we communicate. But our GP volunteers—sorry, Greater Phoenix Volunteers—are well-trained at gathering information. The people you saw me talking to when we first met had already briefed me on most of the information about Bobby and Tracy. Our messengers can move fifty miles almost instantaneously, or 10,000 miles, for that matter, and we don't always need to talk to convey information, so word travels fast. They didn't need to tell me about you, though. I've been watching you particularly closely."

"What do you mean?"

"There are a lot of ex-mortals who have been watching what happened when you stabilized dark matter. We've seen you on the mortals' internet news over the past few days. You had people here helping you in ways you did not understand, and I don't mean mortals. Do you know what the gulf is?"

I shook my head.

"There is a parallel location, related to this earth, where a great many people go when they die. They are not constantly around humans, or mortal buildings. All those things are blocked out, and the place is blissful and at peace. You should be there, not here, and that is why I am so worried about you. In fact, Tracy also should have gone there, and Bobby would have been stuck here, but meth interferes. Almost all drugs do, if they are taken for the wrong reason."

Her eyes softened, and she smiled a little at the look on my face. I was in the wrong place, and I had a pretty good idea why.

"What about heaven and hell?" I asked. "That's what most people expect to see after they die. But you told Bobbie that hell is mental anguish."

"People don't really know what to expect when they die. Yet, it is so much like mortal life. Some people in life are very close to God. Prophets like Moses said they talked to him, but people were left to decide. That's how it is here. There aren't any prophets or angels explaining things to everyone."

"Are you suggesting that drugs can actually determine where we go?"

"When a mortal imbibes drugs, it doesn't just alter his or her physical matter. It also alters their afterlife self. I can't explain the science behind it. Maybe you can figure that out. I think the matter that we are made of right now is present in our mortal bodies during life, and that matter is affected by chemicals in an adverse way. There are other things that alter our structure as well, such as murder, and these changes prevent people from being able to cross into the gulf. It is a common theory that the Zolians can't cross because they are affected by some similar change, not chemical, but something that affects the structure of the matter from which they are made. I'm sure you already understand we are made of very real matter, it just isn't atoms."

"So people who haven't been changed by drugs or other things go directly to another place?" I asked.

"No. Normally some of those beyond the gulf will come and meet them here. They sense the time of death is drawing near. It is instinctive. But it doesn't work for people who have been changed by drugs, or other things. Some things alter the spiritual part of you, so that you become unrecognizable. Think of it this way. You recognize someone's voice, because of its frequency, pitch, timbre, and overall sound. Then, they have surgery and it permanently alters the way they speak. You can't recognize it anymore. That's what's bothering me. You shouldn't be here—not you, of all people. You lived life like you knew what was important."

With everything she knew about me, did she know about my affair? My world was crashing in. It was bad enough that I had betrayed my wife and my children but dying in the middle of it seemed too much to bear.

"And what is it that's really important?" I asked.

"In all honesty, the most important thing I did in my mortal life was to raise my kids—especially one of them. He was handicapped, some would say severely, but he was a person filled with love. Whatever I've become since, I feel like I learned it all from that sweet boy. Love is what is really important, Will. Love is the key, and service is its byproduct. That boy was a master at loving other people. He did so much more for me than I ever did for him. He was sent to the world to help me become what I am now. He was my angel."

Two white-robed people appeared through the wall, and I jumped. Their movements were shockingly sudden, instantaneous in both the way they moved and the way they stopped. I immediately recognized Zinc, and there was a flame of fury in his eyes.

The other Zolian had a round head, thin neck, and squat body. His eyes were cold. "Hi there, Will. I'm Blitzer. It's after nine o'clock."

Charlotte's eyes were wide with surprise and fear, and she stood up, defensive. I moved quickly to my feet. I felt as stunned as I would have if Azzoloft himself had been there.

"Am I to understand, you maggot," said Zinc, "that Azzoloft gave you a direct order yesterday to meet Blitzer at nine, and you just blew it off?" He said "blew it off" with little puffs of air, and I could see little spurts of darkness, almost imperceptible, escaping from his mouth with each syllable. He drew near to me, moving slightly above me, and looking down above my left shoulder, causing me to twist my head to look at him, his body above me in the air.

"You think we are playing at some game, and that you have nothing to fear from Azzoloft?" Zinc was very close now as he hissed in my ear, "How wrong you are." He looked at Charlotte. "Wouldn't you agree, your eminence," he finished the word "eminence" with a nasty hiss of sarcasm.

He and Blitzer squared off in front of me. "Now why don't you come along nicely," said Zinc, "and we won't mention to Azzoloft that Blitzer had to come and get me to find you this morning."

Charlotte raised a brow at the news that Blitzer needed Zinc's help to find me. She moved forward, full of confidence and power, and with a hint of resonance in her voice, she said, "I don't think he's going anywhere with you; not until I am finished with him. I command you to leave."

My already high opinion of her multiplied by ten. Here was a person who evidently could order these guys around. Then it occurred to me they might not leave.

"I was afraid it might come to this," said Blitzer. Zinc silenced him with a glare.

"You might think this is the end of it," Zinc said to Charlotte, "but as you know, I have a very, very, long memory." Then they were gone, as suddenly as they had come.

"It seems, Will, that there are several things you haven't told me." Charlotte did not seem relieved they were gone, but was rather more somber. "You are in deep trouble," she said. "I'll ask you again, what are you doing here? Your death was only yesterday, correct?"

"Yes." I felt like a schoolboy before a favorite teacher, and the disappointment in her voice was more castigating than a whipping.

"And did you, in fact, meet Azzoloft?"

I told her then, quickly, what had happened yesterday, with most of the details.

"Will, you asked me if I knew you before you died. I did. Some of us are able to put thoughts into mortals' minds. You are known to many of us who have this ability. There is a resonance, a wavelength, which allows us to communicate with each other, and sometimes even with mortals, to a limited extent. We know who the mortals are who are best able to hear us, those most attuned to us. Your attunement was remarkable. But, it was more than that. There are whispers among us about things to come. When we cross the gulf, at times we sense other events, things in the future. It is information, almost like prophecies. You weren't just guided to stabilize dark matter, some have sensed that you are to play a role in future events that will occur because of that breakthrough. That is why it is a shock to see here. It seems out of place. It seems like the wrong time."

"Anyone who has a breakthrough in science feels a muse," I said. "Writers feel it, and artists depend on it. It isn't that unusual."

"Will, what was your mission in life?" Her voice was resonant now.

"I don't know, except that stabilizing dark matter was part of it. I feel like I need to do something to stop Azzoloft from succeeding with a retest." I paused. "But I ended up neglecting my wife and children, and then betraying them. I don't see how I can help anyone, now." As I said it aloud, I let the realization sink into me. I had neglected my family. If I hadn't been so focused on my work, would any of my problems with Marie have happened? Would I even have been tempted to cheat on her with Ronnie? I couldn't know the answers to those questions, but I did know that I had failed in one very important thing. The most important thing.

"Actually," I said, "my family should have been my mission in life."

"Your family was the most important thing, just as my son was to me. But there was more to your mission than you probably realize. I'm sure you sensed something about your identity, but you couldn't explain it.

"You were sent to be a powerful force for good among mortals, and you should not be here. Why, Will? I must know why you are here."

An overpowering sense of shame overcame me. Knowing all the good things I had done as a husband, father, scientist, and a believer, and the wrong things I had done, was really painful. "I was unfaithful to my wife. Right before I died."

I could see from her eyes that she at last understood. She understood what Azzoloft could not. Like Bobby, she had just shown me how to enter my own mental furnace, my own private hell. She had shown me that all the good I had done in my life only made the burning heat more excruciating, the pain of lost opportunities was unbearable.

We left the room and went back to the first floor. "Before you leave, let me give you a few final words of advice. Blitzer will come back, and you won't be able to hide from him. But you don't have to do what he says."

"What is the worst they can do to me? I'm already dead," I said.

She gave me a solemn look. "Did you ever feel real despair, true desperation, in your life? That is what they can do to you. They can paralyze you with it, and they can immerse you in darkness. They can imprison you, both mentally and physically. And unless you are able to overcome the huge mistake you made by having an affair, they may overcome you entirely. I don't think the time has come for Azzoloft's full power to be revealed, but things are changing."

I stared at her, wondering what things could happen.

"I believe in God," she said, "but I think that religious language about a lake of fire and brimstone is figurative. It is a warning. It is referring to a state of mind, one you have already experienced as remorse over your affair."

"What I suggest is that you busy yourself with other things. You'll have lots to do if you want to figure out what happened at the strategic test, and how you can stop it from happening again," she said. "Avoid the Zolians as much as you can. You might try going to your family—no one will be more willing to help than them. If fact, we can help you with that right now."

Charlotte pointed around her to the beehive of activity I had seen in the lobby. "Much of what our volunteers do here relates to accumulating information and locating people. It isn't much, but it is the service we can give, and many of us would be willing to do anything to feel useful—to 'have a job,' you might say, even though we don't get paid. We can help you locate your family members, assuming they are not beyond the gulf I mentioned."

"Why aren't you beyond the gulf?" I asked.

"I go back and forth. Many people choose to do that. I spend most of my time here because I want to help people. People like Tracy. People like you."

What could she possibly do for me, now that she knew what I'd done? It was too late; she was just trying to be nice. She knew better than I did how big my problem was.

We watched the groups of afterlifers spread around the lobby. Some of them stayed at each location, while the greeters were taking persons seeking help to particular areas. Some of the volunteers were coming and going with exceptional speed, leaving and arriving as fast as Blitzer and Zinc had.

"Each of these areas around the lobby represents a portion of the Phoenix metropolitan area. Now, who do you want to find?"

"I'd like to find my mother, and my brother."

"When did they die?"

"It's been several years."

"And where were they living before they died?"

"In the East Valley, near the first high school."

"All right, let's start with Kenny, over here. He supervises most of the East Valley."

She introduced me to a black male in a white robe. He was as long and thin as a feather blown in by the wind. I told him I needed to find my mother and brother in the East Valley. He squinted, looking me over.

I could see an escort bringing two men towards Charlotte, and she excused herself and moved towards them.

■ ■ ■

"Okay, sir, what is your mother's name?" Kenny asked.

"Irene Johnson."

"Hey, now that's an easy one. That lady knows tons of people. But I can tell you right now, she's on the other side of the schism."

I took it he meant the gulf. She hadn't come to meet me, and there was nobody to blame but myself.

"There must be hundreds of thousands of afterlifers in the East Valley. You're trying to tell me you know where my mother is off the top of your head?"

He cocked his head to one side and looked at me. "I'm not trying to tell you anything. Didn't anyone explain to you that our memories get a lot better after we die?"

"Uh, no," I said. "Why would that happen?"

"Because you've got nothing slowing you down," Kenny said. "No such thing as Alzheimer's. And another thing: I don't lie. Other people might, but I got no reason to. Okay? So, when I tell you, 'yes, we can remember thousands of names,' and, 'yes, we find people efficiently where possible,' I'm talking about a network of people across the State of Arizona, and this is the hub, right here."

"Is there any way I can see my mother if she's on the other side of the gulf?" I asked.

"She decides if she wants to come here. Any other questions?"

"Yeah. Why don't you use computers?"

He gave me a look for a second before he answered. "Cause how am I going to pick up the mouse? You think I can go recruit a mortal to type on the keyboard for me, is that your idea? It's a good thing our memories are better. No computers!" He calmed down for a second and then leaned closer to me. "I wish we could use them, personally. I really miss my computer."

"You know," I said, "there's another thing I was wondering about. Why don't you all work for the government? If finding people and domestic violence protection is important, why doesn't the government do it?"

"Have you heard about some government out there?" he asked, squinting at me like he'd been looking at the screen on a cell phone too long. "Cause I sure don't know of any government. You know what runs a government? A budget. Can you imagine a politician who's got no budget? That'd be one useless politician. No budget, no government, no kidding. Besides, you want to find your family, or don't you? You think bureaucrats are going to find anyone? I'm here as a volunteer. I'm good at what I do. I'm not a stinkin' bureaucrat. You got something worth doing here, you get yourself some volunteers. Now who else are you looking for?"

"My brother, Brett Johnson. Died two years ago. From the East Valley."

"Never heard of him. Let's see what we can find out. Let me talk to my people here. You can either hang out here, or I'll come find you. It may take a few hours."

In the meantime, I could go back to Marie's house. I told Kenny the address.

What would my brother say when he saw me? Was he even aware I had died?

CHAPTER 10

ELIAS

I WENT BACK to my house—Marie's house—to wait for Kenny. The grass in the front yard was green, the skies were soft blue, and Marie's roses were in bloom.

I stood on the grass of our front lawn, underneath our large pine tree by the roses. It occurred to me how much different they looked than from the inside of my former house. The petals of the roses were so fragile, the colors so vibrant, they were almost glowing with life. By contrast, the walls of my house were dead, as dead as dirt. I looked at the soil underneath the tree and realized that wasn't quite right. Every part of the natural earth, including the dirt and rocks, had that living vibrancy. There is more beauty in them than any man-made thing. A concert harp, or a fine violin, are marvelously beautiful, but for a different reason: it is the craftsmanship and the artistry, not that they are alive. There was a connection among all living things, not an emotional one, but a scientific one, as if we were light bulbs all plugged into the same wireless power source. But, even the walls of my house were made of wood, and the wood maintained the data about where it came from.

As I looked around me at the beauty of every living thing, I noticed a man coming toward me on the sidewalk along the street in front of our house. He was dressed in a black shirt with short sleeves and no collar. He wore tan slacks and well-crafted brown leather shoes. I wondered where he was headed—probably one of our neighbors out for a walk, although better dressed than most.

He saw me looking at him and smiled.

Then I remembered. He couldn't see me looking at him, because he was a mortal, and I was an invisible dead guy. Then I recognized him—the man from the congressional hearing. By all appearances at the hearing, he was just another mortal, although his message was bizarre. He had to be looking for me, if he was here. There was no way he would have shown up at my house, or what used to be my house, by coincidence. He must not be a normal mortal, or he wouldn't be able to see me.

He walked across the grass towards me, held out his hand, and said, "Hello, Will. I'm Elias. You can call me Eli."

I stared at him. Then I realized my mouth was open and I closed it.

He laughed, full of good humor. Gingerly, I reached out and shook his hand. It was just like shaking Leilani's hand, except Leilani was cuter. I felt the sense of pressure, but not the firmness of a grip.

"It must be a shock for you," he said. "I can only imagine. You aren't used to having people who look like mortals able to see you. Of course, that is probably because someone like me is so rare."

"But how...."

"Mortals are easy for you to understand, because you have experienced mortality. You now begin to understand ex-mortals, as you experience a form of existence you had scarcely imagined as a mortal. Your current state is very similar to the Zolians, which is no accident. You even have some concept of indestructible physical beings, which is what Azzoloft was trying to become, when he appeared out of the dust at the NSHC. Obviously, I'm not exactly like any of them. I'm not a mortal."

"If you aren't mortal, why do you look and act like one?" I asked. "How do you know about what happened at the NSHC, and why would you get involved?"

"I go where I want and observe what I want," he said. "You recall, perhaps, there was a security guard who helped you one night at the lab? He left so fast you didn't see his face? Or perhaps I should say, he disappeared from your sight?"

"That was you?"

'Yes. I've been keeping track of your project. Besides, it was on television, once it leaked on national news. I act like a mortal because I can. I blend in. There is more going on than you realize, though. By stabilizing dark matter, you have opened a portal between worlds. Things could happen, fast. People who are religious will see them as a fulfillment of prophecy. But it is vital to stop Azzoloft, which is why I spoke up at the congressional hearing."

"Who are you?" I asked. "Did someone send you?"

"You know my name. Eli Matheson. I'm not going to explain to you who I am. I chose to get involved at the hearing because I've never seen a threat this great. If you want to know whether God sent me, the answer is no. God did not tell me to show up at a congressional hearing. On the other hand, he didn't stop me. I'm looking for a way to help you understand the stakes, because I think you are going to need it. Let me describe it this way. The book of Revelation says there was a war in heaven. That war wasn't fought with spears and swords. You can't kill a spirit the way you kill a mortal. So how was it fought?"

"I have no idea how it was fought, but it was a war of ideas."

"You are a scientist. Put it in terms of science."

"Satan was cast out into earth with a third of the angels of heaven," I said. "That would take powerful technology. Billions of people, or beings, or whatever they are, were forcibly transported from another planet here. Whatever type of beings they were, they could not interact with mortals, presumably because the beings were made of something besides atoms. Religion gave us the hypothesis, and now we have scientific evidence, through observation. I've seen the Zolians. They are reality."

"Right," said Eli. "It seems evident that Azzoloft could be Satan, and he's got billions of followers. But ask yourself this question: Why would Satan be so stupid as to fight against God, if he knew God was omnipotent?"

"Satan must not have known," I said. "He must have thought it was a fair fight. He thought he was arguing with Michael, and that Michael was a fallible person, who happened to be wrong."

"That's right. Satan lost the war," Eli said, "because he didn't understand what the consequences of that war of ideas would be. He wasn't being stupid. He just didn't know of any omnipotent being. He only knew there was going to be a mortal planet. As it turned out, Satan learned the hard way that Michael, or someone, had truly awesome technology at his disposal. Technology like nothing we had ever known."

"At least mortals now have fair warning," I said. "Religion says don't become a liar, thief, or murderer, or you'll go to hell. And by the way, religion says to mortals, God is omnipotent, so don't think you can get out of this. That is a fair warning, but we still have lots of murderers." *And one really stupid adulterer named Will.* "But this isn't really hell yet. According to religion, hell doesn't actually take full force until after judgment day, when those who are going to hell are cast into the pit, with Satan and his followers."

My experience with the light, right after I died, was like that. My soul had been a recording of my life, and I viewed it, enhanced by a radiant light. My mortal body had been lying in an intersection, and I had been in the valley of death, a place in between, where spirit and body separate. The light had the objectivity of a scientist, not a harsh, judgmental God. The judgment was still off in the future somewhere, and I wasn't ready.

"That is where you fit in," said Eli. "By stabilizing dark matter, you opened a door. It has been closed for 2,000 years. And now you are—more than inconveniently—dead. I say inconvenient, because having opened that door, you will play a role in the events to come. You are part of the fulfillment of things to come, prophecies, some might say. Information about the future, some of which I have seen. I assumed that stabilizing dark matter was how you opened the door, and that you were supposed to be alive to prevent Azzoloft from being able to take an immortal form that can interact with humans. It has finally occurred to me that there may be another option. Perhaps your death will turn out as an advantage. What you must do, though, is ensure that Azzoloft doesn't get the chance to finish what he started that day at the NSHC. No doubt, you've considered the implications."

"What I see," I said, "is that people can be made of several types of matter, and those types of matter give rise to a paradigm of the rules of physics, for each matter type. Atoms form only twenty percent of the matter in the universe, and now I see the other eighty percent, as an ex-mortal, and I realize just how real dark matter may be. It has characteristics, a different paradigm, completely different from being a mortal in a world made of atoms. The first type of matter is what I would call *alpha* matter, or spirit matter, like me, or the Zolians. The second is mortals or people made of *mortal* matter. The third is that they can be made of *resurrected* matter. Each of these types of matter has rules of its own. The key characteristic of resurrected matter is that you can't kill it, and it can interact with mortals. Azzoloft wants an indestructible physical form. It would make him very powerful. Right now, he can't kill anyone. If he had a body of stabilized dark matter, nothing could stop him from killing mortals. It isn't only himself; he has billions of followers. Fortunately, it would take time for him to transform them all. The point is, he needs to be stopped."

"You are the one who invented this technology," Eli said. "You understand better than anyone else why it is happening. You can find the information that will help you, but you are going to have to learn how to use it. Do you have any idea why the particles would take the form of Azzoloft?"

"The reason I thought we could stabilize dark matter is that scientists had discovered the Higgs particle," I explained. "I figured there must be a particle like the Higgs particle that would break the symmetry for dark matter and stabilize it. Maybe the form, or bodies, that Zolians have, and that I have, were designed as a prototype. It's like DNA. It is an instruction manual, a blueprint. When Azzoloft entered the particle field, the matter forms into his shape, because his spirit or alpha matter body is a living blueprint."

"That would make sense," said Eli. "The other part you need to know is that Azzoloft has the power to gather light around himself. He does it to show off, but there is another purpose."

I had seen Azzoloft do this when I first met him at the resort. He had been radiant, full of light.

"He borrows the light from his followers," Eli said. "If you are going to stop him, you will need to figure out how he does it. He has a connection with them, which gives him power. Just remember, he is not the only one who could use such a connection."

"Who are you?" I asked. "Really. You look like a mortal, but you aren't one. You aren't like other ex-mortals."

"That information is on a need-to-know basis, and no one needs to know."

"What about Azzoloft? Does he know?"

"He knows exactly who I am. You can ask him, but he won't tell you the truth. He's a liar. It's what he does."

I heard the door to the house open, and I turned to look. Marie was coming outside to get the newspaper. She looked in our direction, but there was no indication that she could see either me or Eli. She had no look of recognition that a man was standing in front of her house talking to me. I turned back to Eli to ask why she couldn't see him. He was gone.

■ ■ ■

It wasn't long before Kenny came to get me. "Brett is here all right," he said, "and right now he's at the mall over in Scottsdale. Get there quick and you should be able to find him. He's in a place called Tony's."

"Great," I said. "I really appreciate your help. But there is one other person I'd like to find, but he's not a relative. His name is Isaac, and he helped me out yesterday when I got here. I really need to talk to him." Isaac was a scientist. I needed to ask him about the portals. I described what little I knew about him, and Kenny said they'd let me know if they came up with anything. It wasn't likely, since I didn't know enough about him.

I thanked him for his help. Charlotte's volunteers were a good bunch of people.

I knew where the mall was at, and my flying skills were quickly improving. I was able to glide about 100 meters above I-17 northbound. The traffic at the 101 interchange near Scottsdale was snarled, and I was glad I wasn't driving in it. When I got to the mall, I circled until I saw the sign for Tony's Bar and Grill, I moved through the wall and inside.

The place had dim lights, a row of slanted mirrors along the ceiling behind the bar, and a plasma TV screen on each end of the row of mirrors. There was a cable sports channel playing nonstop. I got there during happy hour, and the place was packed with mortals, but then this mall always had a lot of people. There were also several groups of afterlifers in white robes, and I saw my brother Brett there with two women I'd never seen before. He was busy kissing one of them, an attractive woman in a white robe who looked to me like she was from Thailand. The other was watching them with a bemused expression. From what I had experienced of touching other afterlifers, I didn't see how he'd get any thrill out of kissing.

"Excuse me," I said, "but I'll have to ask you to stop kissing my wife." Brett looked up and burst out laughing. He actually looked decent in the robe. I'm sure when he died his biggest heartbreak was leaving behind his closet full of shorts and sandals.

"Dang, bro, I heard you were here! How ya doin'? You look great, man! Where have you been? I was looking all over for you!"

"I got distracted by a few things." I glanced sideways at the other woman with Brett, trying not to stare. "Why are you guys kissing, anyway? It can't feel the same as if you were a mortal."

"No," said Brett, "but there is still no better way to show how much you love a beautiful woman."

Talking to Brett was always the same. No matter how serious I might be with my work or whatever else was worrying me, Brett was like a reckless teenager. I felt my somber mood lifting, and it was great. Talking to Brett was exactly what I needed.

"Hey, I heard you finally did it! That thing with dark matter that you were always talking about. They were talking about you on TV. I knew you would. But seriously, why don't you learn how to ride, man?"

"I'd rather not talk about it."

"I hear ya. This has gotta be tough on Marie, and your kids."

The woman Brett was with cleared her throat.

"Oh, I'm sorry," Brett said, "this is Pat, which is short for a name I don't know how to pronounce. Pat, this is my brother, Will."

"Nice to meet you."

"And this," said Brett, pointing at the other woman, "is Shartruze."

I looked at her, relieved that I finally had a reason. Shartruze was truly striking. Her skin was olive-toned, and she had exotic features like an ancient Egyptian queen. She smiled and moved uncomfortably close, only inches from my face, and looked into my eyes.

"Hey, you're not bad-looking," she said. "If we were both mortal right now, I wouldn't mind doing exactly what you seem to have in mind."

This really was a change from talking to Charlotte. My reaction to her looks must have been more obvious than I thought. Maybe it was easier to discern without a physical body.

Listening to Shartruze talk was like hearing air hiss out of a punctured tire. I felt light-headed, and the room got slightly darker. I lost track of time.

Pat said, "I hope you like older women. Shar claims she's over 100,000 years old, but she refuses to tell her real age. She's so funny. She's a Zolian."

Shartruze smiled in a way that soothed me more than Oxycontin could have.

"Really, Will, she's cool," said Brett. "She's the only Zolian I can even stand. Most of them are unbelievably pompous creeps—no offense, Shar. Their big claim to fame is that they go around talking to mortals all the time, like that makes a difference."

"Unlike most Zolians, I don't see any need for hostility towards post-mortals," Shartruze said. "If pressed, I might even admit to the heretical notion that it would be fun to experience the decadence of mortality—you know, a man with a nice tan, lots of muscles, and no shirt. The only problem is that he'd get old, fat, and repulsive, just like they all do. But before that happened . . ."

She looked over and saw a mortal couple entering the bar.

"Ah, there, see what I mean?" she said.

The man had a chiseled face and a perfect haircut. He was impeccably dressed in slacks and a form-fitting shirt. Shartruze moved over to a mortal woman at a table who had looked briefly at the man and then quickly back at her menu.

"Go ahead and stare," Shartruze said to the woman.

I was shocked to see a dark mist exuding from her mouth as she spoke to the woman. At first, I thought I was imagining it, but then I blinked and looked again, and realized it was real; a kind of black vapor extended down from Shartruze's mouth to the mortal woman. It curled around her ear, caressing her almost as if it were alive, beckoning.

"He's worth looking at." The woman looked back up and stared.

"Now if he looks at you, meet his gaze," Shartruze said. "Don't look down; no reason to be modest. Life is short, and he's the kind of thing you were looking for when you came here today—something exciting, something worth being bold for."

The man's wife—they were both wearing wedding bands—noticed the woman staring before he did.

"She has bug-eyes. Look at them," Sharturze said. "Look at those hideous stripes she's wearing. And that leather skirt is way too tight. No wonder she waddles when she walks."

There was a surge of emotion in the room as the two women stared at each other, but neither the mortals nor the afterlifers seemed to be paying much attention to what was happening. The mortals had no idea Shartruze was even there, and beautiful mortal women giving each other nasty looks was nothing new. The man noticed the brazen woman staring at him; then he immediately noticed his wife staring back, and a flicker of a smile tugged at the corner of his mouth, but he stopped it in the nick of time, just as his wife turned her gaze to him. The wife pointedly made her way to some tall stools at a table around the corner, and I thought it was over.

Shartruze wasn't quite through. "Go over by the restrooms."

Shartruze waited and watched while the woman got in position. Then Shartruze moved over by the man and whispered.

Sure enough, the man headed for the restroom. The woman stepped around the corner in time to bump into him, and pretended her heel was twisted, falling into his arms, if only briefly.

"Oh, I'm so sorry!" she said. She brushed back her hair with her fingers.

The man's wife had been watching, and her eyes were narrowed to slits.

The man was blushing, in spite of himself.

Shartruze moved near the woman.

Shartruze's mortal protégé dropped her purse. "Bend over slowly, let him watch you."

The man watched her, too intently, which could only make things worse for him when he got home with his wife.

The woman gave him an exaggerated smile, lowering her eyes and biting her lip. She sauntered back over towards her seat, trying to draw his wife's eyes, but his wife was pointedly staring away.

"Bravo," said Brett to Shartruze. "You accomplished as much as ever. I don't know why you bother, Shar."

She smiled at him and glanced knowingly at Pat. "I know you don't, Brett. You don't see the point because there are things I haven't told you. Lots of things, as always."

I felt a strange mix of attraction and revulsion when she was close. Her features were so stunning, her words so alluring.

She glanced back at Brett. "The fact is, that man works in the same building as the woman I was talking to. I was at that office this morning, urging both of them to be here this afternoon. I went to talk to his wife and warmed her up to the idea. What you and they both think is coincidence was carefully planned. It takes days, weeks, sometimes months of planning to set up an affair."

She looked back at me with a mocking smile, then moved close. Her words hissed in my ear. "Doesn't it, Will?"

How much did she know about Ronnie?

With that, she was gone, a blur through the ceiling and out of sight.

Here was Shartruze, tempting mortals. Or was she? This wasn't a devil in hell tempting someone. This was a person. A person I could see and interact with, after my mortal death. This was real. We were all so far off, so far from understanding, as mortals, and here, in the afterlife, we were still missing it. This was science. This was technology. Mortals are made of atoms. Ex-mortals are made of something else, perhaps dark matter. Eighty percent of the universe is made of something besides atoms. Zolians and mortals had something in common; a lot in common, actually. They were made from the same technology. We could call it spirit matter, but I would think of it as alpha matter, or *type A* matter.

There was an interaction between worlds at the type A matter level. There was alpha matter, or spirit matter, in mortals, as well as atoms. This was a communications technology, with Zolians and people, like Charlotte, able to put thoughts into mortals' minds. This was science, and we'd all thought it was spirituality, or religion. We had it all wrong. We were set up. We were supposed to misunderstand it. Maybe it didn't bother Charlotte, but it bothered me. It was time to find out exactly what we were missing.

■ ■ ■

We left the bar and entered the eatery area of the mall. We stopped in the rotunda. There were so many plants! It was like a mock jungle. A huge American flag hung from the skylight   above.
"So, why do you guys hang out at the mall?" I asked Pat.

"Are you kidding?" she asked. "It is my favorite place in the world, or at least one of them."

"Aren't you a little old for . . ." 1 paused, realizing my words weren't flattering, but she laughed.

"Oh, no, it isn't like that. I'm a designer—houses mostly, but I love nice mortal clothes, as well. This is where you get to see it all. During the mornings I like to go to new houses that the mortals are building around the Valley, and then I come down here and pick out decorations. I also go to some of the stores to look at tile and granite. I pick what I want, and then I impression the aura of my design into morals' minds."

"She's great at impressioning," said Brett. "And she has impeccable taste."

"Impressioning? Sounded like a perfect pile of bull crap to me." Charlotte might be able to put thoughts in mortals' minds, but not this lady.

"I don't talk to mortals as directly as Shartruze can. I wish I could, though—I'd tell them exactly what design they needed, and all the houses would look phenomenal," she said. "But I do get through to them. Bathrooms, kitchens, bedrooms—it's all so fun!"

"Wow," I said, "so that's what we do in the afterlife. I'm really going to suck at this." What a perfect way to waste time. "We might as well douse the lights, hold a seance, and see if we can talk to some mortals."

"No, that's not all we do. Brett can't design anything to save his soul. He just likes to watch sports. That's why he comes here. Right, babe?"

He smiled. "Absolutely."

"Baloney," I said. "That's a great cover story, Brett, but I know very well that you're hanging out here because this is where you find beautiful women like Pat."

It was Pat's turn to laugh. "I don't know about me, but it's true, there are a lot of women afterlifers who like it here, especially at this mall. It's a lot better than most. I'm getting ready to go meet with my fashion club. Once a week we meet here to analyze the best and worst dressed people in the mall. I've learned so much since I died. It's amazing."

Brett raised an eyebrow. "The women in her club are all hot. You should see it. But, sadly, I won't be there. I'm headed over to see the Diamondbacks game right now. Why don't you come along?"

Sounded great to me. I wondered how hot the women could really be, considering they would be in white robes. Brett's idea of "hot" had previously been "scantily clad."

Getting from Terry's sports bar in Scottsdale to the ballpark in Phoenix was fast. No getting in your car, no fighting traffic, and no need to buy tickets. We followed the freeway again, and the mortal traffic had gotten even worse, with cars backed up for miles on the Seventh Street off-ramp to get to the game. For us, there was no looking for a parking spot. We just went straight to the game. We went through the open retractable roof and into the stadium. The weather was great. The ballpark looked like it always had, except for about a hundred afterlifers hanging out to watch the game in addition to the normal crowd of mortals.

While we were waiting for the game to start, I asked Brett, "So Pat was a designer as a mortal, huh?"

He laughed. "No, she was a prostitute. She died of a drug overdose."

I felt stunned. "Seriously?"

"I'm dead serious. This place is like heaven for her. She can be everything she always wanted to be. She grew up with dirt-poor immigrant parents, and had a really rough, short life, but now she finally has her chance to shine as a designer. She loves it."

Her heaven? The same mortal planet and buildings, with a few Zolians for laughs? I wondered anew whether my brother had any clue about heaven, hell, or anything else. Where was God in all this? I looked around the huge indoor stadium and its hundreds of rows of seats rising steeply in every direction.

"You've never seen a baseball game until you've seen it like this," Brett said. "We aren't talking about front row seats. To heck with rows, man. You can watch from any angle, anywhere."

We listened to the mortals sing the Star-Spangled Banner. I noticed most of the afterlifers joined in, their hands over their hearts in their white robes, facing the mortals' huge U.S. flag on the wall of the stadium.

The opening pitch was thrown, and the game was underway. I found the view was great from 100 feet straight up from the field. After several innings, I got excited and moved down closer when the bases were loaded.

"Hey, what do you think you're doing?" Said an afterlifer behind me. "Get out of the way! You're blocking my view!" I moved back behind him. I wondered if he was a Zolian, but he seemed intent on the game. I looked around the stadium at the other people in white robes, and noticed there were dozens interspersed among the crowd, standing above them. There was a roar from the crowd as the batter knocked the ball into the bleachers on the far end of the field, but none of the watchers looked up. They must've been Zolians.

I thoroughly enjoyed what I saw of that game. It was an awesome view, and baseball like it had always been. The couch potatoes heaven. After the Diamondbacks' three hits in the third inning, they took over the game. Brett told me how he had been to every stadium in the country, not just for baseball games, but basketball and football, as well. "All the college games, all the professional games, spring training, you name it. And all free. No tickets, and the best seats in the house."

What was bothering me was that there were no hot dogs, no pretzels, and no popcorn, at least not for the afterlifers. I couldn't pick up a pretzel any more than a mortal could see me. There weren't any pretzels made of the stuff I was made of. I wondered if my tongue even had taste buds still. I stuck it out to check, and Brett looked at me funny.

I could see taste buds, but there was nothing for them to taste. I had a problem with that. And another thing. I'd always liked playing baseball better than watching it. Now I couldn't pick up the bat. I couldn't catch the ball. I couldn't show 'em how it's done. Afterlifers were the ultimate spectators. All watch and no do.

Life in the mortal, physical world was life on the stage, in the spotlight, in the action. I should never have wasted a moment wishing I could leave it early. But that was kind of like Luciano Pavarotti wishing he'd never learned to sing.

Suddenly, all I could see was an ugly face and a sneering grin. Blitzer had found me. "Boo!" he said.

CHAPTER 11

ZOLIAN OCCUPATIONAL TRAINING

"SOME PEOPLE INSIST on learning things the hard way," Blitzer said. He stopped a foot away from my face, invading my personal space. As he spoke, I could see vapors of dark mist, and I felt them touch me, like tendrils of poison. I felt instant anxiety. "You received a personal offer from Azzoloft, and you spurned his generosity. You will regret that. Now Charlotte isn't here to protect you."

What a way to ruin my ball game.

"I was hoping Azzoloft had forgotten all about me."

Brett raised his eyebrows at the mention of Azzoloft.

"Azzoloft isn't in any hurry—he has all the time he needs," Blitzer said. "Zinc, on the other hand, had a few ideas on how to make you regret your lack of respect. He took your obnoxious behavior with Charlotte personally." Blitzer was exhaling black mist as he spoke.

The black mist wafted over me, and filled me with a sense of dread, mostly of Azzoloft. I tried to push the feeling from my mind. The feeling was pervasive and unshakeable. "What is Azzoloft planning to do? What does he want with me?"

"Ah, is this false modesty, Will? You are the man who led

143

the team that stabilized dark matter. Azzoloft has been waiting for that for a very long time. He's been watching you since the earliest stages. He wants your loyalty and support. If you aren't with us, you're against us."

Why should he want more people on his side? Didn't he have enough already? And why was he waiting on us, if he has so much power? It seemed to me that someone who has a physical body has more power than someone like Azzoloft. He needed someone to stabilize dark matter because he couldn't do it himself.

Blitzer started moving away from me. "Let's go."

"No, actually, I don't think he wants to go with you," said Brett. "Do you, Will?"

Brett was right. I wanted to get away. "No."

Blitzer darted towards him, coming within six inches of his face. "Leave us," he hissed.

"Make me, dirt bag," said Brett. "You think you can handle me, or do you need to call in some of your little buddies to help you?"

The slightest hesitation in Blitzer's response made me think that had been his idea.

"I think I'll go with him. Maybe you should leave," I said to Brett. I had of feeling of danger that started when I felt the touch of the dark mist. Something much worse was going to happen if I didn't go.

"I'm not worried," Brett said. "And, hey, I've got nothing better to do. You're my brother, and I haven't been able to talk to you in a long time. I don't care what this fuzzball thinks."

Blitzer's face showed anger only as a passing glimpse. Then his demeanor changed. "Sure, come with us," he told Brett. "It just occurred to me how to put you to good use."

The sun was sinking through the haze towards the

horizon west of Phoenix. We moved high over the city and headed east until we weren't too far from the neighborhood where my family lived.

Blitzer slowed down. We moved through the air about 50 meters from the ground. We approached the freeway that runs east out of Phoenix. There are four lanes in each direction, and the eastbound evening traffic was crawling. There was a swarm of people in white robes above the freeway, moving at the same speed as the cars.

"You're a smart guy, Will. Have you noticed that there are usually one or two Zolians, where they can see nearly every mortal?"

"How could anyone miss the fact that there are hordes of Zolians hanging around mortals?" said Brett. "You guys are dang creepy if you don't have anything better to do with your time."

Blitzer turned to Brett, his tone ridiculing; "Do you really believe that there are a bunch of devils that go all over the world tempting people?"

"Of course not," Brett said. "I'm an American. Haven't you read the polls?"

"It took a long time," said Blitzer, "for Americans and everyone else to figure out how preposterous it is to believe that devils go around tempting mortals. The reality for mortals is the same as the reality here. If mortal religion had any truth in it, you would be calling me an angel, and not a devil, because of the power I have. But I'm going to show you up close and personal what I can do, and why."

We moved up higher, a quarter mile off the ground, so we could see the streets intersecting the freeway and the neighborhoods in between. "You see a lot of Zolians in a pattern, the numbers of mortals and Zolians roughly equal. Mortals are incredibly susceptible both emotionally and mentally."

145

Blitzer closed his eyes and tilted his head back. "I can sense them Will, I can feel the emotions from both mortals and Zolians. I can feel when there are many, or very few nearby. And during rush-hour traffic, there is always angry emotion roiling up from the freeway."

His excitement reminded me of a shark sniffing blood in frothy ocean waters.

"I told you they were creepy," said Brett.

Blitzer looked into Brett's eyes and smiled. "You have no idea."

Blitzer turned toward me. "We are so far advanced over what you could ever understand. The Zolians have many abilities you can't imagine, so much knowledge from eons of existence. Do you know what it was like? Can you even imagine the earth in its pristine state? Before there were any mortals on the earth, it was filled with beauty, its vast forests teeming with animals. There were no buildings, no freeways, and no pollution. It was a paradise.

"Mortals are alien invaders," Blitzer said. "You came and began marring our pristine earth. Certainly, Azzoloft found a way to have your temples, cathedrals, and churches built for him, and your buildings and homes he claims as his, since you all die while he remains. But the truth is we haven't been able to stop you from pillaging, destroying, and polluting our planet. Instead of pristine beauty, we see your slums and ugly architecture. Your war-torn cities occupy country after country. Your fires leave what you call national forests desolate and scarred with scorched earth and trees."

If they wanted to see pristine earth, why weren't they off enjoying the stunning beauty of the icecaps, or the rain forests, instead of here, showing a constant and morbid interest in mortals? If mortals were destroying the planet, were the Zolians so impotent they couldn't stop it?

146

"Why don't you leave and go to some other planet?" I asked.

Blitzer turned on me, his face contorted with hatred. "It belongs to us. We found a haven here, Azzoloft first, and all the others of us who have joined him. We were here for hundreds of thousands of years. Some see this as a war. It's us against you. They would love to see you blow yourselves up with nuclear weapons, until the humans are destroyed from the earth. We could then banish you from the afterlife as well."

I didn't answer. I stood there, watching his face, and then looking down at the hordes of people below, and wondered how much damage his race, with all their hate, could do to mortals, if what he was saying held any truth. I had always believed there were devils who tempted us. The book of Revelation speaks of one-third of heaven being cast to earth, but I'd never imagined it like this, something this real, palpable, obviously evident, and scientifically observed. These beings weren't made of atoms, because mortal scientists couldn't detect them. And they were everywhere. The only thing we still couldn't prove was the religious part, that these beings were Satan and his followers. Everything religious was still unprovable, like it had all been precisely programmed. Science gave us provable truth, and religion gave us unprovable truth. Like a test, with the exam on judgment day. I believed liars, thieves, and murderers were going to hell, but everyone else should get a medal, for having to go through mortal life, and afterlife, without being able to prove God exists. That was harsh. It was hard.

"If we assume you can travel at the speed of light," I said, "the nearest star is only four years away. You could reach the center of the galaxy in 27,000 years, which isn't that much if you've been here for hundreds of thousands of years. Have you explored? I would think there are hundreds of planets like ours, if not thousands. Can you tell us what else is out there?"

"You think you know so much, but you really know nothing." His demeanor was pompous and derisive, but defensive. He wasn't answering the question. Was something holding him here? They said they came here as a haven in space. A haven from what? Why weren't they out dominating the galaxy? How long had they really been here? He didn't fit in the evolutionary process, but he wasn't acknowledging religion, either.

"I think we're done here," said Brett. "Take what you know and shove it."

Blitzer grinned. "Then it is time for my friends to join us, as you suggested."

"Let's get out of here!" I whispered to Brett. I hadn't forgotten how forty of Azzoloft's followers came to get me right after I died.

Brett was looking over my shoulder. People in white robes came at us, surrounding us this time with military precision, boxing us in. They immediately started moving southward. I could see Blitzer moving alongside us, through gaps between our captors. We moved very rapidly south over the desert, until we approached a ravine. There was a hole in the ground, under the overhang of a rock, in rugged terrain. It looked as if there was dark fog misting around the entrance. There were other Zolians guarding the area.

Blitzer nodded to one of the forty. "Seize the one on the left." The Zolian flew at Brett, dark mist spewing from his mouth and enveloping Brett instantly. Through the mists I could see his face contorted as if in pain, his eyes shut tightly, as the Zolian tackled him, moving him out and onto the ground. As the black mist swirled, the Zolian had a crazed look on his face, staring at Brett, who was motionless, his face frozen in a grimace.

"Let him go!" I shouted at Blitzer.

"Come with me, and we might let him go later."

Anger filled me, and I looked down. My fists were clenched, but I knew it wouldn't help to try to attack Blizter.

"If you refuse to come," Blitzer said, "you will join him."

"I'll be back, Brett! Hold on." Brett was wallowing in a mist of darkness, his eyes fixed in a stare, his body motionless. They escorted Brett into the hole beneath the rock, into darkness.

Blitzer moved away, and I followed.

"What did they do to my brother? What did that black mist do to him?"

"It will take a while for him to—recover," he said.

He started moving away, and I followed, wondering if he was prepared to seize me if occasion required. Azzoloft might be sparing me, only so long as it suited his purpose.

"That looks like a prison. How long do you keep people in there?"

"As long as it takes. Hundreds of years, if necessary. This is just one of the entrances. We call it the pit."

"Religion says Satan and his angels are going to be cast into the pit," I said.

"Maybe we should go back and put you in," he said, "so you can go looking for Satan, and see if he's in there."

There was a pattern of deception, twisting things, and now holding my brother hostage. This wasn't magic. I didn't believe in magic. That black mist was real. I wished I could do a chemical analysis on it. It had a real power, like poison. I had felt a fleeting dose of it. It was like condensed sin. But sin was supposed to be inside a person, in the spirit. In the type A matter. Was it a power, like a chemical, to activate my sin and fill me with darkness brought on by my own past? Precision. Technological. Not spiritual. Or yes, spiritual, but real. Not mystical. That was it! Mortals view heaven and hell as mystical. I was experiencing the reality of it, the science of it. The consequences weren't damnation from God, so much as programmed results. The precision was better than computers. We had everything backwards, upside down, inside out. Sin was technological. It had to be. Mortals were like test dummies. Our lives were being placed in cars on the highway of life, and the guy at the controls already knew how we would break and shatter on the barricades of murder and adultery. If there was someone at the controls, and if that guy was God, no wonder he gave us dire warnings.

Why didn't Brett already know the Zolians hold post-mortals in prison? He had acted like he had nothing to fear.

"You locked up Brett for trying to help me. How many post-mortals do you have locked up?"

"Ask yourself how much of a threat Brett was to us before he interfered."

Brett was busy going to ball games and chasing Pat. He had lived out his mortal life a day at a time, finding happiness where he could. As an ex-mortal, he was the same way, and the Zolians evidently thought that was fine. I spent my life trying to follow the religious plan I believed in, which was to continue learning, growing, and serving other people. Too bad I had messed it up right at the end.

Blitzer flew quickly towards the East Valley, over a neighborhood, with houses that looked like they'd been built several decades earlier.

Blitzer approached a house with a red brick front, a shingled roof and yellow-painted eaves. I recognized the house—it belonged to Mike and Alicia. Blitzer pantomimed knocking on the door, even though his fist went into the door with each pretend knock.

"Open up, anybody home? Oh, don't mind if I do." He acted like someone had invited him in and went through the door into the home.

"This is Alicia," he said. "Remember her?"

I did. She was in my church congregation.

He waved his hand towards a mortal woman with lots of curves, dressed in white pants and a purple blouse. Obviously, she was had no idea two non-mortals were present.

"Pretty, young thing, isn't she? Makes you wonder why she and her husband fight all the time, and why he is addicted to pain killers."

"I don't wonder. I know them," I said. "His name's Mike. He's a great guy, and he only takes pain pills because he got injured in a serious car wreck. He's a junior high school teacher, and the kids love him. You had better leave them alone. Let's go find somebody else for whatever you have in mind." I said.

Blitzer looked at me at me and laughed. "We're not going to go talk to anyone else, Will, because I say they'll do fine. I know they are friends of yours. Do you think we only affect people you don't know? Would that help you lie to yourself and feel it less? Or should I suggest, to Zinc, that we pay a visit to your wife and kids? Maybe he already has."

He wasn't just willing to attack my brother; my wife and kids were now fair game.

"So, tell me why Mikey here is still using pain pills after his accident."

"Because he has a permanent injury to his back."

"He's got a pain generator all right, but not the kind you think. Did you consider his emotional pain?"

I knew about emotional pain. Mine was named Marie.

Alicia took her keys off the hook by the door. We followed her into the study at the back of the house, where her slightly pudgy, balding, young husband, Mike, was sitting at the computer listening to songs and downloading them to a portable device.

Alicia gave him a hen-peck kiss. "I'm off to my meeting. Bye."

She left, and once he heard the car pull out of the driveway, Blitzer looked at Mike again. "Let's do some work with Mike, here. Mike is a nice family man, he's got a wife and some little kids. We just saw his wife head off to her book club. I know, because I've worked with him for a long time, trying to shape his thoughts, teach him, and help him understand what mortal life is all about."

Blitzer began talking directly to Mike as he was typing on the computer, even though he couldn't see us. Blitzer's face was next to Mike's looking at the computer screen. "You've got a problem, don't you, Mike?" Black mist started wafting from Blitzer, swirling around Mike's head. "Your problem is pain. Your back is throbbing, and it keeps throbbing, whether you sit or stand. But there are pills. The pills will solve the pain. The pain will go away. You've got to get the pills."

Mike clicked on a new song, seemingly unfazed by Blitzer, and kept listening to music.

"He isn't listening to you. That's awesome," I said. "I told you the guy has brains."

"You are ignorant, Will. Watch."

Blitzer kept talking. After a while, Mike rubbed his back.

"You've got a problem, don't you Mike? You ran out of pain pills. No doctor or dentist in their right mind is going to give you another prescription. On the other hand, you are a resourceful guy, and you scanned in the last prescription your doctor wrote for you."

As Blitzer talked, Mike's eye twitched. He rubbed his back again.

"All you have to do is print it out, doctor it a bit with an ink pen, and you'll have a passable prescription."

A few minutes later Mike had printed and signed the fake prescription.

Blitzer closed his eyes. "Can you feel that, Will? I feel visceral emotion coming from him, just as all Zolians can. You know why? He's looking forward to his fix. His pulse is accelerated, like every addict before a fix. You should see him when he's into pornography, it's the same thing."

Blitzer had to be some kind of perverse person. "Uh, no," I said. "I don't really care to feel Mike's visceral emotions." Especially not if he was into pornography. That I hadn't known.

"I can feel those emotions—hatred, anger, lust—everywhere I go, just as humans experience them."

I thought about the dogs chasing postal workers. A dog can sense your fear. It starts to growl. It doesn't matter whether you pretend you're not afraid, it'll sense it anyway.

"Well, maybe it's my turn," I said. "I know Mike, and I'm on his side." I turned to him, and said loudly, "Don't do it, Mike. You can't abuse drugs. You are going to lose your teaching certificate if you get busted. You'll lose your career."

Blitzer laughed, and mocked me: "Don't do it, Mikey. You'll lose your job."

As I watched Blitzer talking to Mike, I did learn, but I had no desire to be more like him. I didn't think he could read Mike's mind, but Blitzer was extraordinarily adept, no doubt from many years of experience, at reading actions. Blitzer knows Mike uses porn. If Blitzer says type in "XXX," and Mike does, Blitzer knows exactly what Mike is thinking. Mike has a dirty mind.

As I watched Mike, black mist began oozing from him into the surrounding air.

Blitzer was finished. He told me I could go. Before I left, I demanded that Blitzer let Brett go.

"We aren't through with you yet. After the strategic re-test, we *might* let him go. Just be glad Azzoloft hasn't decided to put you in there with him."

They weren't going to let him out. Anyone like me or Brett was a ticking time bomb, with a built-in self-destruct mechanism, and Azzoloft could set us off whenever he chose.

What were the Zolians trying to accomplish? They were exerting control over mortals. If they succeeded, as they did with Brett and me, they could exert control over us when we died. That isn't war. They weren't killing anyone. Well, they did get people to commit murder. For that matter, the Zolians were likely behind wars around the earth, inciting mortals to hatred and violence. If the Zolians waited long enough, judgment day would come. And the big surprise would be that judgment day was going to be technological. That might even surprise Azzoloft.

CHAPTER 12

SKY'S OFFICE

I THOUGHT ABOUT what I had learned from Blitzer. He was able to communicate with mortals. He could clearly put thoughts in Mike's mind. That was a power I didn't have. It was a technology. All of this had to be based in reality, just as everything mortals do can be explained. Gravity, DNA, muscles burning energy, the physics of our bodies allowing us to walk or run, it was all science. Ex-mortals can fly. And Zolians can put thoughts in mortals' minds. I thought about the fact that I could touch my son, even though he couldn't feel my touch. I could go right through a wall, so why didn't I go through people? What would happen with an animal? It was time to run an experiment.

Our neighbors had a bulldog named Buster. I went over the fence into my neighbor's back yard. I saw the dog standing in the sun, drooling as usual. I put my hand on the dog; I was able to touch him, just like I could people. I was glad he didn't know I was there. His favorite pastime had always been to bark at me whenever I went in my backyard. If I could touch living animals, even though I didn't feel the texture of them, there must be something different about them than non-living things.

The dog shook his head, and a big drip of drool danced through the air and then hung from his jowls. I tried to touch the drool, but my hand went through it. There had to be hundreds of thousands of microbes in that drool. How could my hand go through them, but not through the dog? For that matter, what if I was flying by some mortal and he or she sneezed? Would the bacteria in the air stop me midflight, the way the pilot on the plane had?

I went back over the fence into my yard and looked for a spider. We always had little spiders on cobwebs around our windows. I found one and put out my finger to touch it. My finger went through it. That was good. I didn't have to worry about stopping in my tracks for every mosquito I ran into. Must be the size of the living thing—or maybe spiders and mosquitos have no souls. Nasty, biting, blood-sucking organisms. Okay, maybe they are God's creatures, and they have a purpose. Bird food.

I flew up fifty feet from the ground and looked around. I had seen lots of Zolians and post-mortals, but I didn't recall seeing any post-life animals. Did animals stay on earth after they died? Were favorite family pets still here? What if stray cats stayed around after death? They should be everywhere, considering how many feral cats there were in our neighborhood. Worse, we should be positively buried in all the pigeons that had lived in my neighborhood, if they all stayed here after they died.

How could I tell for sure the birds or animals I was seeing were flesh and bone living animals, as opposed to post-life forms of the animals? For a person, we were all in white robes, so post-mortals were easy to distinguish from mortals. A pigeon wasn't going to have on a white robe. Perhaps I could conduct an experiment.

I observed the pigeon for a while, wondering how I could

set up an experiment. Suddenly the pigeon defecated, adding one more spot among many on the roof, and I was filled with a mild disgust. My experiment was over and I didn't have to go beyond the step of observation; if post-mortals don't eliminate waste, post-life animals don't either. This, at least, told me a way to distinguish living animals, but not whether there were any post-life animals here.

Science had always filled me with wonder. I wanted to know everything, and that was why our work on stabilizing dark matter had succeeded. There were a great many questions I had about how things worked for post-mortals, and I was filled with excitement at how much I could learn. This might be a scientist's dream—having a whole new world of possibilities to explore. There must be thousands and thousands of books on the subject—no, wait. There probably weren't any, since post-mortals evidently don't have any paper on which to write. Were we limited to observation, or were there other experiments I could use?

Whatever the excitement of a whole new paradigm of physics in the afterlife, the fact remained that Azzoloft needed to be stopped. I felt a lingering dread, the dread I had felt back at the lab, alone, when I had felt paralyzed. Everything was real. Too real. It was too much like mortal life. People, not angels. Too much missing. Too much unexplained. Too many, as in God, missing in the afterlife.

I had no answer for that, but right now there was another question I wanted answered. The main thing was to stop Azzoloft, but there were other things that might help. Isaac had said he was investigating a murder, and the police told Marie someone had put acid on my brake cables. It was time to go back to Sky Lurich's office.

I flew east. To get to New York, I was going to have to fly much faster than I had before. The plane I had encountered on my way to Ronnie's had moved me faster than before, but even so, it would take hours to get to New York. There was no reason a post-mortal couldn't fly faster than I had before, faster than the jets. As I flew over Weaver's Needle in the Superstition Mountains east of Apache Junction, I realized how different it was to be flying rather than following a road. I increased altitude, and could see that the mountains were vast, compared to a roadway with mile post signs.

The sense of freedom was tremendous. The blue of the atmosphere at the horizon reminded me of flying in planes, but instead of looking out a tiny window from a plane, my view was unimpeded and stunning.

I wanted to find a way to speed up, but just willing myself to go faster didn't seem to work. Isaac had said that our minds control our flight. Maybe focusing on the point I wanted to reach would help. I picked the most distant spot on the horizon and visualized myself as already there. I reached out in my mind, as though pulling myself to that location. This worked, and I reached that point almost instantaneously. I picked another point on the horizon, and another, and another--my speed was much greater, and I tried to move as fast as my thoughts, from one point to the next. The sun was my gauge as I moved northeast.

Finally, I slowed and tried to get my bearings. I suddenly realized I had none. I had seen a rapid succession of vast mountains and hills, and stretches of flat land, with farms and fields, but now I had no idea where I was. I had been so intent on going faster that I didn't know where I was, except that there was nothing but mountains below me, with no cities or even recognizable roads. I picked a distant spot on the horizon again, but I was still lost when I got there.

I began thinking about Isaac and wondering why I didn't ask for his help before I started off cross-country. For one thing, I was confident that I would learn quickly and travel fast. Frustration rose in my gut, and a memory of being lost when I was a child, alone on a mountainside. Isaac could have at least told me how he expected to find me, if I needed him.

I decided I just needed to fly east until I saw a road, follow that road to a town, and then I'd know where I was, and I could follow roads from there. But it was going to take forever to get to New York.

Then I saw a person in a white robe was moving towards me very quickly across the mountains. He slowed as he approached me. It was Isaac. This was impossible; it was preposterous.

"No way!" I said. "How did you find me?"

He laughed. "I love practical jokes, but this one is too good for me to have set up. You are really lost. Even I'm not sure where we are right now." He looked around.

I didn't think it was nearly so funny, but that was only because I felt stupid. I could have found my way out of this, but he showed up so suddenly I didn't have the chance. "Just tell me how you found me." My tone was ruder than I intended.

He didn't seem to notice my tone. He was grinning. "What would you say about the state-of-the-art technology mortals have today, Will? Would you call it advanced?"

"Of course, it is! It is the most advanced it has ever been, mostly due to computers."

"Finding you required a combination of communication and location, both of which feel so natural to me now that I wouldn't think of it as technology. It is as though you had a tracking device on you, and an emergency S.O.S. signal, although it doesn't need to be an emergency. When you are reaching out to someone in your mind, they feel it. As far as location, I'm not saying I had you on GPS, just that I knew which direction you were in, and a sense that you were distant."

"That is impossible," I said. "That kind of tracking requires radio signals and satellites; it is high tech. Why should my thoughts be able to summon you from hundreds of miles away just by thinking of you? And how would you know it is me?"

"I'd say I recognize your wavelength. If you were in China and I called you on a cell phone, it all depends on knowing and dialing the right phone number. I could recognize your voice from thousands of other people I know, which is a function of the wavelength of your vocal sound. To me, the earthly technologies are mere mimicry of more advanced abilities we have as post-mortals. I'm not saying I hear your thoughts, like telepathy. I just feel a connection, a subtle sense, along with a sense of direction. And not everyone feels it."

"Can you prove that? Have any studies been done?"

He laughed again. "I'm a scientist, like you. That is what the Science Association is all about. We've been observing how science works for ex-mortals for years. But I suspect when you start trying to run experiments, you're going to run into some hitches. You haven't got a microscope; you can't dissect any frogs; and you can't build a machine to stabilize dark matter. Just ask Azzoloft. Why do you think he needed a mortal to build one? Anyway, where are you going?"

I told him about my dream of Sky Lurich, and about what the police told Marie. "Why did you say you were investigating a murder last time I saw you?"

"You were murdered, all right. Lurich's men had a remote control device which released acid on your brake cables."

Sky Lurich was willing to kill me? In the dream I'd had of Sky, the Satan figure wanted me dead. I had felt fear, a sense of the foreboding. That wasn't enough for Sky to kill me.

"You know of Sky Lurich?"

"The Science Association has been watching him because he's involved in your project, and he was at the testing. He's not the only one interested in this. I've been watching the particle accelerators in other countries, and some of them are trying to duplicate your result of stabilizing dark matter."

"The information was classified," I said. "We didn't publish it."

"No, but Sky knows about it, and Sky has had contact with China. China wants this technology. They also want to ensure no other country has it." If I'd have gone to work for Sky, I might have ended up with a job transfer to China, as a traitor. Loyalty. Sky was serious about loyalty—to him.

"How long would it take us to get to New York if you helped me?"

He stepped towards me and put out his arm. "I'll show you."

I locked my arm in his. In an instant we were staring into the green eyes of the Statue of Liberty.

We were ten feet from the face of the statue. The view below us, and the sudden sight of New York City, was stunning. "How can you do that?"

"I've been here before, and this is the spot I visualized."

"How did we travel that far instantaneously?"

"We are built for speed. We can get anywhere in the world that fast."

Not a very scientific answer. "How do we compare to the Zolians?"

"They are masters at flight, I can tell you that."

"How do they disappear?" I told him how thousands of them had disappeared when I was with Azzoloft.

"When you travel the distance we just did in an instant, it looks like you are disappearing to someone who stays behind."

I led the way towards Sky Lurich's building, taking in the view as we flew between the buildings. When we got there, I flew up the side of the building, looking in the offices until I recognized Sky's offices. I felt a thrill, a sense of power, as I moved through the glass wall of the building directly into his personal office. His security guards weren't going to do him any good now.

We went through the wall of his office and into the lobby towards the hidden panel. I felt something like electricity run through me. Was the dream real? Was there a room with a bizarre figure of the devil? We came through a wall—and straight into two people in white robes. Sky obviously didn't hire these people—someone else had to put them there.

"Quick, grab my arm!" Isaac said.

I did, and Isaac immediately moved us past the Zolians into the wall, recognizing it from my description of my dream as the possible location of the secret room. They shifted to try to block us. To my surprise, we didn't stop when we hit them. They were knocked aside. We were inside the room.

The room didn't look like my dream; the figures were gone. Instead, there was a conference table, with several people, including Sky, seated at the table. They were looking at a large plasma screen that covered an entire wall, with a map of the world. I immediately realized it showed the locations of particle accelerators, and three of them were lit in red, including the one in Arizona. The others were in Russia and China. I looked around the room and noticed, on one area of the floor, I could see a groove—where the figures had been.

I wanted to see more, but I barely had time to look at anything. Almost instantly, we were surrounded by a wall of people in white robes, forming a box around us. They surrounded us in a formation with computer precision, their bodies blocking us as systematically as steel gates falling into place. Isaac forced his way through them, with me holding his arm. As soon as we were past, we faced another wall of bodies, time and time again, with each wall slowing us; after eight walls of people, there weren't enough Zolians to stop us, and we burst past them. As soon as we were past, Isaac was able to get us, instantaneously, back to Marie's house, in the front yard where he left me last time.

"Where did they all come from?" I asked. "There were hundreds of them in an instant." I felt tense, but not like when I was a mortal. There was no increase in pulse, but it was a tension, a state of alert vibrating throughout my body. Maybe adrenaline, for mortals, was just a use of chemicals to mimic what I was feeling.

"The first two were guards. They summoned the others, who arrived instantly, just like I showed up when you wanted me to. "

"How were you able to knock them out of the way?" I asked. "I tried that when they first came to get me, but it didn't work."

"Part of it is sheer willpower, but it must be more than that, because some of them are really determined, as well. That isn't the only place I've seen guards,though. The Science Association tried to study some of these issues, but all we have so far are just theories. The geneticists in our group think it is determined through something like genes. Why are some genes dominant? It is a function of science. As ex-mortals, we are made of matter. It isn't likely based in atoms, because it doesn't interact with atoms. Genes determine if a man will look like a weightlifter or a marathon runner. Like so many things, we see some evidence, but we can't test the hypotheses. Strength, here, isn't a function of muscle and skeletal strength like it is for mortals."

"The figures were gone," I said, "but the grooves were still in the floor. That was where the figures were attached. Sky got rid of them and turned it into a secret conference room. Where else have you seen guards?"

"They were all over at the strategic test. They were trying to keep members of our association out, but some of us got through."

"Something is really weird," I said, "even though we only got a brief glimpse at that map, I can visualize the whole thing, down to the last detail."

"That's normal. Your mind is better than a scanner now. When you are trying to remember something, you will. The map had all the particle accelerators in the world. Any idea what the red is for?"

"Obviously they are of interest to Lurich. My guess would be he's been planning to expand his access to other accelerators, so he can stabilize larger quantities of matter. Maybe we can check it out some time?"

"Sure, you know how to reach me." He was gone as quickly as he'd arrived.

I needed to find a way to get Brett out. But first, I wanted Charlotte to take me to the Gulf.

CHAPTER 13

THE GULF

CHARLOTTE HAD CROSSED the Gulf. I needed to see how that was done, and I felt she knew more about it than Isaac would. I went back to the room where I'd first met Charlotte. She was talking to several people. She excused herself, and joined me.

I asked, "Would you be willing to show me how you cross the Gulf?" I explained my reasons.

"The places where we cross the Gulf are pretty scattered," she said. "They are mostly places you've already heard of, places of spiritual tension or energy, like Stonehenge. The nearest one is in Sedona, Arizona. Some people call it the vortex. Hold onto my arm."

In an instant, we left Phoenix and were among the red rock cliffs above the town of Sedona. When we arrived at the spot, the air in front of us was shimmering, like heat waves, hardly noticeable. We moved forward into it, and Charlotte's image shimmered before me, and then disappeared. I could see what happened, and the air around me was like a vortex, blurred. I felt nothing, except anxiety at being left behind.

In a moment, she reappeared, and we moved out of the shimmering area, a few feet away.

"See," she said, "I tried to take you with me, but I knew I couldn't. You don't have the connection, the resonance. It is like color or sound, and you are the wrong wavelength. There is a strong spiritual power here."

I didn't feel any spiritual power. What I saw was a vortex, a rift, more than a spiritual power.

"What do you see? "I asked. "Where did you go?"

"There is a buzzing, a noise like being near mortals' electric powerlines. You enter a dark tunnel, and you move towards the light."

It was like dying. I didn't know or remember how long she'd been an ex-mortal, but it hadn't been long for me. "It's like dying!" I said. "Isn't it?"

"Yes, I suppose so. That was a long time ago, for me. But when you reach the light, everything is different."

"What do you see?" I asked.

"The earth, but without any buildings. Without power lines. Without man-made structures. There are no Zolians. But the most important thing is what you feel. There is no contention there. There is only peace. You feel a unity. It feels out of place to think of cares, or the U.S. government, or what the president of the United States is going to do. There is only a memory of the need to help other people, and only when you try to think about it. Otherwise, you have no cares or worries at all. The world of mortals seems gone. Irrelevant."

"This isn't spiritual," I said. "This is technology."

"It isn't technology. It is the gateway to heaven, as simple as it can be. This is everything we were ever promised," she said.

"But weren't you promised Jesus would be in heaven?"

"Yes, I realize that," she said. "I know he isn't there, at least we don't see him or talk to him. But he has to be around us. He is with us. I feel his peace. That is what God is, and he is there. Jesus is going to arrive at the second coming, and we'll be waiting for him."

What she was feeling was peace, world peace, global peace, and maybe God had nothing to do with it. She was a religious lady. She was thinking of this as a passage to heaven. I was seeing a portal.

"Are there any atheists who have crossed the Gulf?" I asked.

"Probably, she said. There are all kinds of people and all kinds of religions. It doesn't really matter, or it shouldn't."

"Something had been bugging me, from the moment I died," I said. From the moment I mistook Azzoloft for the devil, in fact. "God is as absent, or as present, in the afterlife, as he ever was for mortals. We are no closer to seeing him or proving his existence, are we?"

Charlotte nodded. "God isn't here telling us to be Protestants instead of Catholics, or vice versa. From what I've seen, there are good people from every religion, and every manner of thought. What I feel is that it matters a lot that we are unified. That's why I gathered the Greater Phoenix Volunteers. I was looking for ways to improve, to help others."

I thought of the being of light some people encounter in near-death experiences. For me, it had been a little different. It must depend on the perception of the individual. "Even the light I encountered when I died felt nondenominational. It was like someone seeking my subjective reactions to an objective stimulus. If I paraphrased what I felt was communicated to me, it would be, 'Isn't mortal life great? That was pretty cool, huh? Bet you're glad you had that opportunity.'"

"We really don't understand everything," she said, "and I am okay with that."

I wasn't okay with it. We, as mortals and ex-mortals, weren't getting it. None of us were! It was like we had all been set up. This was not what we thought it was. Religious believers thought it was all about God, and atheists thought it wasn't. If everybody was seeing what they believed, then what was real?

"We say the Bible is full of prophecies. What if it is more than that? What if these are visions of the future? What if they are based in technology?"

"I don't buy that," she said. "The choices people from around the world make every day are real. Otherwise, it sounds like predestination, or predetermination. If that were true, we wouldn't have a real choice. I, for one, have a choice."

"Sure," I agreed, "individually we are all making choices, and they are real. But I have this sense, this feeling, that mortals are not controlling the big picture. It is as if it is programmed. Nothing turns out the way we planned. We started out to stabilize dark matter, and then Azzoloft showed up and it spun out of control. I had no idea who Azzoloft was, or that he could use stabilized dark matter to gain a physical form that would interact with mortals. Why doesn't Azzoloft just materialize using mortal matter? What is it about the particle field, and stabilized dark matter, that allows him to materialize in a different form of matter? I have this feeling that we opened a door. In a way, it is a terrifying feeling. Something is coming that we don't understand. But, there is another side— the same something may be good, as well. A mixture of good and evil. Like nuclear bombs, or nuclear power. But, we aren't controlling it. We are like actors in a play, assigned parts we don't understand. It is programmed."

"God controls it, and it will be okay," she said.

"What about World War II?" I said. "Did God make the decisions, or did Winston Churchill, Franklin D. Roosevelt, Eisenhower, and Patton?"

"I agree," she said. "The allies had to do their part. God

expects us to do all we can, and then he makes up the differ-ence."

"Was my part opening the door to the apocalypse? Without knowing what I was doing? I thought it was just another scientific breakthrough, but the world is not ready for Azzoloft. We have to stop him."

"And I'm here to help you. But I think it is more about God, and less about Will."

She just didn't get it. Ex-mortals didn't get how this worked, any more than mortals did. There was a double dose of information. Two world paradigms, mortal matter and whatever matter ex-mortals are made of, both showed the precision around us. They showed DNA, and molecular struc-tures, all governed by stunningly precise equations. Those equations applied, from the Plank scale, smaller than atoms, to the galaxies. How could ex-mortals not see it, when it was all right here, all on planet Earth? Everything was right here. Ready or not, alive or dead, here it came. And Will Johnson has just stabilized dark matter. My apologies, world. I didn't know what I was doing. I thought this was only good news. It was an exciting development. I didn't know I was opening a door to a paradigm shift. But, if there were portals there, ones that Charlotte could use, even though she hadn't figured out what it was, there were others. I needed one that even I could use.

We talked for a while longer, and then I thanked her, and she left. I went in search of another portal.

CHAPTER 14

PORTAL

THE MOUNT OF Olives wasn't hard to find, even though I'd never been there. The Garden of Gethsemane was at the base of the Mount, east of Jerusalem, and that's where I looked for a portal I could use. Charlotte's portal had been the wrong frequency for me. I knew the Bible, and the Book of Revelation. It was the code. The written program. Plain as the sun, and 2,000 years old. What a way to hide it. Mortals didn't get it. Mortals didn't have access to the portals ex-mortals used. Ex-mortals, like Charlotte, didn't get it, either. They couldn't figure out a portal if it bit them in their ex-mortal butts.

Some mortals used portals, though. Two thousand years ago. Three mortals. Peter, James, and John. And Jesus, a man who wasn't exactly mortal, who was killed anyway. Peter, James, and John might have thought it was just religion. They were okay with religion as mythology, not scientific reality. Mortals didn't know what technology was in the days of the apostles. The technological data dump had only happened in the twentieth century.

This planet was technology. Why hadn't I figured that one out? This planet recorded four billion years of data.

Photons, our mortal form of light particles, recorded fourteen billion years of data. Photons recorded how the first sun was created, presumably by God. Or some scientist. A non-mortal scientist. Because mortals had been duped. Mortals had been given amnesia. But someone should have gotten in trouble for that. Amnesia was a lie. Giving someone amnesia without their permission was like a lie. And God wasn't supposed to lie. I was mad at God. I was suddenly filled with rage.

God made me a tool to open the door to the apocalypse, without telling me what I was doing. What if I didn't want to start worldwide terror? That was the difference between me and other people who were filled with rage at God. I was going to hurt a lot of people without meaning to, like the people who invented the atom bomb. But I still understood anger, fierce anger, at God. I tapped into a vast current of anger. Azzoloft's kind of anger. I understood why serial shooters and mass murderers were mad. They were mad at God. They just didn't know it. We were all mad. At God. If he exists. Atheists were mad because they think God is hiding. Christians kept forgiving him, in spite of their pain. Yes, God was pain. He knew the mortal world was full of it, and he inflicted it on us all. Unless. Unless there was some part of this we didn't get. But it was too late for us not to have an answer. In the afterlife, we really needed an answer, right then. We opened the door, and Azzoloft was going through, unless we found an answer about how to stop him. I needed an answer.

I looked everywhere across the Mount of Olives, until I found it. There was the shimmering place, unseen by mortals. It was full of energy. Dark energy, light energy, even as a physicist, I didn't know which it was. There was another portal, right on the mount. But I knew it wouldn't work for me. It didn't look right. It didn't feel right. I was starting to feel something, now, my own wavelength, my own frequency, and it didn't match Charlotte's. It didn't match this portal. It didn't match what it must have been before I died, or even what it would have been if I hadn't committed adultery, and then died. But the Great Program in the Sky knew that. Or God. Or something I didn't understand. But I was going to. It was written. Written in the program 2,000 years ago, by a man name John the Revelator, who found a portal.

Just like Charlotte's portal in Sedona, the portal on the Mount of Olives was useless to me. There had to be another portal. Then it occurred to me, the intuition that it was the Mount of Transfiguration. That would be the portal I could use. Where was it? Sinai. The Sinai Peninsula. I didn't have a map. Where was all this stuff? There had to be a way. Where did Peter, James, and John go? How did they travel to the Mount of Transfiguration? They were with a man who had raised the dead. The man had disappeared out of the midst of a mob when they tried to kill him. The first time. Later, he could have disappeared again, and didn't. Courage. Deathly courage. He knew about odds. He knew about numbers. He had no GPS to find the Mount of Transfiguration. He had something better, programming. He was wired to the Great Internet, the great database in the sky.

I closed my eyes. I spun in a circle, slowly, in the air. Yes. Direction. A sense, a connection, to direction. Magnetic North was a technology, wired into the earth. Obvious enough for mere mortal scientists to harness. A compass, that marvel of science. Magical. Miraculous. Mortals had it all wrong. They couldn't tell the difference. Ex-mortals couldn't tell the difference. Duped. By the Great Scientist. Angry. All angry. Filled with anxiety, because they didn't understand science. It's all science. Almost. The confusion warred within me, the anger and realization, the light and the darkness, the hope and fear of what was happening.

I followed the direction I felt, like a GPS, like a compass. I listened with my soul. Across that barren land I traveled, with its sparse modern inhabitants. Animals were wired. They were connected. Something flowed through all living things. Ex-mortal matter, or non-mortal, it was connected to vast data, technology our internet merely mimicked. Science said evolution was the reason animals have instincts and migration patterns. It was hardwired by the animals' genes into their brains at birth. Static, unchanging, like data on a computer not hooked to the internet.

Nonsense! That made as much sense as giving a duck a map to fly south, instead of planting a microchip in its head, and connecting it to the GPS and the internet. Except there isn't a microchip, it is non-mortal matter, programmable, connectable, in non-mortal matter. Or ex-mortal matter. Or alpha matter. Or type A matter. The matter we were made of, Zolians and ex-mortals, was programmable. That matter, inside a duck, or a mortal, was programmable. No. It was connected to an internet. Not an internet built by mortals.

There were some farms and fields. Houses. Settlements. Muslims and Jews, in the Middle East. An ancient animosity between mortals, mortals who never understood. Live. Or kill. If you wanted to kill, you'd better have understood the program. What did I know? Confusion. I wasn't trying to solve peace in the Middle East. All I had to do was stop Azzoloft.

■ ■ ■

I found the rift. It felt inevitable. It was calling me. Why was I so angry, and so excited? So sarcastic and obnoxious? Warring voices in me. A connection to a war. More ancient than the Middle East. A conflict. Inside me. In my soul. In my mind. A door opened when we stabilized dark matter, letting in light and darkness, understanding and confusion, and conflict. I felt like a prism. The colors crossed the spectrum of good and evil.

As I approached the rift, I was disappointed. It was on a rugged hillside. There was a large old dead bush near it. The same frequency, the same shimmering that had been at Charlotte's portal, and at the Mount of Olives. I couldn't get through it. Impossible! I had felt such a sense of destiny, a sixth sense, listening, darkly, on my own frequency. I had been so certain!

As I approached, anger pulsed through me. Then it happened. The portal changed. It matched my frequency. Of course. I laughed out loud. It was not a good laughter. Instead, it was angry and ironic. This was my portal. It was more than a portal. It was a computer. Portals are run by computers. Everything is. And my precise frequency was wired into this portal. Unless I was wrong. Unless technology had become my religion, and it didn't actually exist. So far, God had remained hidden. I could see his program, but no one else could. I couldn't prove it.

I looked around me in the shimmering light and dark. Where was the computer keyboard? These computers must have had something better than mortal keyboards.

"Where is it?" I asked out loud. It was like asking the air in the midst of the shimmering vortex of the portal. I saw nothing like a computer, but I knew inside me it was there. Intuition. The destiny of programming.

"Where is the keyboard? How do I access the computer?"

Nothing.

Then anger. Blazing anger.

"WHERE IS IT?!" I roared. I felt the resonance then, my anger as a resonance, like Charlotte's, but dark.

Nothing.

I waited. Still nothing.

Then I let go of everything, clearing my mind. A shiver coursed through me. I had felt it before, as a mortal. Some people say it is like someone stepped on your grave. To me, it was the seam, the place where the spirit matter attaches to the mortal matter. It was a sensation and awareness of our soul, a combination of two types of matter. In its more extreme form, I think it is shock. Medical personnel moved quickly when an injured mortal was going into shock, because the person could die suddenly. The shock was the awareness that the spirit matter could, and very well might, separate from the mortal matter.

In that shiver of my spirit matter, I moved into a state or condition like sleep, or unconscious. I couldn't tell whether it was a dream or reality, but I thought it was real. It was part of the deal, this masking or consciousness, allowing God to remain hidden from mortals. Mortals didn't get that, but it was no surprise to me now. Everything was so precise, for ex-mortals as well as mortals, allowing us to have access to some data, but not to everything. We took dreams for granted, unless they were religious visions, and the viewer could never prove the difference between a dream and a vision.

The computer lit up, a vision, surrounding me, not photons, not electricity, but what photons and electricity mimicked. Dark matter. Dark energy. Dark light. No! It isn't dark! God had brilliant light made of something besides photons, a non-mortal form of light. Did it have a speed limit, like photons, the speed of mortal light? Or no limit at all? Or omnipresent light? We should be calling it brilliant invisible (to mortals) light. Dark light is brilliant light, power, and technology. My mind could be creating it, or I could be seeing it. God was hiding, now more than ever. I had no proof. This could all be science, based in technology, or it could be my own thoughts slipping into unconsciousness, the anonymity of God.

Could Azzoloft access this portal? Somehow, I doubted it. I felt it. Programming. Where is the programming? This was programmed to let me in, and not Azzoloft.

"Who are you?" I asked the computer.

"I am Pangea."

Was this a voice in my head? I was immersed in 3-D, so real I couldn't tell.

"Are you a person?" I asked.

"I am not."

"Are you connected to the human internet?" I asked.

"Of course. More accurately, the internet is part of me."

Was this real, or was this my unconscious mind telling me what I wanted hear, like in a good dream?

"Show me," I asked. "Run a search on Dr. Will Johnson." Up it came. A list of search results. A caption with my picture, 3-D so real I couldn't tell if it was in my mind or outside it. It showed my date of birth, and my date of death.

"Glad they got my death date right," I said. "Do you have the Bible?"

There it was, Introductory pages, Title page, Genesis Chapter One. The pages flipped before my eyes, a vision of a book that looked like a video recording of the book. I could flip the pages with my very thoughts. This was my kind of computer. No more keyboard necessary, just voice and thought command.

I explored, then, quickly, hungrily, through the databases of that computer. I asked questions. But I didn't need everything that was already on the internet. I'd had a lifetime of access to that.

"Can you show me the future?" I asked.

I was not expecting the answer. The dream of Sky Lurich

came back to me. It wasn't the part with the Satan prototype. It was the visions of a figure leading a vast army, with modern technology, against Jerusalem. It was a vision of a siege. There was a pervasive feeling in it of chaos, of a world on the brink, of a connection of the forces of evil between all nations and peoples.

It was a replay of my dream. It was data, a video, to be replayed on request. It was programmed.

"Show me more of the future, please. Show me something I haven't seen."

"Access denied," said the computer. Obnoxious twit of a computer. Mocking my amnesia. Withholding important information from the ex-mortal who needed to fight Azzoloft.

"How can I stop Azzoloft?"

"Access denied."

"Do I have a mission? What is my purpose?"

The computer displayed my web page again. Dr. William Johnson. Led the team which stabilized dark matter. Died. Stupid computer.

"Who is Eli Matheson?" A web news article appeared, describing what Eli said before in the congressional hearing.

"Did I exist before I was born?" How was that for a cosmic question?

"Access denied."

I asked other questions, and got the internet answers I expected, the things I already knew. How could I access the things I don't know?

"Show me Daniel's vision from the Bible. The one with the great golden statue." I knew it was in the book of Daniel, but I didn't know the chapter and the verse. The computer could find it quickly.

I was expecting the chapter and verse to appear. A vision opened instead. It was like virtual reality, a waking dream. I saw the great statue, with the body, and feet of miry clay. I saw a stone, rolling from a mountain top and growing, until it smashed the idol, a simple vision.

Then the vision expanded. There were congregations gathering, with the signs of early Christianity. There were martyrs. There were monks, writing as scribes in medieval churches. So many lives dedicated, and so many lost, preserving and protecting that book. The Greek Orthodox, and the Roman Catholic churches, even in the midst of the chaos of human actions, preserved the Bible.

Was this an integration of my memory and knowledge of history, things I'd seen, or data from an objective and accurate outside source? Were my biases and emotions superimposed into this information, or were they objective?

The vision continued. The efforts of the Protestants brought religious freedoms. There were great men and women who sacrificed much. Their sweat, and tears, and the blood of the martyrs, were part of the stone. My emotions as a believer filled me with gratitude, but I was watching data, objective facts. The Catholics and Protestants were all doing so much to further everything, in spite of deadly disagreements and conflict. Everything was working together, ultimately, to bring a final unity. A oneness.

There were nations, England, France, Germany, and Spain. So many good people doing good things, in the midst of many evil things. Everywhere there were good people, people fighting for truth and freedom. As I realized this, I saw scientists, over centuries, from Newton to Galileo, from Curie to Einstein, men and women who wore out their lives seeking truth.

Then I saw the group of men and women who founded America. There was a panorama of scenes of what America is: the best, brightest hope of humans, the best government ever formed. These were feelings, not data, so they must be my feelings, my perspective. America was great. America never stopped being great, not in my lifetime. America was great, not because there was no evil in it, but because the good prevailed against great evil. America was part of the stone. Catholics and Protestants were part of the stone. Jews were part of the stone. Good people, everywhere, in every time, fighting for freedom. Buddhist, Hindus, Muslims, were all better people because of their beliefs and religions.

And all this was programmed. The stone was cut without hands. The stone was programmed.

The end result was going to be a great unification, at judgment day, when religions and nations would be made one. Science and religion would become one. The earth would stand as a utopia, with all sickness, disaster, and war done away.

This is what no one around me understood, what I had felt, but not consciously understood, until now. The door was opened, and the data was pouring through. It felt like data. It felt like everything was coming together, everything I'd ever known, and new information.

To me, the stone Daniel saw was the program, working with greater-than-digital precision, to take the good acts of good people from many religions and nations, and turn them into a better world. The program worked without hands. Good and evil acts of humans were directed by the unseen program to produce what existed in the world at that moment. Anyone who didn't believe in God would see the results through their own filter. Two billion Christians worshiped a man named Jesus who died 2,000 years ago. Objectively, that is an amazing fact. Did it happen because that man was powerful? Because he was beyond mortal? There was no proof.

What other visions could I access?

"Show me the beast, from the Revelation of John," I asked.

"You've just seen it."

The evil. The murder of a martyr; every unjustified killing in God's name; the contention; the racist hatred; religious persecution; thefts; rapes; wars; and mobs, were all part of the beast. Satan personified it, but he didn't invent it. Good and evil exist.

We were approaching a zenith of society, a zenith inevitably programmed into the technology. The United States of America was the pinnacle form of government, the best you could possibly achieve with a mixture of good and evil people striving for progress. If you get nuclear weapons, your society of humans will end, on average, 126.2 years later. No, it isn't the nukes. It is the internet. Not the mortal internet, but the unmasking of an internet built of something besides photons and electricity pulsing among a worldwide connection of mortal computers. That was the door we opened. Then what would stabilized dark matter have to do with it?

If I was right about transfigured beings, this is where Moses and Elijah was said to have appeared to Jesus, Peter, James, and John. "I want to talk to Moses."

"Access denied."

"I want to talk to God."

"Access denied." Good thing. I was bluffing.

I kept asking questions until my mind was numb. I also asked the computer how I could cross the Gulf.

"Access granted."

I was ready to cross the Gulf. Then everything went dark.

CHAPTER 15

CONNECTIONS

DARKNESS ENGULFED ME. There was the sensation of a tunnel, or enclosed space. There was a buzzing. The sensation was very much like what I'd been through after my motorcycle crash, like repeating death. The valley of the shadow of death was a real place, or condition. It was in between states of consciousness and forms of being. Was it a cloaking device designed to keep us from figuring out what was happening, or a natural characteristic of the technology involved? A light at the end of the tunnel. Moving towards the light, and out. And it could all have been in my mind. No wonder ex-mortal atheists didn't believe. There was still no proof.

I was past the gulf. I could see the shimmer of the portal behind me. I looked forward, and saw the planet earth, at the same location, Mount of Transfiguration…. No buildings…. I rose up from the earth into the sky above, enhancing my perspective. The earth was the same as I had seen before, but everything mortal was gone. I could see only the natural earth. I continued to rise into the air, looking at the blue horizon, like the view from an airliner, without the airliner. The earth stretched out below, modern earth. Programmed, to me.

Perfectly deniable, to anyone who hadn't crossed the Gulf. Even for those who crossed, God wasn't here.

There was precision in the mortal earth, precision at the level of atoms. I thought back to college, where I had marveled that you couldn't crash your car without the laws of physics taking over. How much the front end of your car got smashed, every ripple in the metal, the shattered plastic, glass, and wiring of the headlights, was determined with computer precision, seemingly instantaneously, by the laws of physics. I spoke the language of physics.

What physics told me is that this earth was programmed, using the same laws of physics. This place, what religious mortals might think of as paradise, must be programmed differently. I doubted it was made of mortal matter. It must be something different, ex-mortal matter or Zolian matter, and those laws should govern what happened when Azzoloft again went into the particle field. He could change from Zolian matter to stabilized dark matter. That was Eli's warning.

We opened a door when we stabilized dark matter. Eli was not a mortal. Azzoloft was not a mortal as a Zolian. Azzoloft would not be a mortal if he transformed into a being of stabilized dark matter. What would he be? Like Eli? Or something else?

I reached out in my mind to summon Charlotte and Isaac. They'd want to know I had crossed the gulf. They needed to know what I had found out.

I returned to the ground near the portal and moved among the people. Several of them stopped and looked at me. A group of a dozen people gathered around me.

Charlotte and Isaac arrived. Charlotte was smiling and excited when I first saw her, but I watched the joy flee from her countenance.

"Will," she said. "How is this possible? I knew when I felt

your summons that you had crossed the gulf, but this is all wrong."

I looked at those surrounding me, people I didn't know, and at Charlotte and Isaac. They were shining, lit with more light than normal, on this side of the portal. I looked down at my hands, and robe. I wasn't lit up. I emitted a mixture of darkness and light. I was sunshine and dark clouds.

"How do you feel?" asked Isaac. He looked as concerned as the others.

"I feel angry. I also feel exhilarated. I feel confusion, and turmoil. I'm excited that I crossed the gulf, but it is so ironic how I did it."

"That's what concerns us," said Charlotte. "Everyone who has ever crossed the gulf seems to have done so by feeling love, peace, and unity. There is a feeling of connection to each other. Most of all there is a resonance."

"What do you mean when you say resonance?" I asked.

Charlotte, Isaac, and the others joined hands, forming a chain of people. They joined hands. They began to sing. It was a single note, but the light emitting from them perceptibly increased. The connection was stronger than any one individual. The connection increased some power, a light, within. Electrifying, but not with photons. Not with mortal light. There was a noise, like static on silken robes, a type of light and energy beyond mortal, enhanced by this connection. Did they see? Did they know what it was? I looked into their eyes. Time seemed suspended. Joy, in each one. Joy inseparable from light. A connection. They probably thought it was divine, at least the religious ones. Were they all religious?

Wasn't this greatness? Didn't Abraham Lincoln speak with power at Gettysburg? Did he resonate? Don't his words resonate, even today? Or Martin Luther King, Jr.? Or Winston

Churchill? The resonance transcends religion, and even mortality. It is a different type of technology.

They changed notes, a singing, a humming, a buzzing.

Buzzing. Like when I was a child, and I fell off the merry-go-round, or every time I was seriously injured as a child. The buzzing was a connection; a light. It protected children from mental trauma, and comforted them. Time was suspended.

They were using music, a pitch, a tone. A frequency. To them it was joy. It was religion. It was music. I knew what it was. A frequency. Science. A gateway. A key. A lock. A lock that brought me joy, but also anger. I was angry at the person, or being, who created that lock. A programmed lock. A computer lock. Did they get it? Did anyone except me understand what was happening? They were so happy, so joyful, so ignorant.

They stopped smiling. The let go of each other. They were watching me.

I felt awful. I felt darkness and anger increasing in me. Something else. Pride. Yes, pride. I knew more than any of them. I knew more than any mortal, or ex-mortal. I knew more than Azzoloft. I felt like Azzoloft. Angry. Furious.

"You've gone dark, Will," Charlotte said.

"I'm okay. Really." This was awesome. They had a connection, a resonance. I don't think Azzoloft knew how powerful it was. Maybe he did, and he feared it. He should have feared it. It was a real power. It was a technology, hidden from the very people who were using it. Azzoloft understood power. He had power. He had a lot of followers, and that brought power. There was power in numbers. Mathematical, geometric, and military power. Mortals understood that.

Other ex-mortals began arriving. Isaac turned to greet them, dozens of them. "You need to see this," he told them. They were all looking at me.

I looked at my robes, white in color, but emanating darkness, mist. Zolian mist. In paradise. I thought this was paradise, beyond the gulf. A door was opened, and I embodied the darkness coming through. The religious people here were thinking this was evil let loose in paradise. I was evil let loose. The Zolians are coming. That was their fear.

"How did you get here," asked Charlotte, staring at me, concerned.

"I found a portal. On the Mount of Transfiguration. I'm guessing the one Peter, James, and John used, or at least, they watched Moses and Elijah use it." The Mount of Transfiguration. The earth would be transfigured. That's what religions had taught me. But the churches didn't get it. Transfiguration was technology. It was programmed. It was merely changing from a molecular, atomic-based state, produced by Higgs particles, to another state, non-mortal, produced by Johnson particles. Johnson particles were my own little technology. My own piece of science, my favorite part of physics. My totem, no pole needed. Catholics didn't get it. Protestants didn't get it. They fought as mortals, with contentions that had gone on for centuries, and affected nations. Over the Trinity. Over Catholic priesthood. Over apostles. Beings of power. Beings who understood the power, but who didn't know it was technology. Of wars. I'm ready, even though no else gets it. Pride. Darkness. In me. Almost like Azzoloft. Or Satan. My soul in danger of succumbing to permanent, irreversible anger, hatred and darkness.

Maybe the Catholics and Protestants weren't fighting here. Maybe they had achieved a type of unity.

"Hey, how many of you are Catholics, show of hands?" I had a hundred people, light-emitting people, concerned people, staring at the dark guy, the guy filled with conflicting dark and light. Contention. Wavelengths. Frequencies. Science.

Darkness changed me. It made me angry and obnoxious. It made me dark. I'd spent a lifetime fighting it, suppressing it. Just like all mortals do. Everyone had depressed days. Everyone. And nobody got that. Mortals lived in denial. Nobody had raised a hand. Had seconds passed? Where was time? Could it really by slowed by my ability to think, by my mind? My awesome, dark mind? My understanding, dark mind? Einstein explained relativity. Great theory. Great reality. Great science. Let me explain the Johnson particle. The particle that makes transfigured matter happen. It changes ex-mortal matter to transfigured matter. Like Moses and Elijah, appearing on the Mount of Transfiguration, centuries after their mortal lives. People who could use a portal.

"Look at Will," said Isaac, to the other members of his association. "It's happening. This is why the Zolians are gaining power. This is the scientific side. It's what I've been telling you. It is also the religious side. Something has happened, and we are seeing the evidence, the proof. Will's team changed something. If Azzoloft succeeds, he will enter the mortal world, with a human appearance. He will be living proof of an immortal. Science and religion will be united in proof."

"It would be astounding," one of the other members of the association said, "in scientific terms, but it doesn't prove religion was right. It doesn't prove God has anything to do with it."

"No," I said, "but it would show that there is a world of beings, unseen by mortals, and allow them to mingle."

Light was pulsing through me. I felt electricity, but not photons. Not mortal. The power of light, pulsing, but I had darkness as well as light. It was awesome. There was light. There was still darkness, dark power, anger. Terrifyingly awesome. Was it the darkness that terrorized me, or the light?

Searing light. Paul, an apostle, blinded by light. Judgment day, with the wicked fleeing from incineration.

"I asked for a show of hands by Catholics. I'm serious."

Some of them raised their hands.

"Now let's see the Protestants." Different hands.

"Okay, Islam?" Others raised their hands.

"Jewish?" Others.

"I told you, Will," said Charlotte. "They're all here."

"What about atheists?" Isaac didn't raise his hand, but several in his group did.

"That is the biggest debate the Science Association," said Isaac. "Some of us cross the gulf, and others can't. It isn't that we haven't experimented. Some who are atheists cross, others don't. We just don't fully understand it."

"I don't think this is about different beliefs," said Charlotte. "I think it is about love and unity. You can't join the resonance without feeling the joy and the unity. You can't hate anyone in the group, or the resonance won't work. You can't hate anyone on this side of the gulf, or it won't work."

"All of you then, join hands," I said. "I'll show you what I think has changed." They joined into a large chain and began to sing the note. I moved to Isaac and touched his chest with my finger. Nothing. I tried to sing the note. It resonated, but not like theirs. It was dark, a dark pitch. I dropped my hand and moved away. Isaac watched. Everyone watched.

The Charlotte spoke up. "You need love, Will. Love is the key."

She didn't get it! Anger. Anger is what I felt. Love? I had loved Marie. I loved my kids. And I'd betrayed them. I'd experienced the greatest scientific moment of my life, I'd opened the door, I'd stabilized dark matter. And then I'd committed adultery. It was wrong. What kind of evil sense of humor? What God would let me fall, instead of triumph? If I had to die, why not warn me? But, more than anything, I felt anger over the sense of amnesia, of important information being withheld, without a good enough reason. Azzoloft had information we did not have. That was so wrong. He could lie to us, and we'd know the lie, but not the truth.

"I don't feel love," I said. "I feel anger. I've felt darkness, since the time we stabilized dark matter. Even as a mortal I felt it. It is more powerful now. It is growing; multiplying." Exponential growth. Computerized growth. A door opened. We opened a door to darkness. As a mortal, I thought I controlled the darkness within me. But I couldn't. Not completely.

Religion would say I needed to repent. I didn't know if I could repent, or what it would take. At least I wasn't in Dante's hell, burning in lava, amidst demons and devils. Maybe that was coming. Maybe that was judgment day. What did Azzoloft have to do with it? Was he Satan? Or something else? My thoughts were jumbled, random. Demons. The devil. Hell was coming, but not until judgment day. Satan would be cast into hell, with the wicked, on judgment day. Right now, everyone here was either mortal, ex-mortal, or Zolian. Except Eli. Some were doomed. Damned, forever. But not until judgment day. I still had time.

I felt a current of anger. I was tapping into data, and something was allowing that to happen, like a program. What if they were all wrong? The angry current was saying *Jews, Catholics, Protestants, damn them all!* Were these my thoughts as well? Was this some kind of dark internet, beyond mortal technology? Was it mob mentality? The religions were smug, damning each other for unbelief. Damning atheists as unbelievers.

Damn Azzoloft, not just for being a smug jerk, but for withholding information. He didn't have amnesia, but we all did, and he was mocking us. He was telling the world of ex-mortals how wrong we all were, sowing his contention and lies, until the Science Association members were utterly lacking in comprehension. Good and evil were combined. In me. Why was I so angry? Who needed God, when you could have a computer? Crazy talk. Confusion. No. Not crazy. Sarcastic. Snarky. Digitized. Damn right. Damn you all! I hate you all! I hate your smugness, your false beliefs, and your lies! The more you know about the Bible, the more you damn other people to hell. Death is instant damnation. You got it wrong. I proved it. I'm not burning in hell. Yet. So, damn you!

I hoped this anger wasn't me, but it continued to flow through me. This must be what Azzoloft felt, surging anger. Damned ignoramuses.

I found the secret, right after I found the Johnson particle, and the world, a whole world, not made of atoms, is waiting to be revealed. Multiple worlds. And now I'm dead and damned, a vessel of wrath and confusion. I hate everybody, especially God.

I was not past, present, or future. I was not bound by time. I had become, and I hated what I had become. Everyone should hate God. The current of hatred flowed, as if it was the mind of Azzoloft, and I was fluent in the language: God didn't lie to you. He didn't have to. He gave you truth. He showed you visions of hell fire. He showed the power of darkness and evil. He wrote his Bible. No, he downloaded information to his prophets. They wrote the data in the Bible, for people to fight over. Only the ones who stop fighting can cross the gulf. Yeah, God is forgiving. He says he's going to save you all. Whoops! Not all. If unbelievers are damned, God can only save a few of you. Damn everyone, except me. I'll be God now. BOW DOWN, damn you. As these thoughts coursed through my mind, I realized how awful and blasphemous they were. If I was going to spend an eternity in hell, it would be these kinds of thoughts that could get me there, quicker that adultery or anything else. And yet my anger was so powerful I didn't care.

Charlotte and the others looked shocked and terrified. Bunch of stupid ex-mortals, staring at me. Why had they lined up in a chain? Why were they singing that stupid note? Why were they lighting up? Resonance. Yes. Because they want power.

"STOP IT, WILL!" I heard Charlotte. Her lips weren't just moving, she wasn't just yelling, she was resonating at me. Damn her. Bow down. Show respect. Stop talking to me like that. Don't you know you I am? Do you want me to show you power?

"Stop what?" I asked. "I didn't say anything."

"No," said Charlotte, "but you look like you're possessed by the devil, and you just ordered us to bow down to you!"

They felt what I said, even though I didn't say it. But I felt it, really felt it. Bow down.

"I think I know how Azzoloft feels," I said. "He has more anger than anything I've ever felt. Anger magnified by a thousand, by millions."

"How would you know what Azzoloft feels?" asked Isaac.

"Not him, so much as darkness and anger. I feel like I'm tapping into it, a great current, wherever it exists. I feel anger, pride, delusions of grandeur, hatred of God. I think I opened a door, and I connected to everything. I felt it even before I died."

I finally understood. They hadn't been terrified of me. They were terrified for me. They thought I was going nuts, bats, crazy. By nature, I'd always been a kind person. I'd been a loving father. I'd also felt discouragement and darkness at times, as every mortal does. Now, it was magnified. There was a war going on, and I'd swallowed part of it when we opened the door. It was raging inside me.

"There has got to be a way for you to connect to light, to us, and not just darkness," said Charlotte. "There is still light in you, mixed with all that darkness. The key is love. Isn't there someone here you love?"

"I don't know. Yes, I do know. I love you all. You are wonderful people. I just don't know what is happening to me. Right now, the one thing I'm sure of is that I really need help from all of you, if I'm going to stop Azzoloft. You have no idea what is coming." The end of the world. Armageddon.

My mom. Irene Johnson. She was somewhere here, and I loved her most. She had to know I was here, if she was looking. Where was she?

"The Zolians have gained power," Isaac said. "They are more aggressive. Perhaps you did open a door of some kind. They are inviting ex-mortals to join them. They attack those who oppose."

Like Brett. Anyone who gets in their way. Eli had been right. Azzoloft would take on a form that looked like a human body, except that it would be made of stabilized matter. He wanted to take over the world. The mortal world was going to change. I thought of the vision I had seen. Why hadn't others seen it? Someone like Charlotte. I had seen the army, besieging Jerusalem. I had seen that dream before I even died. There was power, dark power. In a computer database, a video of the future. To be revealed. Access Granted.

Dark Access.

"If we are going to stop Azzoloft, we are going to need to gather our strength. Isaac, you were there at the strategic test, right?"

"Yes. The Zolians surrounded everything. There were so many of them we could hardly find our way to get near the building. It was like pushing through a labyrinth."

"Next time there will be even more," I said. "How many

ex-mortals knew that it was Azzoloft who was forming in the dust?" I asked.

"We all saw the camera video that was on the mortal news, but most of us didn't recognize who it was. We'd never seen him. Eventually we figured out it was Azzoloft." Azzoloft was like a famous person. He was a powerful person, with billions of followers. Selective. Few ex-mortals had ever met him. I got to meet him, though. My prize, for stabilizing dark matter, and then dying. Lucky me.

"Charlotte," I said, "you asked me how I crossed the gulf. I found a portal. First, I tried the one you took me to, but I knew it wouldn't work. Then I found one on the Mount of Olives. It didn't work. I knew it wouldn't work. It was the wrong frequency. I think it was programmed. It is a computer. You all have been crossing the gulf using a computerized portal, which controls the frequency of who crosses, with scientific precision."

Charlotte frowned. "The portal has probably existed for thousands of years. It doesn't have anything to do with computers."

There was no point in arguing with her. I had no proof. I crossed by talking to a computer named Pangea. Maybe that was all in my mind. Charlotte crossed using mythology, or God, in accordance with her beliefs. The gulf was like unconsciousness, like sleep. It was so real, we couldn't distinguish. We couldn't prove anything to someone else.

"Anyway," I said, "then I went to the Mount of Transfiguration. I knew it would be the right frequency for me, even though I am not who I was. I felt it. I sensed it. That's how I crossed here. And when I go back, we're going to get organized." The portal was programmed to let me through, whether she believed it or not.

"What kind of organization are you thinking of?" she asked.

"We need to persuade the president not to proceed with the strategic test. If that doesn't work, we're going to need to outmaneuver the Zolians. They are going to use everything they have to keep us away from the strategic testing."

We talked for a while longer. Everyone said they'd help if they could, and then they left. I asked Isaac to stay and help me. I needed to know whether this side of the gulf was paradise, or a technological paradigm. Or both.

CHAPTER 16

SCIENTIFIC PARADISE

ISAAC AND I were in paradise, at the Mount of Transfiguration. At least, it looked like the same mountain I was on when I entered the portal. The old dead bush that was near the portal wasn't there anymore. I looked around. There weren't any other dead plants.

"The vegetation here looks similar to what we saw on the other side of the gulf, in the mortal world. This earth looks the same, but I notice the dead plants are gone," I said.

"Correct," said Isaac. "The earth here looks very similar, but the plants here are living. We've never found any dead plants here, which indicates these plants are not made of atoms. They are immortal, probably made of type A matter, like we are."

A bird flitted past us. I moved to a live bush and tried to pluck a branch. I couldn't move it. I tried to swipe my hand through the branches. They moved in a natural motion, like a mortal bush would. I could move them, but not mar or damage them.

"The Science Association has studied this side of the gulf," he said. "Our botanists tell us the plants here are similar species to what is growing on earth at this location."

"What about animals, like that bird?" I asked.

"Animal species are here, and the species are generally located in the same places they'd naturally be found on earth."

"How is that bird flying," I asked, "if there are no air molecules? Flight requires atmosphere, and gravity."

"How do you fly?" he responded.

"We don't really fly," I said, "we move through the air, like photons through a wave of light. Our physics are different. But the flight of that bird looks natural, the way a mortal bird would fly. On the other hand, right after I died, I was walking the way I did as a mortal, because I was used to it. Maybe that means these are the ex-mortal animals. I wonder if people's pets are here, like if the family dog died, will it be here somewhere?"

"Possibly. But if all the animals that had ever lived on earth came here when they died, we'd be hip-deep in rabbits. We haven't found any baby animals, nor seen animals die."

"What about extinct species?" I asked.

"They aren't here."

We moved rapidly over the landscape, towards Jerusalem. I saw no mortal buildings. The terrain was similar to what it had been on the other side of the gulf. When we got to the area where Jerusalem should be, the city was gone. There were many ex-mortals in white robes, some alone, and others talking in groups.

"Where did the city go?" I asked.

"There are no mortal buildings on this side of the gulf," he said.

"Instead of a city, there is just natural-looking vegetation," I said. "It's like a computer filled in the vegetation where the city used to be, to make everything look natural. What does the Science Association make of that?"

"It doesn't have anything to do with computers," he said.

"It is a parallel evolution. This side of the gulf is made of type A matter, the same matter ex-mortals are made of. The type A matter continues to evolve and change, even as the mortal matter of the earth changes. There doesn't appear to be any mortal matter on this side of the gulf."

I looked at the sun. It looked the same as it had when I was mortal. "What if we are seeing the mortal earth through a type of filter," I asked, "one which removes everything mortal, or made of atoms? The problem would be that the sunlight we see as mortals is from photons, a type of mortal particle. How are we seeing sunlight, if mortal particles and atoms are filtered out?"

"What we might be seeing," he said, "is a type A matter version of the sun and earth. We aren't necessarily seeing photons."

"In other words, there could be multiple types of light," I said, "just as there are multiple types of matter. A whole different paradigm.

"Why are all these people here?" I asked. There were many thousands of people.

"Those who are on this side of the gulf can go anywhere in the world. The area of Jerusalem is a popular spot."

"Why are they all standing around talking?"

"You can listen in," he said.

I went down near a group at the Mount of Olives. There was a man speaking to the group. It turned out to be a lecture about Christianity. I visited other groups. There were many different topics being discussed. Some were Jewish, others Christian, and still others Muslim. There were differences of opinion, but no contention.

"Is this it?" I asked. "This is heaven, paradise, where people just stand around and talk?"

He laughed. "What else did you expect? I mean, once you

realized that we don't meet God here, this makes sense. The people on this side of the gulf are in perfect peace. They are learning, by teaching each other. We don't have books, but we remember well enough the things we learned as mortals. It isn't all religion. We can go to the areas of Oxford or Cambridge, and we'll find discussions focused on science, instead. That's where many of the members of the Science Association are."

"How about eating food? What is paradise, without food?"

I went back to the Mount of Olives and tried to pick an olive. I knew they aren't necessarily good to eat straight from a tree, that's why mortals bottle them first. I couldn't pick the olives. They were part of the tree, inseparable.

"We can't pick olives," I said to Isaac. "I'll bet we can't pick wheat either. No pancake breakfasts here. No food, not even apples." This wasn't the garden of Eden, it was different.

"How many people do you see starving here?" he asked.

None.

"I see," I said. "We don't get hungry. Which means to the extent we are expending energy to move around, that energy isn't coming from the metabolism of mortal food. What are we, electric-powered people?"

"Maybe so," he said. "Although, electricity is for mortals. We likely have an energy source similar to electricity; some other type of light or energy."

"I assumed," I said, "the reason we didn't eat on the other side of the gulf was that all the food there was made of atoms, i.e. mortal matter. That was only part of it. If you ate an apple, you'd have an apple core. An apple core is garbage. It dies, and rots, once it is removed from the tree. This is a whole different paradigm, a world where the laws of physics prevent evil."

"I don't think they prevent evil. It is just natural, a

different natural law of physics. You can't pick an apple. So, what?"

"Okay," I said, "all these people stand around and talk, or bask in the sunlight, or whatever they are doing. We have a world here made of very real type A matter. Why aren't we building houses out of type A matter?"

"To build a house, you need materials," he said.

"We can't mine iron here, can we?" I said. "We can't make a nice steel axe, so we can chop down a tree, and build a log cabin. We are all stuck cabin-less. And who planned it that way? This was all done with better-than-computer precision."

"Why do we need cabins?" Isaac asked. "Houses are for mortals. Mortals need privacy. They must bathe, and they don't want anyone to see, so they build a bathroom. They have kitchens for cooking food. We don't have food. That is why our scientists say we have a parallel evolution on this side of the gulf. It wasn't planned or designed, it is natural."

"I think this entire planet is digitized," I said.

"I admit this could very well be the work of God," he said. "I'm not an atheist. However, I don't agree that it is digitized. God is all-powerful. He doesn't need computers. I am confident that nothing here proves there is a God."

"No," I said. "But there could be an astounding level of science that makes everything look so natural. It looks, to me, like science perfected. Mortal scientists had 6,000 years of documented history. Give us a million years, and where would we be?"

"At the rate we're going, we wouldn't necessarily progress," he said. "We can't experiment effectively after we are dead. We can't effectively study type A matter. We can't take it apart, or break it down, or make a microscope."

"I know," I said. "We're stuck here watching mortals perform science."

"We all watched you building a particle field generator that could open the door to a new paradigm of technology. Well, Dr. Johnson, now you know how it feels to watch."

"Yes. All watch and no do." *But we had better be able to do something*, I thought. We needed to stop Azzoloft.

We rose high over the earth. We could see the vastness of the ocean, the animals moving, and hosts of people in many parts of the planet. I wanted to see if the landmarks were there. We went to the Grand Canyon. I'd been there several times as a mortal, since I lived in Arizona. It was there, and it looked the same as it did to mortals, as far as I could tell.

"Why is it that the Grand Canyon would show up here," I asked, "if this side of the gulf is type A matter? The Grand Canyon was caused by water erosion from the Colorado River, from water made of atoms. The physics of type A matter should be different. Temperature changes cause the water condensation that makes rain, and I haven't felt any temperature fluctuation since I died. Rainfall is caused by gravity. Flowing rivers come from either natural springs, rain, or snow packs. I want to see the source."

We went to the north until we saw the Grand Tetons. There was snow there, melting, and flowing in rivulets and streams. I looked for thunderclouds, and found some. As we moved into the rain. I did not feel the impact of the drops. They just glanced off me. My robe didn't get wet.

"Just as I thought. The laws of physics are different. I'm not getting wet in the rain. This rain shouldn't be causing erosion, or canyons."

"Most of our scientists believe this side of the gulf evolved on a parallel plane. There is a connection between the two places, which is why the Grand Canyon develops here, even though there is no water erosion. We don't understand the connection. The earth, as seen on both sides of the gulf, is virtually the same, except that the Zolian side allows ex-mortals and Zolians to see mortal matter, and the other side of the gulf does not show anything mortal."

"Religious scientists in our association have a similar view, except that they believe God created this planet out of type A matter, as a paradise, a place of peace and rest."

What I'd seen on this side of the gulf was extraordinary. It could be pure science, or it could be God's creation—just like earth, with different laws of physics. It was beautiful, peaceful, and even joyful, with all peoples, nations, and animals in harmony. No more sickness or death among plants, animals, or people. No more crime, or hunger. A utopia. At last, a world at peace. Everything any of us could have expected from heaven, except God wasn't here to meet us. Yet.

■ ■ ■

Now that I had seen what was on the paradise side of the gulf, I had more questions about the Zolian side, particularly the connection between the way the earth appeared on each side of the gulf. We went back to the portal I had used. Once across the gulf, we returned to Arizona. We went to a park in the East Valley, near some office buildings.

"What if the connections between the two sides of the gulf were similar to the connection between type A or spirit matter, and mortal bodies?" I asked. "Take a look at this."

I placed my hand against a live tree in the mortals' park. My hand would not go into the tree. "See? This is how it is with most living things we see, living things made of atoms. But, now, let's go into that office building across the street and compare."

We were there in instant, inside the building. "Here's a desk, made of wood." I swiped my hand through it. "The tree this desk was made of is dead, so that fits the notion that there is a spirit in the living tree, and the spirit is gone after death.

There is scientific matter in the tree—dark matter, scientists might call it—which blocks us from moving through it. But it doesn't work for gnats, mosquitos, bacteria in the air, or a lot of other living things that should have spirits. How do we draw the lines? How do we know where the parameters are?"

"Members of the Scientific Association have already looked at many of these issues. This isn't news to us," he said.

"What have you done with it?" I asked. "Are you building new particle accelerators? Better telescopes?"

"Of course not. We can't."

"And yet we need to figure out why the stabilized dark matter took the shape of Azzoloft," I said. "Ex-mortal science isn't solving that practical application. How does Azzoloft get the particles to form in the way he wants them? There must be a scientific explanation, and I think it has to do with the power of connections, both light and dark. The laws of science are just as present for ex-mortals as they ever were for mortals."

"Maybe I can help with that," Isaac said. "For years, members of the association, mostly neurosurgeons, have studied how ex-mortal bodies work. You should talk to Dr. Yee. She's usually at the neurological institute. It's close by. Let's go over there."

We moved from the East Valley, heading west into Phoenix. We approached a hospital complex with many buildings. One was a white eight-story tower, with the regular patterns of windows indicating scores of patient rooms in a hospital.

"Why would she be in Phoenix?"

"This neurological institute is a teaching facility and a hospital, one of the best in the world. Ex-mortal scientists congregate around mortal areas of science and learning. Archeologists go to mortal digs. Boston and Cambridge, and cities with other major universities, are full of members of our association. Physicists, including me, watched you and your team discovering how to stabilize dark matter. But if you want to know about neuroscience, Dr. Yee is the person to talk to. She had dual degrees in neuroscience and psychiatry—as a mortal, of course. She spent her mortal lifetime in this field. She's continued to study and learn from both mortals and ex-mortals, so her knowledge is state-of-the art."

A woman in a white robe came out through the building. Out of mortal habit, I almost expected her to be old with white-hair, but as an ex-mortal she looked thirtyish, with dark black hair.

"Hi Isaac," she said. "What can I do for you?"

"Hi, Amy. This is Dr. Will Johnson," he told her.

"Oh, hello. I recognize you," she said. "You've been on mortal TV recently, until you . . . oh, I'm sorry . . ." She looked down at the ground, and then back at me. "I hope I didn't offend you."

"Not at all," I assured her. "I imagine I haven't been on mortal TV since I died."

After the introduction, Isaac explained why he thought she could help me. Then, he excused himself, and left.

"Let me show you around the facility," she said.

We moved through the side of the mortal building into the lobby area, cafeteria, and administration on the first floor, and then to surgery on the second floor. There were mortal doctors and nurses in the surgery area. There were some ex-mortals, who greeted Dr. Yee as we passed.

On the other floors we saw the neuroscience back and spine unit, the oncology unit, and other patient rooms. As we went, she described to me the work the mortals were doing, as well as what the ex-mortal observers had learned.

I told her my theory about why ex-mortals can pass

through non-living things, but not through living things, including mortals. We went back to the operating room area, and we found a surgery in progress. They were working on a man who had a spinal injury in a car accident. He'd had one leg amputated just below the knee.

"Shortly after my death," I said, "I got in the way of a mortal airplane. I realized I could pass through the plane, but not through the mortals in the plane. There has to be a scientific reason why I go through the glass and metal, but not through a person. Religion suggests a reason: There is a spirit, i.e., non-mortal matter, inside a mortal body, and we can't go through that matter any more than I can go through you as an ex-mortal. I would call it alpha matter, or type A matter. We can't fly through a mortal tree, or other living things. Because they are alive, the type A, or spirit matter, blocks us. There is a dual form of spirit matter and mortal matter in living things, and the two appear identical to us. When we look at a mortal person, we see the mortal matter, but the spirit matter is within."

"I'm not sure exactly what you mean by spirit matter," she said, "although in the Shinto religion, there is a belief in spirits. We can see that we still look like people after our mortal death. We have observed mortals die, in this hospital. We see their type A matter form come out of their mortal body. It is a very natural and beautiful thing, although the mortals grieve for their loss. In terms of science, the results are immediate and observable. There are two types of matter, one is made of atoms, and the other isn't, but both are in every mortal. There is nothing mystical about it."

"Why is it that an ex-mortal can't pass through a mortal," I put my hand on the shoulder of the surgeon while he was working. Then I swiped my hand through the green cloth and table where the man's amputated leg would have been. "It is obvious that when this man dies, he'll have his leg back. Every mortal deformity is cured when we see the person outside their body. Doesn't that mean the ex-mortal form of body is essentially a digitized blueprint of that mortal, as precise as DNA?"

"I've never heard anyone suggest it is digitized," she said. "It looks perfectly natural to me. The two types of matter are connected, and they evolve together, a symbiosis. When the type A matter is inside the mortal, it conforms to his bodily shape. That's why, even as ex-mortals, we don't see this man's type A matter leg sticking out of his mortal body. Everything has a scientific explanation.

"It doesn't surprise me," she continued, "that an ex-mortal can't pass through a mortal's body, or another ex-mortal. I think the reason you can't pass your hand through a mortal person is related to the electrical charges. Mortals generate electricity. The nervous system runs on neurons firing, and signals moving as fast as light through your brain and body."

"Yes," I said, "but electricity is a mortal phenomenon. Electrons are a type of matter, and photons are mortal energy. Mortals don't see us because we are essentially made of dark matter, photons don't interact with, or bounce off us. So why would an electrical field prevent an ex-mortal from passing through a mortal?"

"That's a good point," she said. "It probably does have something to do with type A matter. But there is more to it. As mortal scientists and physicians, we believed our minds, emotions, and thoughts are generated by the human brain. Yet, when a mortal dies, we see her mind and emotions are intact. That means there is more to the interaction between mortal matter and type A matter in the human brain and mind."

"I met a lady named Charlotte," I said, "who told me drug addictions changed an ex-mortal enough to keep them from crossing the gulf. Couldn't that change be a part of the connection between the mortal brain and type A matter? In other words, the type A matter is recording and changing based on what is happening in the mortal brain?"

"Yes, and it isn't just drug addiction that remains," she said. "Depression is a function of the human mind, of chemicals in the brain. But a person who is depressed may still be affected by as an ex-mortal. As ex-mortals, our illnesses are gone. An amputee is whole as an ex-mortal. But our personalities don't change just because we die, nor do our basic attitudes.

"The ongoing nature after death," she said, "of the mind, personality, and attitudes after death is part of the evolutionary process. We are evolving into a race of immortals. The number of ex-mortals is many times the human population of seven billion."

"Are you suggesting that this is the next step of human evolution?" I asked.

"In a way. Humans are a population-generator for ex-mortals. That's how we all began. It's the way we came into existence. We want humans to continue to thrive. The only way to get an ex-mortal is to have them born as a human. But ex-mortals don't die. Our population has been increasing for thousands of years. You spend eighty years as a human, and then thousands, even unlimited, time as an ex-mortal. That is our future, and it is a far better one than most mortals imagine."

"Won't we eventually run out of room on the planet?"

"Ask me that in 30,000 years, and I'll let you know if I'm concerned."

"What about Zolians. They aren't ex-mortals," I said.

"How would we ever know?" she said. "They are all liars. They may be pretending to be something they aren't as a psychological means of distinguishing themselves from the masses. I like to joke that they are the Neanderthals—lower brain capacity. As you can tell, I don't like them much. The reason we continue to teach, learn, and study as ex-mortals is partly because we enjoy it. But the practical side of it is psychology. How do we rid ex-mortals of hang-ups like guilt and depression? That is the healing we are doing. It's the only healing ex-mortals need to do. And the Zolians don't understand it."

"It's more than that," I said. "Azzoloft is trying to use stabilized dark matter to form a physical body so that he can interact with humans, but I don't think he'd be mortal. Having people who are non-mortal would certainly qualify as a new step in evolution. If we are going to evolve, though, we don't want Azzoloft to be in control of it," I said. "We've got to find a way to stop him."

"I couldn't agree more," she said. "What do you have in mind?"

"Here's what I know so far," I said. "Azzoloft is able to form stabilized matter dust into a physical form. His physical form, if he succeeds in getting a physical body made of stabilized dark matter, will look like his Zolian body. That is true for ex-mortals. For example, I saw my brother here, and he looks like he did in his mortal prime. That suggests that type A matter might be a blueprint. It may contain a set of instructions for a more powerful being, like DNA does for mortals. The stabilized dark matter is taking Azzoloft's form because his type A matter body is a blueprint."

"Why would it make any sense for a blueprint to exist after a person dies?" she asked.

"In religious terms, it is so that person can be resurrected. If there is a code like DNA for what a mortal is going to look like, maybe the spirit form is the blueprint for what a resurrected being is going to look like."

"You think that might work for Azzoloft, if he has never been mortal?"

"Maybe. It might work differently for him, though," I said.

"Then why doesn't mortal matter take his form? If he can gather stabilized dark matter particles into a form, why doesn't he just use dirt?"

"From a physics standpoint," I said, "the reason mortal matter exists is because of the Higgs particle. What I discovered, which allowed us to stabilize dark matter, was what I'll call the Johnson particle. It performs the same function for dark matter that the Higgs particle performs for mortal matter, by breaking symmetry. The machine generates a field of Johnson particles."

"Even if Azzoloft's type A matter bodily form is the blueprint, how does he get the particles to assemble?" she asked.

"I don't know, but I think it has to do with his connections to his followers. When I crossed the portal, I felt the dark connections, as well as the light. I think it is digitized, in a way. Better said, our digital data, moving through the internet, mimics a higher technology he is using. I think there is a power source, a type of light, which he is tapping into. It is giving him the power to draw the particles to him, gaining a human appearance. Like a fiber optic cable, it carries data as well as being a power source."

"I agree, there do seem to be connections we don't understand yet," she said. "Primarily, the fact that the human mind outlasts the mortal brain. I just don't see how we could study that. People think of psychology as a soft science, but that is what we do best here. We can't run MRI's on ex-mortal brains. I wish we could. We're left studying human MRI's. To me, studying what the Zolians are doing isn't science. I think their makeup is the same as everyone else's, they just have a remarkable commitment to claiming they are different. I'm not sure how we're going to cure that psychosis. I'll admit, I'd hate to think we may move 30,000 years into the future of evolution, and still have Zolians refusing to admit they are ex-mortals. But you may have changed all that."

"How's that?"

"Because you opened up a new possibility by stabilizing dark matter. There may be people who are not mortal, but who can be seen by, and physically interact with, mortals."

Dr. Yee was pure science. It wasn't about good and evil. There was no devil. Azzoloft was a mere ex-mortal psychotic, whom death didn't cure. There wasn't a vast current of flowing data, making connections of good and evil. Evolution. Darwin started the notion, and now it was at a whole new level. Evolving to immortality.

"Well, let me know if you have other ideas," she said. "I'd be happy to help."

■ ■ ■

I left the hospital, trying to understand how we were going to defeat Azzoloft. What if the light we were talking about was a third type of light, not usually visible to mortals or ex-mortals? Resurrected light, some light we thought was mystical, but which turned out to be the highest technology yet. That could mean a different kind of interconnectedness. Our internet could be the low-tech version of a vast connection of another type of light, which carried information and data to, and among, us all.

I went back to the tree in the park and put my hands on

the trunk. I reached out, trying to feel the connections, the light, the life within the tree. I sensed a connection, the data, the DNA, the recording of all things, the experience of cells in a tree, a wondrous sense of organization. A living thing was a recording of data, but it was more than that. It was an interconnection from cells to trunk, at every level, a tree as an organism, each cell alive, and the whole tree alive. There was no way to prove it, any more than a mortal with a near-death experience can prove what she saw.

I thought of Marie's rose garden and went there, by her house. Looking at the beauty and delicacy of the roses, a wondrous awe of the power of life, the connections, and the data, the information filled my mind, like a vision. There was a vastness in the organism of a tree, every cell a world unto itself, and innumerable cells combined into a living thing. Surely, God was a scientist! He had to understand all of this, far better than me. How many billions of ex-mortals were there, and how many of them had seen this connection among living things? If a tree is a recording of data, what of a person, or what of the earth itself?

There was more information, more life, and more connections, than I'd ever dreamed possible. There was a living sea of data in the earth, and in all physical matter. How many ex-mortals here had ever thought to ask for, or to look for, this information?

There was more—this was one tiny planet in a universe. And all of the data and understanding was in mind, beyond proof.

Yet, in that incomprehensible connection, there was light, a searing power. It brought joy to almost everything, but not to me. That was what I felt when I was filled with dark energy after I crossed the portal. Even now, I felt fear, fear of the brilliant light. I couldn't cross the portal like everyone else had. Having an affair had changed me. That wasn't just religious, it was scientific. I could feel the energy and power of the darkness, and of the light. If I went into that brilliant white light, I might be destroyed, incinerated, even as a post-mortal, by a type of burning mortals had never understood. It wasn't just mortal burning, your molecules being turned to carbon, to ash. I didn't have the information. Access denied, you ignoramus. God isn't going to tell you, except that you know that light sears you, and you have an overwhelming desire to flee, to hide in the rocks and the caverns with the damned. I was going to be forced to choose, with insufficient information. I was being asked to trust God. I most certainly did not. I'm not Abraham. He passed his test. I failed mine. What I felt was hurt and anger, irreversible.

Azzoloft understood the connections between himself and his followers. He fed on their power and their support. Forty billion and one is more powerful than one alone. I doubted he understood the light behind the connections, but he knew how to use it. I could use it as well.

Darkness was coming. A powerful darkness. If I couldn't use the light against Azzoloft, I'd use the dark energy I felt. Embracing and using darkness shouldn't make any difference, I was going to hell anyway. We had to stop Azzoloft. We had to make sure there was no retest; and if there was a retest, the connections could be the key. Azzoloft didn't understand how the science was going to work. He didn't know how DNA played into it. He didn't believe in programming, like I did. I couldn't prove my theories, but they might work. I'd be gambling, but so was Azzoloft. Azzoloft was going to accelerate judgment day, and some people weren't ready. Like me. Or my brother, Brett.

If darkness was coming, I wanted Brett to be safe. I wanted him to be away from the Zolians before the next test.

CHAPTER 17

DOMESTIC VIOLENCE

I NEEDED TO figure out how to get Brett away from the Zolians. Shartruze seemed to be friends with Brett, as much as a Zolian can be. She could help me get him out of the Zolian prison, or at least persuade Blitzer to let him go. I wasn't certain if I could find her, though. Maybe I could focus on her and find her the way Isaac had found me. Would she have to be thinking about me? Or, maybe Isaac could help me find Shartruze—for that matter, Isaac might be able to help me rescue Brett, although if we got him out, there wouldn't be anything to keep the Zolians from putting him back in, unless Isaac stayed around him to protect him. I focused on Isaac, trying to concentrate. After several minutes, he still hadn't come.

Based on what Isaac had told me, I tried to focus my mind on Shartruze, in hopes I could locate her.

It was easy enough to focus; Shartruze's features were exquisite. I didn't know what direction she was in, but as I closed my eyes and focused, I thought I knew which direction to go. I felt a flow or alignment, like particles of light moving between mind and what I recognized might be her mind. I opened my eyes and moved in that direction. Within minutes I was above a neighborhood full of expensive tan-colored stucco homes in Paradise Valley, northeast of Phoenix. I slowed as I sensed I was nearing her. I entered a large home and saw Shartruze talking to a mortal woman in the master suite on the second floor.

I immediately recognized the mortal woman. She was the woman from the bar where I met Brett and Shartruze.

Shartruze looked busy, but I didn't wait. "Hi, Shartruze," I said.

Shartruze moved towards me, uncomfortably close, putting her arms around my waist, instantly putting me off guard. She spoke in my ear. "Oh, Will, it's nice of you to come see me. It's so touching to know you care." Her tone was beguiling, spiced with coyness.

"How are you so open about attraction, when the other Zolians are so hostile?"

"There are so many luscious mortal men with whom I would love to engage in a heated embrace. That's why I so greatly admire your courage for being with Ronnie. What a wonderful relationship. And she's an impressive woman. Smart, beautiful, and witty."

I wasn't blushing red, only because I'm a post-mortal, but she no doubt felt my emotion anyway. Brett shouldn't have told her about me.

"I do my homework, Will. Of course, that's because I like you, and I'm not afraid to say so."

Suddenly she moved away from me, and back to the side the mortal women, who was wearing a pink satin robe and putting on makeup using a mirror on her vanity.

"But really, I am sort of busy right now. This poor woman is about to shoot her husband, and the S.O.B. really has it coming."

She started talking to the mortal woman again.

"You really told him off that time. Who is he to be asking about the pool guy, after he just had an affair? If he comes back up here, you'll get the beating of your life. No more punching you in the head, where your hair covers the bruising. This time he'll bash in your teeth, he may even strangle you. Your pistol is in the closet. Get it and keep it close. Self-defense."

I watched the woman get her pistol, and then I went downstairs, where a Zolian was talking to her husband. He was sitting at his desk in the study with his hands covering his face. He looked up, and I recognized him. He must have followed through on what he started at Tony's bar, and his wife hadn't taken it well.

I could see what Shartruze meant. The guy was a jerk, but he didn't deserve to die.

I went back to Shartruze. "How long have you been working on these people? They are the same ones from the bar where I first met you."

"Ah, Will--this kind of event takes years of work, every-day persistence, a mix of violence, adultery, mental illness, whatever we can use. I don't think you have any comprehension of the planning and hard work that goes into something like this."

"Why go to all the trouble?"

"We speak to and influence mortals because we have a talent for it. We are virtuosos. When you have that kind of talent, why wouldn't you use it to benefit others? Do you think we want to sit around playing harps on clouds? What a bunch of nonsense. We don't need to have a talent, like mortals, for jamming basketballs through hoops or painting pretty pictures. In a non-mortal world, persuasion and ideas are all that matters."

"Sure," I said, "maybe adultery brings excitement and fulfillment, but how is her shooting him going to benefit anyone?"

"Some people take years of work, although I must say, your adultery was rather sudden. Admirable work on my part, a person of faith becoming an adulterer."

"What!?"

She laughed. "Don't you recognize me, after all my work? I spent years putting thoughts in your mind. You were my favorite mortal, my biggest project. You know how hard your life was. Life wasn't just hard for you. Most of the mortals on this planet view their lives as being almost more than they can bear. They feel overwhelmed, drowning in their own self-pity. They take pills for their anxiety—and they all feel anxiety. Your mind was like mine, and I could turn it. At the point where you realized that even the success of the strategic testing wasn't going to make your life better, and that Marie was going to divorce you, you finally got some common sense. The best thing you did was to sleep with Ronnie. It made you whole, complete. And you act like you didn't recognize me. I was the voice in your head. There were several of us. In fact, Azzoloft himself had quite an interest in you. Your project to stabilize dark matter held his attention."

I felt an awful recognition spread throughout me. Shartruze's ideas and mine probably were alike, which was why I was attracted to her. It wasn't just her striking appearance and beauty, it was familiarity. I felt comfortable—too comfortable—with her. Anger surged through me. The Zolians were ugly. They were ugly on the inside. Maybe this was hell, because they were pure evil. I wasn't angry at God now, I was angry at myself, for what I had done. I had listened to Shartruze. Mortals were still listening to her. And there was nothing I could do about that. Shartruze would keep on doing what she did best. But at least I didn't have to listen to her anymore.

I watched the drama unfolding, going back and forth between the two spouses. Shartruze had no doubt done her job. We watched the woman push out the cylinder and check, yes, five bullets. She placed the gun in her lap, inside her robe. I wondered if she knew how to shoot straight.

Suddenly, we heard a door slam downstairs. I left Shartruze, and went downtairs where I could see a male Zolian talking to the husband in his study. "Unbelievable. The pool guy just walked in, like he lives here. He didn't know you would be home this morning. That is why you keep your gun in the drawer." I felt shock. The Zolians were double-teaming, going for a murder. The pretense was gone. I watched the husband slide the drawer open. He stopped for a second when the drawer squeaked. They each had a gun. Hers was a Smith and Wesson, with a brown handle and a short barrel. Now he pulled out a black handgun, like the ones police would use. The family that shoots together, just might die together.

I moved to where I could see the pool guy. He was looking in the fridge. He called out "Deb?" He grabbed an apple from a bowl of fruit on the counter and took a bite.

The husband walked in, the gun pointed straight at the pool guy. "You've got a lot of nerve," he said.

"Hey, I'm really sorry," said the pool guy. "I-I had no idea you were here. I'm just here to clean the pool."

"You aren't going to be cleaning the pool anymore."

Suddenly shots rang out. The first one missed, and both men tried to duck. Then more shots, bang, bang, bang, bang. Deb was shooting from the staircase. One of the shots struck her husband in the chest, and he slumped to the ground. Her husband raised the gun, aiming at the pool guy, the gun wobbling, blood spreading down his shirt. Deb pulled the trigger again, but the gun just clicked.

Deb's husband shot the pool guy in the head. The gun dropped from the husband's hand. His eyes didn't close, and the look of shock never disappeared.

I felt myself twitch with surprise as a black mist spewed from the lifeless bodies of the two men. Every Zolian in the room, including Shartruze, rushed towards them, inhaling the darkness, their mouths agape, swirling and churning around them. The Zolians spewed forth darkness of their own. I caught a glimpse of the husband after he left his body, in the same form as the rest of us, but he was covered in darkness so thick I could not see through it.

Deb ran to the pool guy. As she reached to embrace him, the darkness was swirling around them. She began sobbing.

The swirl of blackness grew, now obscuring the Zolians and the two men, now ex-mortals, who are all inside the swirl. The group moved through the wall of the house we'd been in. I followed through the wall, and the Zolians with their captives moved more quickly. I followed, wanting to know where they were going, as they moved miles across the city and out into the desert.

CHAPTER 18

POSTING BOND

THE SWIRLING ZOLIANS, in a frenzied ball of dark mist, moved quickly towards the pit where the Zolians cast their prisoners. There were Zolians guarding the entrance. Brett had to be in there, somewhere. Inside there must be swirls of darkness, in chaos. I didn't know how many prisoners they might be holding in there.

The guards stood aside. The swirling Zolians moved through the mouth of the pit with their two captives.

"Hey, my brother is in there." I said. "I need to get in!"

The Zolian guards near the pit laughed. "What kind of idiot are you? Nobody invited you here. Get lost."

Shartruze had gone in. I had assumed she would help me. I looked around at the landscape. The pit was in the desert south of Queen Valley. They weren't going to let me get to Brett.

Then I saw Shartruze and the other Zolians who had been with her come back out of the pit. They headed back towards Phoenix. I caught up with Shartruze as quickly as I could.

"Hey, what is that place?" I asked, trying to sound casual.

The Zolians turned towards me. I could see the dark mist still clinging to them, like blood froth around sharks. The others glared and left us.

Shartruze's eyes looked crazy. She came directly at me, spewing mist. Her face was touching mine, and she kept spewing.

"Hey! Stop it!" I twisted and tried to fly away from her, but she stayed with me. It felt horrible. Her eyes were full of hatred.

"All I want to do is get my brother out of that place!" I yelled. She continued attacking me for several more seconds, but the mists were not clinging to me. As I struggled against her, the mists became thinner. Finally, she backed off. I was glad I decided to stop listening to her. Maybe that was why the black mist wasn't affecting me like it had before. There was still information I needed from her, however. At least half of what she said was usually true.

"Why did you take those two men to this place, but no one took me? It is some kind of prison?" I asked.

"Because you isolated dark matter, that's why!" she said. "You have no idea how rare it is for Azzoloft to have a personal escort take someone to him like they did when you died."

"Is that place supposed to be hell? Those men have been surrounded by darkness since the moment they died. How could they even see where they are?"

"Come on, Will. You are a scientist. You are here. You see the same planet earth you always have. God isn't here. Why are you asking me about religious nonsense?"

"Is the black mist some kind of chemical, made of the same matter we are?"

"Chemicals that affect mortals are just an imitation of what we do. Our power to paralyze those two unfortunate gentlemen isn't a mere chemical. You'll have to figure it out for yourself." Her tone was sharp and impatient. She had been in a foul mood since the frenzy.

"Why would you put those two men who just died into a prison? If that isn't hell, what is your reason? I don't believe there is no heaven or hell."

"This isn't heaven, because you aren't happy. When you have been around for thousands of years as a non-mortal, everything becomes so obvious. Certainly, I could go sit on a mountain top and enjoy the beauty and isolation, but, as you might guess, I don't enjoy that. I do enjoy helping persuade mortals about the principles that govern them. I doubt you see the complexity of it, or understand that your life, any mortal's life is a drip-drip-drip of a leaky faucet, until the bucket of their life's experience is full.

"The sum of life for any mortal is this: You had better enjoy all the good things you can, as long as they last. I believe in adultery, early and often, or better yet, no marriage at all, because physical relations are one of the most powerful things that mortals can feel.

"Some things are compelling—they raise life above the mundane," she said. "In fact they become addicting because they are so exciting; they bring a rush. Sex. Drugs. Pornography. Gambling. Even murder. These things are bigger, better, and more exciting than the misery of daily mortal life. You can't possibly get enough of them in one mortal lifetime. Inhale these opportunities, use them up, make the most of them. Mortality has pleasures, so bask in the hot tub of life with as many young, buff, nude people as you can fit in it. And when the excitement ends, leave mortality on your own terms. That is what I helped you see. That is why you slept with Ronnie. You finally got some sense."

"You've got to be kidding me! That husband just

murdered their pool guy over adultery. I feel rotten about what I did because it is wrong. It is immoral."

"You and your religious nonsense! This is reality. What actually happens is reality. The reality is that we paralyzed that murderer, and that adulterous pool man, from the moment they went unconscious. You saw your surroundings when you died, even though you were an adulterer. You should have ended up paralyzed in black mist from the moment you arrived. You escaped that fate because Azzoloft has other plans for you."

What a horrible experience it would have been, if from the moment of your death, instead of seeing a beautiful woman like Leilani, as I had, these men were going to see nothing but black mists. They could probably feel the Zolians around them in the darkness, full of hatred and frenzy. The black mists would be what they had perceived. I had felt the depression, despair, and self-condemnation in that darkness. How long could they remain like that, perhaps not even knowing where they were? For years? Centuries?

Shartruze left. I didn't try to follow. The frenzy I had seen in Shartruze, and the other Zolians, wasn't rational. It was evil. It looked like hatred. Was it science, or religion? Certainly, the rules for how the Zolians could spew out black mist on some ex-mortals had a scientific basis. Perhaps these black mists were the scientific form of emotions, the horrible feeling of powerlessness for someone, like Brett, who had made a lot of mistakes. Or someone like me.

■ ■ ■

When I left Shartruze, I focused again on Isaac. This time he arrived.

"Where were you? I need you to help me get my brother out of a Zolian prison."

"I've been following Sky Lurich," he said. So that was why he didn't come the first time I'd tried to reach him.

"You're going to want to hear this," he said. "You remember the map we saw in his office, with locations marked in red. He's been working on international deals. Something to do with your machine. He wants a greater production base for dark matter."

"There's only one machine, and it would take months to duplicate the set-up we had."

"I'm not so sure. He may have already been working on this. You remember the map of the world?"

Sky didn't have authorization to duplicate our machine, but he could have accessed the technology, particularly if he had help from the inside.

"Hey, let's get my brother out, and worry about that later."

I explained to him what happened with Blitzer and Brett, how I had located Shartruze, and what happened.

"She's probably right, they will try to put him back in again."

"I don't care. We can't just leave him there."

We discussed our strategy, and then moved together to the area where the Zolians were holding Brett. He summoned a group of his friends. It took a few minutes for them to gather. They were from the Science Association. I summoned Charlotte, as well. After introductions, we set up a plan, in which Isaac and I would go in and get Brett, and the others would stay out of sight until Isaac and I summoned them. After we found Brett, they would help us push past whatever Zolians were at the entrance.

Isaac pushed past the guards at the mouth of the cavern, with me following, The Zolians weren't expecting anyone to try to get in, which gave us the element of surprise. Inside the entrance, we were in a cavern, but the only light was from the entrance. The cavern had a sharp drop as it got deeper, and there was a tunnel 10 meters high. The floor was piled with inert figures, and in the dim light I could see they were covered in dark mist. I saw the faces of some of them. Their eyes were fixed, as if they were blind. I knew what it felt like to be near Brett, and I reached out in my thoughts to sense where he might be.

"I can sense where he is," I said. Isaac and I locked arms, and we moved swiftly forward into total darkness, until we got to the place I felt Brett was being held.

"Brett," I said. "It's Will. I'm with Isaac. Can you hear me? There was no response.

"I can feel him here," I told Isaac, "but he's not responding." I reached out, and felt the form of his head, and his shoulders, in the darkness. How could we get him out of here, if he wouldn't respond? I placed my hand on his cheek and reached out with my mind. It wasn't with my voice, it was with my thoughts, connecting to his thoughts, his essence. I sensed his mind and made a connection. It was like an electrical connection, something I'd never felt before. With that connection, I spoke the thought, "Come with us."

"Will," Brett said. "Will, is that you?"

"Yes, and I'm with someone else. Isaac. You need to come with us. We need to get you out of here." I took his arm. We began moving towards the entrance.

"The Zolians are going to be waiting for us," I told Brett.

We saw the light at the entrance and moved towards it. There were Zolians blocking it. Isaac and I summoned his friends and Charlotte. Isaac pushed through the Zolians, but there were too many. Zolian guards were making a wall. They swarmed us and moved in to form a smaller box so as to leave no spaces. Their precision was uncanny, computer-like. They were forming box after box around us, as they had at Sky's office, with Isaac forcing his way through with Brett and me. This time there were more of them, so that they continuously recycled to form new boxes, and Isaac was unable to break through them fast enough. In addition, they began spewing dark mist. It was like acid on my soul, filling me with dread. Brett stiffened. Isaac seemed unaffected by the mist but holding onto Brett was slowing him down.

"We need help!" he yelled.

Isaac's friends arrived and locked arms with Isaac and us. Together they were able to push through wall after wall of the prison guards, but we were moving slowly, as they regrouped almost instantaneously. The Zolians were vicious and angry. If they needed more numbers, they could summon them. Perhaps they could stop us entirely.

Charlotte came bursting through towards us. The Zolians were startled to see her. She grabbed my arm, and, together with Isaac and the others, we were able to surge through the walls of Zolians to freedom. We headed in the direction of downtown Phoenix, and the administration building where Charlotte's volunteers had their headquarters.

"Man am I glad to see you," said Brett. "I can't take being in there."

"What happened when that Zolian tackled you?" I asked. "He was covering you in a black mist, and it looked like you were being tortured."

"It felt like they had taken everything I ever did wrong, and everything I was ever afraid of, and magnified it. I couldn't see anything. I was paralyzed, sinking into darkness, like a bottomless pit."

"I've heard a lot of people say the same thing," Charlotte agreed.

Isaac and I explained to Charlotte what we had seen in

Sky's secret conference room, and Isaac's suspicions about Sky's international plans.

"Sky Lurich isn't the only one up to no good," she said. "Our network of volunteers is reporting the president is going to have a meeting at the White House the day after tomorrow, and they are going to be discussing whether to proceed with a re-test. The Zolians usually have their people blockading the White House to keep our people away."

We decided to meet the next day. Charlotte was going to try to influence the president at the meeting, with anyone else who wanted to be there to help.

Isaac, Brett, and I left. Isaac and I remembered the locations on the map, and we needed to see if we could figure out what Sky was doing. We decided to visit the hadron colliders in China and Russia. We found the location in China. We avoided the main entrance to the hadron collider, hoping to avoid any Zolians who might try to stop us. We searched through the rooms of the underground complex for a place similar to the facility where we had conducted our strategic test.

It didn't take long to find it. Sky's company logo was on the door leading to a room, and there was a machine in it, similar to the one we'd used. The lights were on, but no one was in the facility.

We went from there to Russia, and found another machine. The room also had Sky's company logo on it. We needed to get organized, if we wanted to have any chance of preventing Azzoloft from having a second chance at a strategic test. Now things were that much worse. He had multiple options.

I was glad the meeting with the president wasn't the next day. I had a funeral I wanted to attend. My own.

CHAPTER 19

PUNCH AT A FUNERAL

MY FUNERAL WAS held at our church. Maria scheduled with our church leader and the funeral home to have a viewing on the day of the funeral, an hour before the services.

I went to the church early on the day of the services. I was pleased to see that the photos of me on the table in the foyer were some of my favorites. It showed my mother, with Brett and me when we were younger. There was another photo, our last photo together before my mother and Brett died. There were my favorite pictures of me with Samuel and Emily; our most recent family photo; and the wedding picture of Marie and I at the church. There were some of my scientific awards, and some newspaper clippings. I enjoyed seeing the display. Mine was a life well-lived---for the most part. There was not a photo of my team from the strategic testing. I could imagine Marie getting one and cutting Ronnie out of it.

I went to Marie's house, and Samuel was playing the piano. He was dressed in his Sunday suit. He was playing a very brisk piece on the piano. His cheek stuck out where his tongue was, the way he did on the toughest parts of the song.

Marie was in the bathroom with Emily, the door open,

putting her hair in a braid the way she did on special occasions. Emily was chatty, almost excited. Emily hadn't been to funerals much, other than my mother's and my brother's. "Will Sarah's kids be at the luncheon?" she asked. The women of the congregation always provided a meal for family members after the services.

"Yes, they'll be there. All our family will be there."

Samuel's piano music was loud, even from the other room.

Marie looked in that direction and opened her mouth to yell, then slowly closed it and finished the braid.

After a few minutes they were ready, and I followed them to the chapel. The director from the funeral home gathered them by my casket and opened it.

I wasn't prepared for what I saw.

I felt complete revulsion looking at my mortal body, the waxy remains. It was someone else lying there, it didn't look like me at all.

Emily had tears running down her cheeks, and she backed away. Marie held her.

Aunt Sarah arrived, with her family, and others started coming into the room for the viewing. The room filled quickly, as many people from my congregation came in. Many of them shed tears, as they embraced Marie, and looked at my body. Their grief was strong. It wasn't my time to die. A motorcycle crash was sudden and unexpected.

Marie hugged them, accepted their words of kindness, and was gracious. To them, she showed the face of a loving wife who had lost her husband. None of them would know I'd had an affair; she wouldn't have told any of them.

Seeing the members of the congregation that I had been a part of for years made me think of how proud I would have been of my life—if I hadn't ruined everything by having an affair. I had done so many good things, and I'd loved these people so much. They'd loved me. Word had probably gotten around that she had served me with divorce papers, but that would only have increased their sympathy.

Several ex-mortals approached me.

"Hello, Will."

"You two look familiar, but you probably look a lot younger than when I last saw you."

"I'll give you a hint. You were at my funeral."

Tom. I recognized him, but he looked 25 years old. "Hey, it's so good to see you," I said. "You look great."

"I'm Bob Grover."

Sure enough, it was a young version of Bob. "Okay, I recognize you now," I told him.

"I'm so sorry, Will," said Tom. "I can't believe that right after your big science breakthrough, you died. That was rotten timing."

Unless he knew about Ronnie, and I couldn't see why he would, he had no idea how rotten the timing was.

There was a commotion by the door of the room; Senator Strong had just come in. Our church leader had gone over to greet him. Dr. Griggs was with him. Then I saw Ronnie. I looked at Marie, and saw her stop talking, then resume.

While the church leader greeted the senator, Ronnie turned and moved back towards the doorway. Dr. Griggs moved towards her. I moved close enough to hear their whispered conversation.

"I'm sorry, Charles," she said, "but I'm not feeling well. You go ahead, and I'll just wait in the hall."

Her face was pale, and she looked ill. It occurred to me that she probably wasn't sure whether Marie knew about our affair.

"The senator will be more comfortable with you here. It will only take a moment."

"I really shouldn't have come---"

"Nonsense, of course you should have."

She hadn't told Griggs about it either.

Senator Strong raised his bushy eyebrows and turned towards Ronnie and Dr. Griggs. Dr. Griggs took Ronnie by the arm.

Ronnie tried to force a smile, but it came out a grimace, as she moved toward the front of the room with the senator and Dr. Griggs.

Marie glanced in the senator's direction, and the elderly couple she was speaking to politely moved on to make way.

"Mrs. Johnson, I am so sorry. Your husband's accomplishments were most extraordinary, and we all mourn his loss. You have our deepest condolences." The senator's eyebrows were low, his face somber.

She thanked him, and then shook Dr. Griggs' hand.

"Charles, thank you so much for being here. It means a lot."

"You know how much Will meant to us. I just can't believe this happened. Please, if there is anything we can do, let us know."

Marie had not so much as glanced at Ronnie.

Ronnie had been waiting, her face frozen. Then she looked past Marie, and saw my face, for the first time, in the casket. Her face contorted with emotion, and she hiccupped as she tried to swallow a sob.

Marie heard it. She turned to Ronnie, raised her fist, and punched Ronnie in the mouth.

Ronnie staggered back and fell into the first row of chairs.

The senator watched, his eyebrows pumping up and down several times.

Dr. Griggs looked at Marie and took a step back.

Samuel and Emily watched, their eyes wide.

Everyone else in the room froze for several seconds, staring.

Marie folded her arms and glared at Ronnie.

Ronnie licked her lips, tasting the blood from a cut on her lip. She wiped the blood away gingerly, but it continued bleeding. She got up and walked towards the door.

Dr. Griggs mumbled "I'm very sorry" to Marie, from a safe distance, and backed away to follow Ronnie.

Senator Strong followed Dr. Griggs, his eyebrows twitching several more times.

My church leader walked to Marie, put his arm around her, and asked if she was all right, and everyone else in the room tried to act as if nothing had happened, except that Emily kept stealing glances at her mother, glances of wonder.

"What was that all about?" asked Tom. I could see the shock and concern on Tom's and Bob's faces.

What could I say? I loved these two men, as much as I'd loved anyone in my congregation. They had always treated me, as a mortal, with the utmost respect. All I could say was, "Marie had her reasons." There was consternation in their faces, but I didn't have an answer, not one I was willing to say out loud. "Excuse me," I said.

I moved out into the hallway to see where Ronnie had gone. She was walking towards the chapel. She went in and took a seat. She had a Kleenex, and she dabbed at her lip. She looked straight ahead, saying nothing as the Dr. Griggs and the senator sat beside her. I hated the look in her eyes, the lost look, a look somewhere through grief and beyond.

As great as the pain Ronnie felt might be, or the pain Marie and my children were feeling today, there was something worse coming. If the president decided to proceed with a retest, the world would change. At my funeral, I was the only one who seemed to realize how much. I needed to protect these people, the people I cared about. I needed to find a way to stop Azzoloft.

■ ■ ■

I spent time near Marie and my children after the funeral, but I couldn't keep my mind off what still needed to be done. There had to be a way to stop Azzoloft. It would be easy if the mortals decided not to do the retest. Charlotte and I would go there when the president made the decision and try to dissuade him.

If the president decided to proceed with the retest, Azzoloft had several advantages over us. He had billions of followers. The Zolians would likely try to keep me and any other afterlifers away from the lab. They would not want us interfering with the test, nor did they want us trying to get in Azzoloft's way.

We had succeeded in getting Brett out of the Zolian pit, but the Zolians hadn't been fully prepared. We had the advantage that Isaac and Charlotte, and those who had crossed the gulf, could push past the Zolians, but we needed more people. We needed to recruit numbers.

The other thing Azzoloft had was knowledge. He'd been watching mortals for thousands of years, and he'd been experiencing this phase of non-mortal existence, as well. I'd been here a matter of days. More importantly, Azzoloft knew why the stabilized matter dust shaped into his form in the particle field.

Tomorrow we'd know what the president would decide.

CHAPTER 20

THE WHITE HOUSE

THE MORNING AFTER the funeral, I met Charlotte at the Greater Phoenix Volunteers building, as we had arranged.

"Hey, you look good in white," I said.

She smiled. "Wish I could say the same for you."

I took hold of her arm, and we moved almost instantly to the front lawn of The White House.

"I take it you've been here before," I said.

"Yes, but that doesn't mean the president ever listens."

I was watching to see if the Zolians would be surrounding the place, given the importance of the meeting today. Sure enough, there were several posted around the outside of the building. They looked at us but remained still.

Charlotte led the way through the front wall directly to the oval office. The president was there alone, looking at some papers at his desk. His face was somber. After a few moments, he got up and left the room.

"Come on," Charlotte said. She moved through the walls to a conference room.

Azzoloft was there. I felt an electric shiver go through me; the kind I used to feel as a mortal. Some people said it was what happened when someone stepped on your grave. I felt an anxiety, and an urge to flee.

Azzoloft looked at us only briefly, and then gazed intently at the mortals in the room.

The room was full of mortals, and several quiet conversations were taking place. I recognized Dr. Charles Griggs, Senator Strong, Sky Lurich, and several others. Some, including Sky, seemed to have a lingering dark mist around them, the kind Brett had when he was in the prison.

The room grew quiet. I turned to see the president enter. He walked to his chair and sat. He was followed by a secret service agent, who closed the door and stood by it.

Azzoloft moved instantly to the president, emanating a dark mist, which washed over him.

The mist did not cling to the president, however. It almost immediately evaporated.

"I want to thank all of you for being here today," the president said. "As you know, we need to make a final decision as to whether we are going to repeat the strategic test at the National Strategic Hadron Collider. You are all aware of the importance of this decision. I've discussed this with many of you, and I'm aware of your opinions. Most of you are anxious to move forward. I'd like to hear from those who aren't, starting with the Secretary of Homeland Security."

The Secretary was petite, her black hair peppered with gray. Charlotte moved over to her and whispered in a resonate voice, "The being in the strategic test is evil. Eli Matheson told the truth. The testing must not proceed."

Azzoloft watched Charlotte. He smiled.

His smile unnerved me more than anything else could have. He was smug, utterly confident.

The Secretary spoke, "Some of you are aware that I am a religious person. We had a warning from a man named Eli

Matheson, and though many people did not take it seriously, some did. Religious believers are strongly divided on this issue, but in my heart, I must say I have had a foreboding, and it has never left me. Perhaps some of you think I should set those feelings aside in making decisions on behalf of our nation, but I do not agree. I do not think we should proceed."

Azzoloft laughed out loud.

"I certainly hope it is not a foregone conclusion that the testing should proceed," a general said. He was thin, with white hair. "I'm a religious man also, and there are a great many of us who feel uneasy about exposing ourselves to a totally unknown being. Putting that aside, however, from a purely strategic standpoint, why would we intentionally expose ourselves to a potentially powerful enemy?"

Azzoloft moved next to Sky Lurich. Black mist spewed over Sky, as Azzoloft hissed, "Do they know how stupid this sounds? Since when did a cabinet member make decisions based on her 'forebodings?' That lady is a nut. She is absurd."

"I am glad you are willing to set aside your religion, General," Sky said.

He was wise enough to be civil, although it must have been hard considering he was covered in the venomous mist of hate.

"I haven't had any feeling of foreboding," Sky said, "religious or otherwise, and I think Mr. Matheson was a quack. From a strategic perspective, the point is, if we had an alien spaceship hovering over our planet, and they contacted us, saying, 'We come in peace,' we'd all be thrilled to talk to them. In fact, for many years, we've been beaming radio into space hoping to make some kind of contact. We wouldn't tell them to go away, nor would we start shooting missiles at them."

Azzoloft began moving quickly around the room,

spewing dark mist as he went. He was in a flurry of motion, visiting every mortal in the room. I was filled with a dark anxiety, and with despair that Charlotte or I could make any difference. The room seemed to echo with taunting and hissing, and I wondered if I was hallucinating.

"I agree to some extent with the points each of you are making," the president said. "I have felt forebodings, and they may well be religious. On the other hand, it is also important to consider the science. As some of you may be aware, I've appointed Dr. Charles Griggs as a special advisor in this matter." He looked at Dr. Griggs.

"I think I speak for most of the scientific community when I say that this should not be a difficult decision," said Dr. Griggs. "The vast majority of those in science and academia do not understand the concern. The scientific method we have used for hundreds of years is based on advancing knowledge. We built the hadron colliders precisely for the purpose of gaining more knowledge. This should be one of the greatest scientific breakthroughs in history. We wouldn't miss it for anything."

The conversation continued. Azzoloft and Charlotte moved around the room.

"Thank you all for your input," said the president. "There is another matter which we need to address. Mr. Lurich, I've become aware that you have arranged to have equipment placed at hadron colliders in two other countries, and I believe that equipment is nearly operational."

There were murmurs around the conference table.

Sky met the president's gaze. "I wouldn't care to comment on that, sir," Sky said.

"No, you probably shouldn't, although I doubt it would matter," the president said. "The evidence we've gathered against you is pretty convincing."

Charlotte and I looked at each other and smiled.

"I'm glad that cat's out of the bag," she said. We were already aware of this information, but we didn't know the president was aware of it. The president should have him arrested on the spot. Our technology was classified.

The president nodded to the agent by the door.

The agent opened the door, and four men in suits came inside. They approached Sky.

One of them showed his law enforcement badge to Sky, then bent over and whispered something to him. Sky got up, and they escorted him out.

Azzoloft watched but did not react. Nothing seemed to surprise him.

I went through the door and watched, just long enough to see them advise Sky that he was under arrest.

"On what charge?" He pulled away from them.

I wondered if they were going to say, "For the murder of Dr. William Johnson." They didn't.

"Illegal disclosure of classified information."

Sky scowled. One of them grabbed him, and this time he wasn't able to pull away. He went with them down the hall.

I moved through the wall back into the conference room.

"Why did Mr. Lurich even show up today?" The general was asking. He ran his fingers through his white hair. "The man has a lot of audacity."

"I think he had the utmost confidence that no one knew," the president said. "I only found out through a very unusual circumstance. I have met with the leaders of the countries where those colliders are located. They are in Russia and China. I persuaded Russia to cease cooperation with Mr. Lurich, but China made no agreements. I know that most of you feel strongly that we should immediately proceed with the strategic testing. Now we know that China may proceed, even if we do not."

Azzoloft was moving around the room again. "It changes nothing," hissed Azzoloft. "We need to do the test first. We must trust no one, particularly not Russia." His words were surreal echoes, as he moved swiftly from one side of the table to the other. The dark mist was surrounding almost everyone now, except the president, the secretary of Homeland Security, and the general. The mists simply evaporated away from them.

Charlotte moved close. "Mr. President, having someone else get there first isn't the issue. You must stop all the tests. You must try again to persuade China of the danger."

"The fact that Mr. Lurich has been able to effectively work with other countries is warning enough," said the general. "He was able to do it without us knowing about it. This could be the greatest threat we've ever faced. It is something beyond our comprehension. We should consider all options."

The president frowned. "What options are you referring to?"

"We know precisely where the hadron collider in China is located," said the general. "We could easily destroy it."

"Mr. President, I think that is going way too far," said Senator Strong. His bushy eyebrows drew together, and his face was solemn. "It would be an act of war. We cannot allow China, or anyone else, to seize this opportunity before we do. But there is no need for a military strike; once we've completed the test, if this figure appears, it won't make any difference what China does."

The debate continued, with other people commenting.

Finally, the president spoke. "I've carefully weighed all viewpoints. There is one thing holding me back. I mentioned earlier that I only found out about Mr. Lurich's actions through a very unusual circumstance. Eli Matheson asked to meet with me. He proceeded to provide me with enough details about Mr. Lurich's actions so I could verify them. He drew for me the layout of the location of the equipment. When I contacted the leaders of Russia and China, his diagram was so specific I was able to convince them I already knew everything. I did not disclose Matheson as my source. But I'll tell you this; Matheson knew things I didn't. Before we finish here, I want you to hear from him again."

He nodded to the secret security agent by the door, and the agent opened the door. Mr. Matheson came in. He was dressed in a suit and looked as if he fit in with the members of the cabinet and others around the table. The agent moved a chair up to the table for him.

"Thank you for coming, Mr. Matheson," said the president. "I've explained to everyone the information you provided me about Sky Lurich. We are ready to make a decision about proceeding with the strategic testing. Nearly everyone here still wants to move forward. They view this as an opportunity to move science forward as never before."

"I understand that. It is the rational response," Eli said. "I have given much thought as to what I can tell you, and I myself am amazed at how limited my options are. First, let me say it plainly: You should avoid further testing, like the plague. You would, without question, if you had a concept of what it means. The being you saw in the initial strategic test is evil. His name is Azzoloft. He truly intends to destroy the human race. You have seven billion mortals. He has many times that many followers."

Eli looked at Azzoloft.

Azzoloft sneered at him.

"Why hasn't he destroyed us already?" asked the general.

"That's what I don't understand. If he is so powerful, why is he waiting on us?"

"The simple answer is that he will gain the power to destroy you only to the extent you open the door and let him in. Once you do that, I am quite certain you will not be able to stop him."

"You have to understand this sounds like a complete fairy tale," said Dr. Griggs. "We are talking about science. You are talking about someone out of a comic book."

"Perhaps this will help you, then. I am a scientist. It is fair to say that I know more about science than any mortal in this room. Did science keep Rome from burning? Did it prevent the Bubonic plague? Suppose someone like me had showed up in 1340 A.D. with a vaccination against the plague. I'd tell everyone that 50 million people would die in the Roman Empire. Would we get the vaccination out to everyone, or would they tell me I was insane?"

"Then give us some evidence," said Senator Strong.

"I already thought of that, and I decided it was a reasonable request. I gave the evidence to the president."

He turned to the president.

"Mr. President, did you explain to them the evidence I gave you about Sky Lurich?"

"Yes, sir, you did. I will tell you gentleman, that I am convinced he has ways to gather information beyond what I understand. He told me one other thing I should mention. He told me exactly what Sky would say at this meeting."

"He said he wasn't going to comment," said Senator Strong. "Anyone could have guessed that."

"No senator, he told me every word Sky would say in the entire meeting. Word for word."

"Senator Strong, and Dr. Griggs, is that evidence enough for you?" Eli asked.

They both stared at the table.

Eli shook his head slowly. "I already knew the answer. If Azzoloft were in this room right now, I could not show him to you."

Azzoloft put out his hands, his face wrinkled sarcastically. "So why are you wasting everybody's time?"

"There is no possible proof," Eli said. "If I disappeared from sight, right now, it would not prevent you from going forward."

He looked at the president. "I am asking you, sir. I have the utmost respect for you, as the president of this country; more than you know. I have done everything I can. I plead with you. Please believe me."

The president closed his eyes, and leaned forward, in thought. Finally, he looked up. "You almost have me convinced."

CHAPTER 21

ZINC'S REVENGE

THAT EVENING AFTER I left Charlotte, I went to my house to see my kids.

A patrol car was parked in front of the house, its lights flashing, and my son Samuel was being taken out of the car. His hands were cuffed, and his elbow was bloodied. The neck of his t-shirt was ripped and stretched. Samuel had his head down, staring at the ground as the officer silently led him up the walk.

When Marie opened the door, her mouth dropped open. "Samuel! What happened?"

"Is this your son, Ma'am?" The officer's voice was businesslike.

"Yes."

"He was caught shoplifting at the grocery store over on McKellips Road. He also tried to run away from a police officer, which is why he is scraped up. If he weren't a juvenile, he would have been charged with a felony for resisting arrest. I will release him to you as his parent if you are willing to take responsibility for him. Otherwise he'll spend the night in juvenile detention."

She nodded, silent, looking at Samuel. He was looking down, his lips tight.

It took a few moments for the officer to remove the cuffs and get the paperwork signed. The officer excused himself and Samuel walked toward the kitchen table as Marie closed the door and followed. He sat down, staring at the table.

"Look," Marie began, searching for words, "I know you're in a lot of pain, Sam, but I . . . I can't believe you'd do something like this."

As I watched my son's face, I heard a voice hissing behind me. "What about you, Will? Do you believe your son is a thief?"

I recognized Zinc's voice and whirled on him. Blitzer was by his side.

"Did you know your son has a serious tendency towards depression?" Zinc asked. "At least recently, anyway."

"Stay away from my son." I faced him squarely, my fists clenched convulsively.

"Let's see how much power you have, Will. You love your son, I can see that. Let's see if you can stop me from what I am going to do."

He was moving around me as he spoke, and he suddenly lunged at Samuel, spewing an almost imperceptible black mist as he moved inches from his ear and hissed out his words.

"It's her fault! She's the one who did it. She needs to hear it!"

I leapt forward and swung my fist at Zinc's face, but it stopped the moment it touched him. My other blows also had no impact. I tried to put him in a headlock, but I was as effective as a mortal trying to choke a stone gargoyle. I didn't move so much as a strand of Zinc's impeccable hair.

I saw my son tense as he felt Zinc's thoughts, and he

glared at his mother. "What do you know? You're really one to talk."

I hadn't ever seen Samuel like this. Marie looked as if she had been slapped, and tears came to her eyes.

"What do mean, Samuel?" her voice was quiet.

"There is one person who could have kept Dad from getting in trouble, and that was you!" I heard Zinc saying the words, and heard my son repeating them like an eerie echo.

Marie bit her lip and stared at the cold mashed potatoes in a yellow bowl on the granite counter top, that we had put in when we replaced the cabinets. Large tears were rolling down her cheeks.

Samuel kept staring at her, and the seconds dragged by.

"Dad would never have done anything wrong if you had treated him the way you were supposed to. I know you were fighting with him, treating him like dirt, before this ever happened. All you had to do was show you cared about him. He missed my birthday. So what? He's going to miss them all now."

Marie could hardly have been more stunned than me.

My son was blaming my wife.

Marie looked up with pleading in her eyes, hoping he would back off, but he met her gaze.

Emily had come out of her room and was standing there, peeking around the corner, watching them. Slowly she stepped out, listening.

I was standing there in a white robe, totally unseen, unfelt, and unknown. Right now, it was a rotten feeling. If my wife wouldn't say it, I would. I shouted, "It's my fault, not hers! Do you know what I did?" I couldn't help saying it, even though it was obvious they didn't hear me. My son kept staring at Marie. Zinc was standing back, his eyes intense.

Finally, Marie said softly, "You're right, Sam. I made

mistakes, and I'm not going to get a chance to take them back." She put her head down and stifled a sob.

Samuel looked angry, like he still didn't forgive her, like he never would forgive her. It dawned on me that it wasn't anger at her, it was anger that he had lost me. He couldn't yell at me, so he was yelling nonsense at her. She wasn't to blame. I had made my own choices. She had told me to leave, but I had no excuses for what I'd done. I never hated Marie. In fact, I was still in love with her, which made what I had done that much worse. Sure, Ronnie was beautiful, and sure, I had admired her for a long time—so perfect, always well-dressed, always composed, always witty. That she was vulnerable enough to be interested in me surprised me. I knew Ronnie had a lot of pain in her life, and why she was so vulnerable, but I didn't pass up the opportunity. For a while I was delighted that she'd responded to me. But the reality remained that it was needless.

I couldn't blame Samuel for being angry at me because he knew I had flaked out. I had become a person who was willing to betray the trust of those closest to me, my own wife and children. He didn't just mourn my absence, he mourned my fall. He knew me as one of the best men he had ever known, the man he loved most in the world—a man of wisdom, knowledge, and faith. He loved me as the world's best dad, at least for him, and he mourned that I had crashed, not only my motorcycle, but my life.

My daughter, Emily, had been watching from the corner, her eyes uncharacteristically wide, but now she spoke up. "I heard dad had a girlfriend. That's why you punched her at Dad's funeral."

Marie closed her eyes and put her head down, shaking her head, still crying. I had never seen her in such pain.

Samuel shouted, "Oh, shut up!" Emily looked like she

had been slapped. Samuel ran to her and pushed her, probably harder than he intended. She hit the wall and fell down. She burst into tears. He ignored her. He looked back at Marie.

"You know what?" he shouted. "I hate you!" He was angry, intense, and his words were daggers in the heart of a woman who had done nothing wrong; they were also daggers in the heart of the man who had. Sam stormed to his room.

I turned back to Zinc. Blitzer had moved over near him. "Stay away from my family. Stay away from them, or I'll . . ."

"You'll do what, Will?"

Fury boiled in me. Anger, raw and terrible, coursed through me. I was so sick of Zinc, and Azzoloft, and their smugness, their lies. And I was afraid. Terrified. That Zinc could tempt Sam? No, my son had been through some rough times, especially losing his father, but they had no more power over him than they had over any other mortal. My son could handle himself, just like every other mortal does. I was terrified of what was coming: Azzoloft was going to become a person who could kill my family, and my stabilizing dark matter had made it possible. God knew that, and it was his fault. It had to be. I was too stupid to control it. Not stupid, just ignorant. God can withhold information from us, he can hide, and we are the ones who suffer for it. And our families.

I embraced the rage, and the darkness, that I had felt when I crossed through the portal. I let it fill me, and burst from me. As I did so, swirling light and darkness pulsed into the room, although not visible to Marie or our children. In that instant, my daughter looked up. Her face was tear-streaked. She mouthed the word: "Dad?" Her face didn't show joy. It showed fear. Looking down, I could see a mix of light and darkness in my body, as the raw power surged through me. Emily had felt my anger and energy, even though she couldn't physically see me, just as Charlotte and the others had, when I had commanded them to bow down without using words.

I lunged at Zinc, intending to seize his throat, using my power to strangle him, to kill him. Instead, he was brushed out of my way like a cobweb.

I faced him and Blitzer. Zinc cursed in fury at being moved aside. As he watched me, shining with swirling darkness and light, he smiled, his eyes filled with hatred, but now mixed with satisfaction. "Look at you, filled with dark energy. It must be delicious to push me aside as if I were nothing. Feed on it. Fall into a frenzy with it. You have joined us. Azzoloft will be so very pleased." He left, and Blitzer followed.

Marie was crying. Emily left, and walked slowly to her bedroom. She took my picture from her nightstand, and carried it to her dresser. She put it in a drawer, face down. On her nightstand, the unicorn remained.

A unicorn isn't from this world. It isn't so much a fantasy, as a hope for something better. Like a hope for a father who didn't die, or a hope for a father who wouldn't be sent to hell.

CHAPTER 22

AZZOLOFT PROPOSES

ZINC AND BLITZER had gone. Azzoloft was coming. Azzoloft didn't know how much I knew; I wasn't sure how much I knew myself. When I had crossed the portal, I felt the coursing current of connections. What I had, though, were only still theories. God remained hidden. I believed, but I didn't expect atheists from the Science Association to take my word for anything. I could openly confront Azzoloft, with no evidence, and reveal the things I thought I knew; or I could play along. There may still be things I could learn from Azzoloft. Actually, there was a lot I could learn from him, if he wasn't such a liar.

Azzoloft appeared by my side. I was startled by the suddenness of it, even though I'd been expecting him.

"Time is short, Will. I think you and I need to have a discussion. Grab my arm." He held out his arm. I loathed the thought of touching him. Reluctantly, I grabbed his arm. I had decided it was better to play along.

Azzoloft and I were moving west, with astounding acceleration, a mere blur.

We began slowing, and I could see a complex of the

NSHC below us, with its modernistic design of steel and glass. We plunged through the side of the central building and down, underground into a man-made tunnel with gray-painted concrete walls. We stopped on a lookout platform above a complex of machinery, which looked like the place where they give tours of the particle accelerator.

"What the scientists were trying to do here, and what you spent the early part of your career doing," Azzoloft said, "was to find the smallest possible particles, the stuff quarks are made of. I watched the mortals build this complex, and I understand more about its design than any single mortal does. In fact, I understand this technology comprehensively, just as I understand nuclear reactors and nuclear weapons. There is so much more happening than any of you understand."

"We stabilized dark matter," I said. "Give us some credit. The thing we couldn't study here is what particles afterlifers and Zolians are made of. Mortals need to understand there is life, a paradigm, made of particles besides atoms. There is light besides photons. I've seen you shine with light, brighter than any ex-mortal I've seen. Yet, mortals don't see that light, but they would if the light were photons." How could he control that light, and the darkness? In me, they were a swirling mixture, like lightning in dark clouds, uncontrolled. How could he bear the searing pain of brilliant light, and I could not? If he was subjected to enough of it, would it destroy him, like it would me?

"That light is one of so many things you don't understand," he said. "The important thing is that we already know what happens after mortals die, don't we? You understand, as few mortals or ex-mortals do, the tremendous advantage it is to have experienced the afterlife, to see that you are still a person, made of a different type of matter. The particle accelerator is child's play compared to seeing a being like you, made of a different type of matter.

"I want you to come with me again." He held out his arm, and I grabbed it. We accelerated straight up, and then we came to a stop many miles above the earth, with its brown and green and blue colors, and white clouds drifting across a few areas in swirls. We looked over the vastness of the planet.

"Did anyone ever tell how beautiful the earth was after it was formed," he asked, "when the animals filled the earth, and it was teeming with life, before there were any humans, or even any of their evolving predecessors?"

"Yes, actually. Blitzer talked about it. He said that many Zolians feel they are at war with humans, and that humans are alien invaders."

"Well, there is certainly some truth to that," he said, "but I try to discourage that sentiment. It sounds so politically incorrect, don't you think? Still, there is a great deal of truth in it. I'm not particularly fond of mortals.

"I was the first one to come to this beautiful planet," he said, "and it has been mine ever since. I gathered my followers out of the reaches of space, and taught them to be a glorious race, and to serve me obediently. But as we watched humans being developed, and being born, and coming forth in the earth with their wars and bloodshed and pollution, I felt great pain. I don't tolerate pain.

"As you know," he said, "what intrigues me now is the idea of indestructible physical beings. Do you know why?"

"I'm afraid not," I said. I didn't want to say what I really thought. He had to know that I was aware of what he could do. I'd invented the particle field, and I had seen, since, the potential for a combination of physical matter and alpha matter.

"I know you are holding out on me," he said.

"Okay, well, let's say it is because you would like to obtain immortal, perfected bodies for you and your followers, because you've always wanted bodies and never got the chance."

"Go on." He said it as if I were standing on a cliff, and he wasn't sure exactly when to push me off.

"Because religion teaches that God cast you out of heaven, and prevented you from ever having bodies, and, in your bitterness and misery, you make war with the mortal children of God."

He threw back his head and laughed, a resounding laugh filled with derision and contempt. "Those kinds of comments make me angry, because your religious ignorance is so painful. I usually allow mortals to believe whatever nonsense they choose, no harm done, but what you said is disrespectful to me."

"I still believe in God," I said. "Most humans believe that when they die, all of religion is going to be explained to them. What I see is that God is using all types of technology, and different types of matter, to build worlds. He has bigger plans than mortals have comprehended, and they aren't just religious. I see now that God is a scientist. Heaven and hell could be very real."

"Does this look like hell to you," he asked, "the planet earth, inhabited by Zolians and ex-mortals? You really believe I am the devil?"

"No, this certainly isn't the typical view of hell," I said. "What I didn't realize, and what no one else seems to get, is that judgment day has not happened yet. Heaven and hell may not even begin until judgment day. We could see technological changes that would create heaven and hell. This planet is supposed to be scientifically transformed and upgraded. What I see here is that everything is digitized, with a precision that exceeds the astounding data in the DNA in a single cell.

Satan is supposed to be cast into a pit called hell, and I think that has everything to do with technology, even though it is explained in religious terms. That explanation was given 2,000 years ago. I think I am just now beginning to comprehend it. None of the mortals I knew had any idea. I don't think the ex-mortals comprehend it either."

"The question is," he said, "do you think I comprehend it? Do you think I exaggerate when I say there is so much more happening here than you understand? You are playing at a game bigger than you know. The answers lie in what mortal scientists are now beginning to discover: how much of the real matter is not made of atoms, and how little mortal scientists understand. That it is possible that I, as a superior being, have a superior body and power unknown and unseen by humans. That even you, as a pathetic shadow of my power and glory, have a body and an appearance after your death. I already know not only everything that mortal scientists know, but so much more. But even you, lowly ex-mortal that you are, can see the value of my followers having perfect, indestructible physical bodies, human in appearance.

"I am still wondering," he said, "whether you can be of any use to me, or whether I should destroy you."

"Maybe you could just let me go, and I'll promise to keep my mouth shut?" I suggested.

He laughed, and there was real mirth this time. "In some ways I still like you. And you will join me . . . or perish."

Since when did he have the power to destroy afterlifers? Perhaps that time was coming. At judgment day, maybe I was going to be cast into hell, right along with him, because I had committed adultery. Or I could join him now, which would guarantee I would go to hell.

"Frankly," I said, "it isn't me I'm worried about. If you have the power to destroy me, I haven't seen it."

"Ah. Then who are you worried about?"

"Well," I said, "Let's start with the President of the United States. You will materialize in the particle field. He'll come in to meet you, the first ambassador science has ever witnessed who wasn't born a mortal from a mother's womb. You'll reach out and snap his neck. His bodyguards will shoot you. Will you die? Shockingly, no. You'll be demanding to be the supreme leader of the world within ten minutes of arrival."

He chuckled. "You really think I would be so violent? That is coming from the evil in your mind, not from me. Mortals can be so very violent. I agree though, it was unfortunate that I didn't obtain a body the first time I appeared in the dust," he said. "I would greatly have preferred catching everyone off guard. Now they've had time to think about it, and to weigh the option of not allowing me to return. But they will allow me to return, because they want to know who I am. And of course, they'll still be off guard. They have no clue how to prepare for what is coming. I want you to help me make sure the transition is permanent this time. Permanent. Irreversible. Do you understand?"

"Why would you need my help?"

"I don't", he said. "There is nothing you can do. I want you to help yourself. I want you to be on the right side."

"The right side of what? What is it I don't understand?"

"Evolution. You are going to see science leap to the next level, not to evolved mortal forms, which are all degraded. Human evolution progresses to people who aren't made of mortal matter. They live in utopia. They live forever. The great human dream. You opened the door so that could happen. Do you want to help us fulfill the evolutionary process?"

"It can't be that simple. What happens to all the mortals living right now? I watched Shartruze and others attack two mortals. One of them had just murdered the other. I watched Blitzer attacking my friend, Mike. I watched Zinc attacking my family. You are evil."

"You understand so little," he said. "Let me try to explain it to you: Evil comes from mortals. Zolians have never been evil. We don't steal. We don't murder. Your morality is based in mortality. Why do mortals punish murder? Ex-mortals don't have to deal with the evil anymore. They are freed from it."

"How can you say that?" I asked. "I watched the man who committed murder. Shartruze and the other Zolians drowned him in black mist and took him to a pit."

"Where he will be able to withdraw from the evils of mortality," he said. "He is at peace. He is at rest. When mortals are gone, you will stop being tortured. Mortality is torture. Mortality is misery, it is pain. Mortals are the reason there isn't utopia. You are inherently self-defeating organisms. You wonder why mass-murders and shootings exist. It is because of great pain and anger those mortals feel. They are lashing out at other mortals. They would lash out at their God, if he were around. He doesn't exist, so they take out their anger on their fellow mortals. Mortality is a horrible option.

"There is another way," he said. "If you have the technology to have a body that can interact with mortals, a body not subject to pain, suffering, and mortal filth, that makes sense. No evil is required. That is the technology which exists. You introduced it to mortals. I will use it to create a better world, a world ultimately at peace, with all evil done away. No hunger, no war, no disease. You are personally invited. Join me."

"You know I won't do that."

"On the contrary, I am confident you will," he said. "We'll get to that in a minute. But let me ask you this. When I had you brought to me after you died, you asked me if you were in hell. If it turned out that your religion was right, and that you do end up in hell for your adultery, with your God condemning you, how long is that supposed to last?"

I stared at the ground, and felt my eyes narrowing. "A thousand years, at least. Probably forever."

"Doesn't that make you terribly angry? You've never been a patient sort. Suppose you could figure out the technology for instantaneously restoring a body that can interact with humans—would you use it, or would you defer to your belief that God wanted you to be in hell?"

I continued to stare at the ground.

Azzoloft started laughing. "You would use the power. You wouldn't sit around waiting for the judgments of your supposed God.

"You should understand," he said, "that you have accomplished a great thing. You have helped me finish my work. You led the team that stabilized dark matter, as you call it. You did it all for me. You are among my greatest servants, and I would like to reward you."

"I did nothing for you! Our discoveries were for the benefit of mankind, and for science."

"You did nothing for others. You did everything for yourself. You neglected your own family, your wife and your children. You are mine. Join me."

"I'll never join you."

"You already did. You committed adultery. Embrace what you have become, and I will give you the respect and honor you deserve. When they turn on the particle field again, I will have a physical body. But it won't be mortal. I've never been mortal. I've always been immortal, and I will continue to be. We will cleanse the earth of mortal evil. Ex-mortals will join us, voluntarily, if they are smart."

He didn't get it. We were a prototype. Our ex-mortal

bodies looked like our mortal bodies. That was no accident. It was programming, it was digital information. He might also be a prototype, since he looked like a mortal. But we also had DNA as mortals, and that wasn't something Azzoloft had, if he had never been mortal. What if DNA was an essential part of the code for having a permanent, immortal body? I didn't know how to stop him, but he didn't know everything either. His claims to be God, to be omniscient, were hollow.

"I will give you the immortal physical body that I and my followers will have, as a reward for your faithfulness. If you want your wife or children to live through what is coming, you had better join me. No one else is going to protect them. And things are going to get ugly."

There it was, the final threat. He'd kill my family if he succeeded in getting transformed into physical matter.

"You will never triumph," I said. "Someone will stop you. If it isn't me, someone else will. And judgment day is coming."

"No one will stop me," he said.

I hated to think he might be right. So far, everything seemed programmed, and prophecy was part of the program. Before judgment day, comes the antichrist.

Azzoloft left me. I went home to guard my family.

■ ■ ■

Our street was silent. The tall pine tree at the corner of the house blocked the glow of the street lamp from down the street. I went through the wall into the master bedroom, where Marie was asleep in our bed. The moonlight came through the mahogany-stained blinds and illuminated her dark hair strewn across the white linen pillowcase. Her white hand rested on the side of the bed I had designated my own, wherever we lived, whatever bed we owned, even if we were only sleeping in a motel for the night. We always understood that my place was on the right side of the bed.

I moved to Emily's room. She was up late, reading a book, *Dragon's Lair*. On her pillow was her favorite porcelain unicorn, perched near her cheek, as if reading with her. Her eyes began to close, and the book slipped in her grasp. She shook her head and continued reading. If only I could be there to hold her as she fell asleep. Her eyelids drooped again. This time, she got up. She went to her dresser drawer, and took out the picture of me she'd placed there. She kissed the picture, and then put it back in the drawer. She got back in her bed. The unicorn stayed perched on her pillow, watching over her, until sleep finally swept me from her consciousness.

I could still see her, but how long would it be until she saw me again, and not just a picture? Seventy years? Eighty? I remembered the conversation I had earlier with Azzoloft. I didn't want the world to end. I couldn't believe it ever would. That night, I wanted Emily to live a long, very normal, happy life.

My son Samuel's room was next to Emily's. I wished I could turn off Emily's light. I went through the wall into Samuel's room. Samuel was reading in bed as well. His telescope was in the box, under his bed. I wondered if he would ever use it again, or if it would just bring bad memories—of me. I moved close to him. "Don't wait for me," I said. "I didn't show up in time for your birthday, and I'm not showing up now. Remember me but use the telescope, anyway. Enjoy it." There was no sign he heard me.

I stayed there with him, until he finally closed the book. He eyed the light switch across the room. He picked up his tennis shoe and threw it in an arch. It bounced off the wall about six inches above the switch. He picked up the other shoe and lobbed it. I knew it would never work. I used to do the same thing when I was a kid. It's wonderful having a physical body, but sometimes getting out of bed to turn off the light is more than we can handle. I could have blamed it on one of Azzoloft's followers, Blitzer maybe, but the fact is Samuel and I were the only ones there. My son was just being lazy.

Watching my son, I remembered what a privilege it was to watch this young man grow up. Being lazy didn't matter much. Being mortal mattered a lot. Being a good person mattered a lot. Azzoloft was threatening me with my family's funeral the week after my own. Who was I, but an ignorant ex-mortal, a pawn in the program? The test was tomorrow.

CHAPTER 23

INTO THE PARTICLE FIELD

THE MORNING OF the test I was at Marie's house.

The realization set in. I was damned. Adultery, for a spiritual man, a believer, was the gateway to hell. It was the ultimate lie to your spouse: I said I'd be faithful to you, but I lied.

Now my actions were standing in the way of confronting Azzoloft.

I thought I was better. I didn't just hurt Marie, I hurt Ronnie. Ronnie deserved a punch in the mouth at my funeral, because what she did was wrong. She got much more than she deserved, in the worst way, when I died. Whatever she gained from our affair--the love from me, and the comfort she felt, was gone. Not just gone, though. Her loneliness had to be worse than before. She had to have seen that she'd made things worse, at what turned out to be the worst of times for my family. Maybe she blamed herself. It had to have been awful. Until now, I had been blinded to it. I was lost in my own remorse, unable to clearly see what was happening to Ronnie, and to Marie.

The thing that was worse than what Ronnie did, ten times

worse, was what I had done. I betrayed my wife's love, even more that I'd betrayed Ronnie's admiration. I'd abandoned my children to the shame of my actions.

My mortal accomplishments were important. My children had loved me deeply. I hoped they still did. Stabilizing dark matter had been a profound achievement. Yet I had felt like a failure. Marie had been in the process of divorcing me. It meant a lot to me to be part of my church. My faith was important to me. When I fell, my fall was precipitous. A drug addict slides downward for years until he hits bottom. I had jumped off a cliff and shattered.

I moved out into the front yard. I looked anew at the vibrancy of the colors, the light that emits from all living things.

My wife's rose garden was alive with color, and with radiant beauty. When I recognized the source of the connection, it felt as though the light particles in me began to resonate, at a wavelength that I now recognized as familiar. With it came fear and pain.

I wasn't ready. Darkness and anger were still very much part of me, just as they had been when I crossed the portal. I was allowed to cross the gulf because I had been programmed to. Me, not Azzoloft, nor any of his followers. At least not yet.

We had opened a door by stabilizing dark matter, but that door was programmed. It was controlled. It let me through; an exception. We, as individuals, were making choices, but all the circumstances and experiences of our lives interact with everyone with whom we have contact. The result is a programmed world in which none of us fully control our lives. We were making individual choices, and the program integrated all our individual choices, carrying us forward in a current towards judgment day.

The worst choice I had ever made, an individual choice

to commit adultery, had played a part in what was happening. My death played a part. Everything seemed to have gone wrong, first my adultery, and then my death. The program was working things out, in all the wrong ways.

When Azzoloft entered the particle field that day, I still had the choice to be a good person, or an evil one. The dark power I felt when I crossed the portal could become my choice, become who I was. I could connect myself to the darkness and join Azzoloft. Or I could connect myself to the light, the connections between wood and steel, plants and minerals, animals and people. But that light wasn't just data, it was power, searing power. It was the power of judgment, the irrevocable wrath of God.

■ ■ ■

As I moved, faster than an eagle, towards NSHC, I wondered if Azzoloft had already transformed. I had stayed longer than I should have in the rose garden. When I reached NSHC, the sky was filled with Zolians. Azzoloft had gathered a tremendous number, far exceeding the post-mortals.

The Zolians saw me, and a shock wave went through their ranks, as they moved to block my way. I saw Leilani, Brett, Isaac, and Charlotte, trying to outmaneuver the Zolians, to get to me before the way was blocked.

The Zolians swarmed to block my path, a solid block of bodies, arms linked, with no space, and swarming around and behind me, not just forty, but a million bodies, in layers, the nearest ones spewing more black mist than I'd never seen. If they were trying to block me, the second test must be about to begin.

I knew it was possible to push past Zolians, because I had been able to brush Zinc aside, after what he was doing to my son. To do it, I had filled myself with dark energy and power, driven by anger, fear and hatred. I didn't want to fill myself with dark energy right now. It would help overpower the Zolians, but I would be playing their game.

Still, I felt fear. The Zolians were swarming and smothering me in thick darkness. I yelled for those around me. "Isaac! Charlotte!" They pushed through, with Leilani, and joined me. Then I saw my mother, Irene. I had never been so glad to see anyone on my side. She was radiant and pushed past the Zolians with ease. We moved forward. The Zolians were swarming around us.

"Reach out with me!" I shouted. "Reach out to everything and everyone you know to join us!"

There shone a light and a radiance, and then others began joining us, the people from Leilani's church, Charlotte's volunteers, Isaac's Science Association, and everyone else who had helped us.

I saw my grandparents, and they were with hundreds of others, and I realized my mother must have been thinking of them, reaching out to our ancestors, friends, and everyone we knew.

I looked at my mother. She was smiling. She was joyful.

It was then, I felt sure. There were more of us than there were Zolians. It wasn't just the people I knew, it was all the people any of us knew, and more. It was a connection among people everywhere, a connection to all living things. All living things were good; only people choose to become evil.

Maybe this was it. Maybe this is how judgment day was going to happen. We would reach out, all connected as one, and God would answer.

The searing came. Even in trying to connect to these people I loved, the knowledge of my affair was there. I felt pain, almost unbearable pain. I could see the joy in others, and connect to the light, without the darkness. Without anger. But not without pain, and a knowledge of what I had done, a filth I couldn't fix. I ignored the pain.

The way opened up before me, like the parting of an ocean, the mass of all my loved ones and friends, and the millions upon millions who were hearing this event, this vortex of power, pushing aside the Zolians, and the dark mist. But I didn't see God. It was the people I knew, and everyone who loved good, filled with light. I felt God was there. He was in the light. He was the light, and the light was in the people, in all of us. In that thought was my pain. God was in the light, and so I could not be. It would destroy me. I wanted so much to be part of it, to feel joy with all these people I loved and with all creation. Instead I felt remorse, and searing pain. The light was destroying me. I felt an overpowering urge to flee, to hide from the light, and from the people who were helping now.

Instead, I followed the path, a tunnel of people in white robes, filled with light, until I could see the buildings of the NSHC. Irene, Isaac, Leilani, and the others were with me. We accelerated through the buildings and underground, towards the testing area. The wall of people in white ended, and a wall of Zolians blocked our path. Zinc, Shartruze, and Blitzer were at the front, facing walls of Zolian bodies, oozing black mist and darkness.

I looked at those around me. We smiled.

I flew straight at Zinc and watched the fury on his face as we pushed past him. My mother and the others were with me. Shartruze saw my mother coming, glowered, and moved out of her way.

We pushed into darkness so thick I couldn't see the mortals in the testing area. I could feel the Zolians in the darkness, but I couldn't see anything. Then the Zolians began screaming. It was loud. It was piercing. I instinctively placed my hands over my ears, but it didn't help. I was suspended in darkness, drowning in the screams, the screams and darkness of the damned.

But I wasn't damned. I could move. I still had a choice. I moved quickly, through the darkness, hearing the Zolians screams, as they were pushed aside. I ran into something, and it didn't move.

"Mom!" I shouted. I reached out into the darkness to embrace her. We held each other closely, and our light increased. We could see each other now, in spite of the darkness, a space of light between us.

"We can reach the others," I said. "Hurry!"

We moved in the darkness, and grabbed each person we found, Irene, and then Isaac. As we touched them we could see each other, and we joined hands, forming a circle again, a circle of people, standing in light. Above our heads, and beneath our feet, and at our backs, there was a wall of darkness so thick we could see nothing, but we could see each other. United in a circle, no darkness came between us.

I could still feel the overwhelming piercing of their screams, and hear the Zolians swarming, screaming, in the darkness. I looked at my mother and Charlotte. They looked calm. Everyone was calm, except me.

"Can you all hear me?" I shouted.

"Block it out, Will," Charlotte said.

The resonance! It was that same resonance she had used when I first met her, the resonance I felt after I crossed the gulf. I could feel it, now, and could see light and darkness, churning from me.

"Hold on to the resonance, inside yourself," Charlotte said.

Charlotte began singing, starting with a single note, a pitch, and I could feel it inside me. I reached out to the light again, and connected to other lights, ignoring the pain the light brought me. This was music. I recognized it, the power of it. I had felt the power of music before, many times as a mortal. Everyone has, some during Handel's Messiah, or during a favorite concert, and others at a Memorial Day Concert at our nation's capital. Music was a communication power, and it wasn't just mortal. Mortal music was a fleeting connection, a wondrous and beautiful thing, when it tapped into the real power. Music enhanced the connections among us, and caused the power to flow faster and stronger. And the stronger it got, the more pain it brought.

The others started singing with Charolotte, not just a note, but connected melodies within a note, resonating inside us, a frequency.

"Can you hear me?" They could.

"We may be out of time at any moment," I said. "If we move quickly through the darkness, we'll run into mortals, because we can't go through them, and we can't push them out of the way like we do Zolians. We'll know the perimeter, based on where the mortals are. From there we can move to the center, where the test is happening, to stop Azzoloft."

We moved swiftly in a circle. I remembered how big the testing room was, from the first test. Sure enough, moving through the dense darkness, we traced a rough circle of mortals, who were watching the test, even though we could see nothing except each other in the darkness. We crisscrossed the area, still moving in our own circle, like a ping pong ball. We weren't stopping anywhere in the middle, and I couldn't be certain where the particle field was, where Azzoloft would be materializing. The good news was that he must not have succeeded yet, because I was pretty sure we were going to see him once it happened. But all this time, he had to be here, hiding like a coward in his darkness.

Suddenly we stopped partway across the testing area.

We had run into Eli.

Eli was standing there, with his back to us, watching something in the darkness. As soon as we touched him, we could see him, sharing our light.

"Eli! Why aren't you in the booths with the mortals? Didn't the president invite you?" I asked.

"I declined his invitation. Getting in here was simple. Going through walls isn't any more of a problem for me than it is for you. I can also remain unseen by mortals, and that would allow me to be free to assist you." I remembered how Marie couldn't see him when I talked to him by Marie's rose garden at the house. There was also the fact that he had been able to see me, as an ex-mortal. He had the appearance of a mortal, but he wasn't one.

"But what about the darkness, and the shrieking Zolians?"

"What I see are the mortals in the room, and the test is going to start in a few seconds. I also see the Zolians. The Zolians are in a frenzy, flying everywhere, and swirling around Azzoloft and the area of the particle field, so he is alone in it." He was in a different paradigm from the rest of us. He seemed able to see both worlds, and interact with both, in ways he chose. He was living technology, better than mortals and ex-mortals combined. The mortals couldn't see the darkness or the Zolians. The darkness obscured the way of the ex-mortals. Only Eli could see everything at once. There was no one better to stop Azzoloft.

"Why don't you stop Azzoloft?" I asked.

"I am not able to interfere with the events further," he said. I did what I could by going to the president. It was his decision to make. I don't know what is going to happen now, but I'll help you if I can." It was like the portal, programmed to let me through in spite of the darkness in me. Eli's choices were bound by the program, and he didn't know the future. He knew the prophecies. He knew the book of Revelation. He just didn't see the gaps, the way it would unfold. Neither did I.

Eli lowered his eyebrows in concern. "They just started the test. The particles are beginning to move!"

I was still standing in darkness, in the circle; Eli could see, and I couldn't. I moved toward him and grabbed his arm. "Guide me over to where Azzoloft is!" I said.

Eli and I moved forward through the darkness. Once we were close enough, he stopped. I moved forward and entered the particle field.

As soon as I was inside the particle field, I could a sphere of light around Azzoloft. Azzoloft was majestic, surrounded by light in the midst of the particle field, surrounded by the Zolian's darkness. Particles of stabilized dark matter were forming in the field, and moving toward him, coalescing.

As he saw me, his eyes narrowed, but he did not move. His concentration seemed intense.

This was the power of light, the power of connecting to light from other things. He must be calling in the light from his followers. They couldn't have very much, because they were mostly evil, but they had some, and with billions of them connected, he had enough. Why didn't it sear him, destroy him, as I felt it would destroy me? Maybe it did sear him, and he just didn't have enough of it to destroy him. I had seen him gather light from his followers the first time I ever met him, at the resort, when I thought he was the devil.

This was Azzoloft's plan, his failsafe, even if I did show up at this test. He had his followers do their best to stop me. He used their darkness and their screams to distract us. He was using everything he had, and now he was counting on his own knowledge. He knew connected light could give him

271

power here, in the particle field. He knew the science of it. He felt the reality, the first time he was in this particle field, when it had shut down. He knew it wouldn't shut down this time, because they had adjusted the shut-down level. The mortals wanted him to materialize. He met my gaze, his face forming into a new immortality in the stabilized particles. He looked triumphant.

He knew I had figured out the power of dark energy. Zinc told him what happened when I was trying to protect Sam. Azzoloft must think I didn't know enough about the connections of light to make the difference.

He was wrong.

I reached out with all the yearnings of my soul, searching for the resonance, and the brilliant light. I pled for help. I reached to my mother, and my circle of friends, and felt them start singing, somewhere in the darkness. I reached past the walls, reaching with my soul, my own light, towards all those who had helped me get to the testing site. I felt power coursing through me as I reached further, calling, pleading for help, a cry of soul. It wasn't for me, it was a cry for the many who seek freedom, a cry for a better world.

I felt the connection to those around me again, and the light around me began to increase. The particles stopped moving towards Azzoloft and streamed towards me.

Azzoloft looked stunned. Finally. Served him right. He didn't understand the programming. Something or someone was helping me, and had been. I was the key. I was the password. I had DNA. That was what Eli had said. I was to open the door, and maybe not just by stabilizing dark matter.

With the light came blinding pain. I felt terror. The light was judgment, and there was too much darkness in me. I felt like my soul was being consumed, tormented by the power of the light. It was hard to think straight. My thoughts went random. This wasn't God, it was high-tech power, a current that was going to electrocute the darkness in me. I was about to burn, not like a mortal, but as an ex-mortal.

Atonement. That was the word. Only I had none. I had no atonement. I had no religion. I had adultery, and a scientific, technical, ex-mortal darkness, with no atonement to save me. Was it science, or God? The effect was the same.

Azzoloft's jaw tightened, as he saw I was absorbing more of the particles. He breathed towards me, a thick blackness issuing from his mouth. As it reached me, I felt it overpowering me. My will was bound to his mind. A flash of realization hit me: I was frozen as I had been in the lab, that very first night, alone, when I had seen the particles start to stream upward. The same power, the same being, paralyzing my mind. The particles started streaming away from me and towards Azzoloft. My doubts were magnified. I would be destroyed by the light. I was an adulterer. I was dead. I couldn't ask forgiveness. It was too late, the moment I died.

NO. God could not abandon me now. God could not refuse to forgive me. The light blinded me, and seared me. There was too much darkness in me. Azzoloft had power over me, and over my mind. God had to save me. No he didn't.

This was a program. This was I TOLD YOU SO. This was what happened if you don't listen to God: Judgment. Irreversible. Programmed. Azzoloft was going to slaughter my family because of what I did.

Anger coursed through me, and power, and dark energy. God could not let my family be destroyed. He could damn me, so long as he saved my family. They were innocent. Azzoloft was damned. God should destroy him, not me.

Darkness and rage exploded from me, in a pulse of terrible power. Lightning and clouds of darkness lit me up, and surged from me.

MARK HAWKINS

Azzoloft laughed, an echoing surreal sound. The lightning crackling from me moved towards him, a surging, technological power, programmed. I felt I was being sucked towards him. This was a technology I, a mere physicist, did not understand, an otherworldly power. A power beyond my comprehension. Azzoloft was pulling me in, and as the darkness in me increased, the excruciating pain caused by the light decreased. I looked into Azzoloft's eyes. All I had to do was flee the light, and the pain would stop. I was damned either way. That was part of the program, and it had better-than-computer precision. Searing pain came from connecting to a vast current of light which had been programmed not to forgive me, but I saw now the terror of my hellish fate with a technological devil none of us comprehended.

Anger, rage, and hatred, whether at Azzoloft or at God, made me like Azzoloft. Dark energy was not the answer. Using dark power, I could only join Azzoloft, not beat him.

In a flash, I saw and understood the program. Pangea was not just at the portals, the computer was data flowing in the connections of light, and that data flowed selectively to those who were programmed to receive it. I saw the fate of liars, thieves, and murderers, and adulterers like me. I saw the apocalypse to come. I saw the antichrist, and he was technological. I saw, as a physicist and as a damned believer, science and religion joined, transcendent, in a figurative pillar of heaven, hell and technology. With or without a God, this program would execute. It wasn't about churches or religion. It was never about atheists and believers. It was about conscience, the morality programmed into the light. Each of us was connected, in our inner selves, the matter inside us not made of atoms, to receive and understand what was right or wrong. We didn't have to believe in God. Any atheist could repent, and be forgiven. If they hurt someone they loved, they'd ask forgiveness. They'd feel remorse. And then they'd feel the relief, the burden lifted. That was the universal experience of mankind, programmed as conscience, and the condition of forgiveness. God never made himself the condition. That is why we could be forgiven, even without believing in God. Judgment day was to be a condemnation for those liars, thieves, and murderers who stop listening to conscience, until it becomes too late. Everyone else would be glad to see God, thrilled that He finally stopped hiding. God was supposed to save all his children, including Thomas, who didn't believe until he saw.

The only things not programmed were our individual choices. That was the only thing we controlled. That was freedom. We made our choices, and the computer integrated them into the program, with everyone else's choices. Prophecies were data, and the program executed, the way it was supposed to, and sometimes our little choices and our little lives made a difference to the program. More often, our choices made a difference only to us, and those we served, lifted, or loved.

Azzoloft wanted to materialize as a being of stabilized dark matter, and he had threatened Marie, Sam, and Emily. They weren't the only ones he would kill, if he went through the technological door we had opened into the mortal world. The President of the United States was here, and he might be the first casualty. Azzoloft wasn't trying to become mortal, he was going to be something more. Transfigured, or resurrected, those were my guesses, but I was dealing with something beyond my comprehension. Access denied. Pangea guarded the tree of knowledge.

The only thing I had left was my freedom, my ability to choose, and I chose the searing pain of the light. I would protect my family, at whatever the cost. I, a mere ex-mortal, was left with the decision to do right or wrong, without knowing what the outcome would be. Ex-mortal sacrifice, in ignorance. I would protect every mortal I knew, from what Azzoloft was planning. I would do that, even if it was fruitless. I would give what I could. That was the only choice I had left.

With all the strength I had left, I surged with the current and power of the brilliant light, accepting the burning of my soul, my own private sacrifice.

In spite of blinding pain in my soul and mind, I reached out, to the entire planet, imagining every living thing, feeling for them, reaching for them, calling them to my aid.

Azzoloft had his billions, but I knew then, as the connections of light resonated with the song of many voices, that they with me were more than they with him. The only problem was that there was darkness in me. I was inviting my own destruction. I should flee and hide in a cave. The terrible light of judgment was coming, right now, and it would destroy me, because of what I had become. I knew what I was. A liar. An adulterer. Today was my own personalized judgment day. It had come sooner than I thought. Like a thief in the night. Time to receive what I deserved.

As I filled with the brilliant light, connecting fully with it, the particles streamed out of Azzoloft, from head to foot. He fought, concentrating as he reached out to the strength of his followers, combining their light and their darkness, but he could not stem the particles that were leaving him. When he saw he was losing particles, I saw in his eyes a glimmer of an intense rage, which suddenly burst forth from his mouth in a visceral roar. It was a terrifying sound, and darkness spewed forth with his breath again, as he concentrated more intensely.

Then I saw legions of ex-mortals, in white, pushing past the Zolians in the test area. When I reached out, and connected with light, they knew the way through the darkness.

The light was leaving Azzoloft, the support of all his followers draining from him, and the darkness dissipating. And with the light, so much pain I felt weak, fading.

Azzoloft stopped roaring and began shaking with the intensity.

I was filled with light, and my mind and soul were burning in the torment of a thousand suns, like the wrath of an angry God. This was how it would end, with my mind consumed by the blazing light. When my mind and my identity were gone, would the darkness of my mind be extinguished? Would I be annihilated? Where nothing exists, would my sin finally be erased?

No. That was not my religion. I had never believed in annihilation, and didn't now. I believed in hell. Hell is flames of torment, a lake of fire and brimstone, caused by the glory of God, and by remorse that conscience can no longer heal. I was blinded by the terrible light, and the unbearable pain was eternal torment. Starting, for me, right now.

Through the brightness of the light, I could vaguely see Azzoloft was trembling. He reached out his hand towards me, and the remaining particles streamed from him en masse towards me. He issued a final bellow, the scream of the damned, echoing with thousands of years of rage, and billions of Zolian voices raised as one, "NOOOOOO!"

■ ■ ■

Beyond consciousness or understanding, I watched, like a vision, until the particles stopped moving towards me, and began drifting. The moment the particles stopped moving towards me, the pain stopped. I had become something else, something the brilliant light no longer seared.

The darkness of the Zolians was gone. I could see the mortals again, behind the glass surrounding the particle field area. I could see my friends, and my mother, and the Zolians, and Eli. I could see everything.

The President of the United States was there, his face was inscrutable, intent. The general's mouth was hanging open. Every mortal in the place was staring at the particle field, awestruck. But it was Ronnie's voice that broke the silence, over the intercom from the booth she was in.

"Will?"

CHAPTER 24

GENESIS

MOST OF THE people in the booths began rapidly exiting. There was a hallway behind the booths, leading away from the testing area. I looked down at my arms and hands. I looked normal. Someone had turned off the test, and there was stabilized matter on the floor. I was wearing a white robe, thankfully. It felt like cotton. The Zolians, and my ex-mortal friends, and Eli, were no longer visible to me, and I saw only as mortals saw.

The door to the room burst open, and the president came in, followed by several secret service agents. One of them said, "Mr. President, it isn't safe for you to approach him." An agent ran ahead of the president, and tried to block him. The president pushed him out of the way. The agent's jaw set, but another agent put his hand on the first agent's chest and let the president keep going.

The room was quickly filling with people flowing from the hallway, everyone who had been in the booths. Someone else was pushing and shoving to get through. It was Ronnie, but the agents stopped her.

The president stepped forward, and I reached out and shook his hand.

"Will, I speak for us all, I think, when I tell you how much it means to us to see you again. I think we'll have a lot to talk about, but now isn't the time. Welcome back."

We talked briefly, and the president left. I went around the room shaking hands, and embracing those I knew. My embrace of Ronnie was one of joy, joy to be back.

No one understood where I had been. They'd held my funeral, and now I had returned. No one knew who Azzoloft was. To the mortals, he'd just been the other figure in the particle field. As soon as I thought of Azzoloft, my vision expanded again. I saw not just the mortals around me, but the Zolians, and my mother, and Charlotte. Was I mortal? No. Was I like Eli? More likely.

Azzoloft was watching me. All the Zolians and the ex-mortals were standing, staring, watching me, as if I'd forgotten them, as if I couldn't see them. Azzoloft moved towards me. Emotion rippled briefly on his face.

Azzoloft got close to me. "Tell them who I am, Will. Tell them I'm here."

I knew they could see me, but not him.

"Should I tell them you are the devil, or just a person who has never been mortal?"

Ronnie grabbed my arm. "Will! Will! Who are you talking to?"

All the mortals in the room were silent, staring at me.

Azzoloft smiled and disappeared from my view. The Zolians followed.

Charlotte placed her index finger over her lips and pointed to the mortals.

I turned away from my mother and ex-mortal friends, and told Ronnie, "I'm sorry. No one. I just want to see my family. Can I get out of here?"

A general approached, with several of the soldiers who

were keeping the area secure. "Just come with us, Will. We'll get you to your family. We do have a request, though."

■ ■ ■

The general wanted a debriefing, and he asked for my full cooperation. He said I could be with my family tonight, and we'd start in the morning. I gave him my word, and based on that, he had me driven back to my home and family. The general offered me a change of clothes. I said it might be easier for my family if I showed up in the robe I was wearing. Either way they were going to be in shock. I was dropped off in front of my house, and I watched as the vehicle left. In my white robe, my family wouldn't know whether I was a mortal or an angel. I wasn't shining. The skin tone on my hands and arms looked mortal.

As I approached the house, I saw my mother, Irene Johnson, standing on the porch. She was young and radiant, dressed in her white robe. "Mom."

"I'm glad you can see me," she said. "I don't know what to think. You look like a mortal again, but you can't be."

She reached out to touch my face, uncertain. She was an ex-mortal, yet Her fingers touched me, and then we embraced, for a long while. I wondered if any of my mortal neighbors would see me, standing in a white robe, embracing a person they couldn't see.

"Something is very different," I said. "I am able to see ex-mortals like you, when I want. I also don't feel like a mortal. I don't feel mortal aches and pains."

"I am glad to see you," she said. "I need to tell you though, that I have never, in mortal life or after, been more shocked than when I learned that you'd had an affair. You were never a liar, Will. You were the child I always trusted to tell the truth.

"I am so sorry for what I did," I said. "I've felt tremendous shame."

"It was an amazing fall, Will. A person so good, a person who had served so much. You were a leader in the scientific community. You were a man of faith. You were a strong man. Hundreds of people looked up to you, and they all saw you fall."

"I know Mom, I really am sorry."

"Will, I know you are sorry. I've already forgiven you. But you need to hear it. You need to know what I felt as I watched you. From the day you died, I've been here at your family's side, unseen. I've helped your son and daughter overcome some of their resentment. I've given strength, encouragement, and comfort to your wife. There is a power I have been using while I have been with them. There is power in knowledge. I know how to communicate with them. At times they feel me near them. They feel the communication. It resonates in them."

"I watched Azzoloft's followers putting thoughts in mortal's minds," I said. "I can't prove they are able to do that, but it certainly looks to me like they can. It isn't mystical, it is scientific, but the rules are different from mortal science."

"Would you like to imagine a world, an afterlife, in which evil people like Azzoloft and his followers can influence mortals, but good people cannot? Do you want to leave your son, your daughter, and your wife to the likes of Azzoloft?"

"No."

"Then you need to be cautious, now more than ever. I didn't come to you when I heard you died, because I felt you weren't ready. There is still darkness in you, and Azzoloft will try to claim you as his. Fight with everything you have. Fight against his lies. Fight against his evil."

"What kind of fight can ex-mortals have?" I asked. "There

are no swords, or guns, or tanks, and no one can kill a non-mortal like Azzoloft, even if there were."

"It has never been about guns or tanks, Will. It has always been about persuasion. Guns and tanks are merely a means of persuasion. Men have a strong tendency to think of power in terms of force. You know what mothers think, Will? Mothers think about persuasion as a soft voice, a caress, as your mother calling your name.

"Love is the key," she said. "Can you see it? Can you comprehend? Mothers persuade with love. Fathers can be very strong, even great, when they love.

"Now that you are back, I think it is time you reached out to your family, this family, your wife and children." She grabbed my hand and squeezed it, looking in my eyes. "I love you, Will. I'm proud of you, again." Then she was gone.

I rang the doorbell. It was a strange feeling, being at the door of my home, like a stranger, without a key. A man in a white robe, knocking.

Marie answered. Our eyes met.

"Will?" she said. She reached out her hand and touched my face. Tears streamed down her face, tears of joy. "How?" she asked.

I took her in my arms. My wife. Until death we did part. I was dead no longer.

Sam and Emily saw us. "Dad?" Emily said.

I gently released Marie and held out my arms to Emily. She came forward, hesitantly. I wrapped her in my arms. My child, my beloved child.

Next, I turned to Sam and reached out to him with all the energy in my soul. "I love you, Sam."

After I embraced Sam, the four of us joined in a group hug. I looked in Marie's eyes. I realized what she had been going through since my death, and why her pain was so deep.

She was afraid I had gone to hell, and that I would never, ever, ever, come back. She believed, with the faith of a child, that if that was God felt should happen, then it was okay. But it didn't make her happy. It wasn't what she wanted. She wanted to believe in life after death. She wanted to believe we could be together again. She didn't want to lose that. She wanted to believe that I could be healed, clean, whole, and handsome, like on our wedding day, not the corpse she had wept over at the morgue. The damage to the body was nothing compared to the mangled spirit of a man whose last hours were spent in betrayal of his wife.

I was back, but I was not mortal, any more than Eli was mortal. We had stabilized dark matter, and we unknowingly opened a door. It was a door between mortals and ex-mortals. Good and evil were warring in me, and in us all. We'd crossed a threshold. I still believed what was happening now was programmed, like everything else. Religion said the end came swiftly, like a thief, when everyone was asleep, unconscious, unable to tell dream from reality, until it is too late.

I thought of my Emily, and Sam, and how much I loved them. I thought of what had happened. I thought of how we had raised them, since birth, and how, at the moment of destruction, I would rather go to hell in a blaze of light than forsake them.

I was a father. To live, or not to live, that was the question. We could not help but be. Life began with wonder. Our early months were marked by light: we were swaddled and suckled. We heard voices of music, words of love sung in our praise, not merely for being, but for living. In the beginning, admiration of us was inevitable. Time passed, and one day we became a voice of music, singing our admiration for the living. That day I sang, with joy burning so bright it scorched me.

I put my arm around Emily's shoulders, and guided her

to her bedroom. Marie and Sam followed us. I went to Emily's drawer, and took out my picture. I placed it back on her nightstand. "I'm back."

She picked up the unicorn, which had always been there. She kissed it. "I know."

AKNOWLEDGMENTS

Three editors assisted me, and I am grateful: Cecily Markham Condie, Daniel Friend, and Stephanie Clarke. Heather Moore, thank you for your help.

Those who read and made suggestions were: Susan Hamblin Hawkins, Lynette Kelley, Lonnie Clark, Bob and Sharon Maddock, Mary Ellen Kerr, David Hays, and Brad Denton. Thanks for your help, and your support.

Mark Hawkins was born and raised in Cody, Wyoming. He obtained a bachelor's degree in Business Management—Finance, and completed his Juris Doctorate in 1990.

Visit his website at markwhawkins.com